What Others Are Saying About ~~Laura Hilton~~ and *The Snow Globe*...

This fall will find *The Snow Globe* hot off the presses, in more ways than one. The romantic tension between Viktor and Esther is palpable. Laura Hilton has once again proven why she is an award-winning author. She had me hooked on page one, with "Kiss Viktor for me." Most definitely a book to add to your reading list this fall.

—*Cindy Loven*
Coauthor, *Swept Away* (Quilts of Love series)
Book reviewer, cindylovenreviews.blogspot.com

Laura Hilton writes an idyllic Amish love story as enchantingly settling as the flakes inside a shaken snow globe. Her storytelling allows readers to "feel" all that her characters endure.

—*Alan Daugherty*
Columnist, Angelkeep Journals, *Bluffton (IN) News-Banner*
Author, *THE flood: A Bluffton History Novel*

Laura V. Hilton shares an intensity in *The Snow Globe* that leaves the reader breathless and craving more. Her knowledge of the Amish life is praiseworthy, and her characters are exceptionally well described and genuine. An unforgettable and enticing story!

—*Nancee Marchinowski*
Reviewer, http://perspectivesbynancee.blogspot.com

The Snow Globe is not just a story that readers of Amish fiction will enjoy. The clever wit and family dynamics will appeal to anyone who enjoys a good, clean romance. Sparks fly from the very start of this intriguing romantic adventure!

—*Rachel Miller*
Amish fiction author

This is a story of what happens when one's world gets shaken up, like a snow globe, and everything feels topsy-turvy and out of control—until, eventually, everything settles and falls into place. Laura Hilton weaves all of these elements into the story. Nothing is overdone; the balance is just right. And she is a master at crafting tender, sweet, toe-curling moments of romance. It is indeed a beautiful story.

—*Dali Castillo*
Reviewer, Goodreads

Laura Hilton's *Snow Globe* is a fast-paced, riveting story. The reader is instantly pulled into the action, living the characters' problems and dreams with them. It is a book that's difficult to put down and clearly deserves five stars. I highly recommend this book—not just to those who enjoy Amish fiction, inspirational novels, or romance but to anyone who simply wants to read a captivating story with a wonderful message.

—*Susan E. Simpson*
Author, *Ginger & the Bully*

Author Laura V. Hilton has a way with Amish fiction stories that will capture your heart and mind for the duration of a book. I am in awe of how her books keep getting better and better. I was so engrossed in this book that I couldn't pull myself away from it. When I had to put it down, I couldn't wait to pick it up again.

—*Judy K. Burgi*
Reviewer, The Book Club Network Inc.
www.bookfun.org

Laura V. Hilton is a very accomplished writer. I stayed up late to finish this book in one day. Enjoyed it very much.

—*Cliff Hall*
Retired riverboat employee

THE Snow GLOBE

LAURA V. HILTON

WHITAKER
HOUSE

THE SNOW GLOBE
The Amish of Jamesport ~ Book One

Laura V. Hilton
http://lighthouse-academy.blogspot.com

ISBN: 978-1-62911-174-2
eBook ISBN: 978-1-62911-175-9
Printed in the United States of America
© 2014 by Laura V. Hilton

Whitaker House
1030 Hunt Valley Circle
New Kensington, PA 15068
www.whitakerhouse.com

Library of Congress Cataloging-in-Publication Data (Pending)

1 2 3 4 5 6 7 8 9 10 11 ⨆⨆ 21 20 19 18 17 16 15 14

Dedication

In memory of my parents, Allan and Janice;
my uncle Loundy; and my grandmother Mertie,
who talked about their Pennsylvania Amish heritage.

Acknowledgments

I'd like to offer my heartfelt thanks to the following:

The residents of Jamesport, Mississippi, and the surrounding areas, for answering my questions and pointing me in the right directions.

My husband, for traveling there with me and helping me make observations, as well as for beating the starter to get the minivan running again when it had decided enough was enough and had a meltdown after being driven through Kansas City.

The amazing team at Whitaker House—Christine, Courtney, and Cathy. You are wonderful.

Tamela, my agent, for believing in me all these years.

Cliff Hall, for answering my questions about working on a riverboat, and Donna—a woman I met in chemotherapy—who works as a cook on a riverboat and sparked the idea in the first place.

My critique group—you know who you are. You are amazing and knew how to ask the right questions when more detail was needed. Also thanks for the encouragement. Candee, thanks for reading large amounts in a short time and offering wise suggestions.

Again, my husband, Steve, for being a tireless proofreader and cheering section.

Jenna, for reading over my shoulder and editing as I wrote, as well as for naming the horses.

My children, Michael, Kristin, and Loundy, for taking over kitchen duties when I was deep in the story. Kristin and Jenna, thanks especially for help with the household chores.

To God be the glory.

Glossary of Amish Terms and Phrases

ach	oh
aent(i)	aunt(ie)
"Ain't so?"	a phrase commonly used at the end of a sentence to invite agreement
boppli	baby or babies
bu	boy
buwe	boys
daed	dad
danki	thank you
dawdi-haus	a home built for grandparents to live in once they retire
der Herr	the Lord
dochter	daughter
dummchen	a ninny; a silly person
ehemann	husband
Englisch	non-Amish
Englischer	a non-Amish person
frau	wife
Gott	God
großeltern	grandparents
grossdaedi	grandfather
gross-dochter	granddaughter
grosskinner	grandchildren
grossmammi	grandmother
gross-sohn	grandson

gut	good
"Gut morgen"	"Good morning"
"Gut nacht"	"Good night"
hallo	hello
haus	house
"Ich liebe dich"	"I love you"
jah	yes
kapp	prayer covering or cap
kinner	children
kum	come
maidal	an unmarried woman
mamm	mom
maud	maid/housekeeper
morgen	morning
nacht	night
nein	no
onkel	uncle
Ordnung	the rules by which an Amish community lives
rumschpringe	"running around time," a period of adolescence after which Amish teens choose either to be baptized in the Amish church or to leave the community
schatz	dear
schön	beautiful
ser gut	very good
sohn	son
süße	sweetie
to-nacht	tonight
verboden	forbidden
"Was ist letz?"	"What is it?"
welkum	welcome
wunderbaar	wonderful

Chapter 1

K *iss Viktor for me.*

Esther Beachy frowned at the bedroom she'd just finished cleaning—*his* bedroom. Freshly laundered sheets on the bed, tucked under the tumbling blocks quilt; the pillows plumped; the dresser dusted; the floor swept and scrubbed. Even the walls washed down.

Kiss Viktor....

That wouldn't happen. Not even for her cousin.

Besides, Viktor was unlikely to let Esther get that close to him, even if she wanted to. Which she didn't. Want to, that is.

She rested the broom against the wall next to the bucket of sudsy water and went to open the window to let in the fresh spring air. Viktor had been on the Mississippi River for a month, and the room smelled stale, though now with subtle hints of lemon-scented Lysol from the scrubbing she'd done.

Her fingers shook as she unhooked the latch and pushed up the window. It stuck a little, so she shoved harder. It slid open grudgingly. Reluctantly. As if it had problems with Viktor coming home, too. Home for thirty long, excruciating days.

He'd probably be upset to find that she'd been hired as a helper for his grossmammi. More likely, he'd be indifferent to her presence and only upset that in the four weeks he'd been gone, his grossmammi had deteriorated to the point where she needed a caregiver.

If Lily wanted to kiss Viktor, she should've stayed home instead of going to another cousin's wedding in Pennsylvania, where she planned to remain for six weeks. She was the one who had a crush on him. Lily, and every other unmarried female in the district. Esther pursed her lips. She was the sole exception. Viktor Petersheim had been the *most* annoying bu in school, and she couldn't imagine he'd changed much since then. Even as a teen, he'd lured the pretty girls behind the barn during singings....

She shook her head and spun around on her heel.

She would *not* think about Viktor Petersheim any more than she had to.

Unfortunately, that'd still be too much, with his coming home today.

Her stomach churned.

Kiss Viktor....

It was mean—hateful, really—of Lily to make her think about kissing him. Because maybe, just maybe, she really did want to. Maybe she was envious of those other girls.

Her vision blurred.

Nein.

She plowed into something hard. Something thumped on the floor beside her, then strong hands closed around her upper arms like vises. Shock waves pulsated through her.

She blinked. A firmly chiseled jaw came into focus. She lifted her gaze. For a stunned second—minute—hour—she stared into brown eyes. Eyes that looked tired at first but then became increasingly... amused.

Viktor.

Her heart pounded into a gallop.

Kiss Viktor for me.... Her gaze dropped to his lips.

Ugh!

She planted her palms against his chest and shoved. He didn't move. Didn't even budge.

His mouth twisted into a smirk. "Didn't think I'd kum home to find a girl in my bedroom." His hands loosened their iron grip on her arms and slid down to her wrists, leaving sparks in the wake of his touch. "And who might you be?"

He didn't recognize her? Didn't remember the girl who'd sat a couple of rows ahead of him in school? Of course not. Why had she thought he would? He'd been indifferent to her. She might as well have not existed, for all he cared.

Esther jerked away and pushed past him. She grabbed the broom and bucket on the way to the steps. Water sloshed out of the pail and onto the floor. Lovely. Another mess to clean up.

"Where are my großeltern?" All amusement had vanished from his voice.

"Your grossmammi is napping. Your grossdaedi went to the neighbors' to help get the fields planted." Nein need to say that the neighbor had recently undergone surgery and that everyone in the community was working together to help him. She'd already said enough. She started downstairs.

A step creaked behind her. "And why are you here?"

Irritation washed over her. Mostly at herself for not being immune to him. She turned around. "Your grossmammi's been sick. They hired me to take care of the haus and the cooking." Esther continued down the steps and went to the back door. She propped the broom in the corner and then, leaning over, rescued the wet rag from the rim of the pail before tossing out the water, aiming in the general direction of the flower bed. Then she lowered the bucket and turned toward the haus. Her steps faltered when she almost ran into Viktor again. "Why are you following me?"

"Sick how?" His voice had lowered into a growl.

Esther trembled. "It started out as the flu, but then it went into her lungs, and she got pneumonia and was hospitalized a few days. She's been pretty tired and weak ever since."

His mouth set, and a muscle ticked in his jaw. "And nobody notified me? I've been on the river, not overseas. I have a cell phone, I have e-mail, I have…." He must've noticed her eyes widening, because he fell silent. He seemed to study her. "So, who are you? Seems I'd remember a beauty like you."

Her heart skipped a beat. But then…obviously not.

"Esther Beachy," she said before pushing past him again.

Esther Beachy? He turned to watch her go, but he didn't follow this time. What had happened to the thin, gangly girl he'd gone to school with? She was a few years younger, but...well, obviously he hadn't seen her much since he'd left home. She'd filled out, developed curves where there'd been none. He shook his head. Had she always been this pretty, or had he been too shallow to ever look beyond her beanpole shape?

He didn't need to think about that answer. His mouth twisted in self-derision.

He rolled his neck, trying to ease the tension caused by the long drive home to Jamesport. Then he looked toward the neighbors' farm to the east. He didn't see any sign of Grossdaedi. With a shrug, he headed back inside. Movement sounded in the kitchen, so he went that way.

Esther stirred something on the stove. He sniffed. Chicken? "What's for supper?"

She glanced over her shoulder but didn't quite meet his eyes. "Chicken and dumplings."

Made Grossmammi's way, he hoped, with lots of chicken and vegetables in the cream base. Not something they ever served on the riverboat. His stomach rumbled.

"Are you leaving after supper?" He realized his question sounded rude, but it unsettled him to have her in his house.

She laid the wooden spoon on a ceramic holder. "Nein. Your grossmammi will need help getting to bed. I live here."

She lives here? A lump formed in his throat. He couldn't think about that. He'd be outside working. Wouldn't have to be around her much. Except for every morgen, noon, and nacht. He swallowed. "Grossmammi needs that much help? Thought you said she's recovering from pneumonia. What aren't you saying?"

"She was falling a lot." Esther looked down. "She has nein strength in her legs and can't seem to take more than a couple of steps without collapsing. She's...in a wheelchair."

His head began to ache as he mentally retraced his steps to the house. He hadn't noticed a wheelchair ramp at either the front door or the back. "Which neighbor is Grossdaedi working for?" He would head over and see whether they needed him. If they didn't, he'd find out what needed doing at home. Building a wheelchair ramp would be on that list, if what Esther Beachy had said was true.

Esther raised her arm and pointed to the west. "Noah Graber."

The fabric of her dress had swirled and strained against her with the movement, and his stomach tickled like a swarm of humming-birds flocking for the sweet nectar in Grossmammi's feeders. He'd been away from feminine charms for far too long.

He managed a curt nod and headed out the door.

Esther watched as Viktor disappeared into the patch of woods separating the farm of his großeltern from the Grabers'. She'd not been prepared for him at all. And as much as she wanted to blame Lily for making her think of kissing him, she couldn't. Not entirely.

He was too handsome for words. His dark hair was styled in some sort of crew cut: super short on the sides, longer on top. And his eyes…like dark chocolate. Her heart skipped a beat, and her cheeks warmed. She shouldn't think of him like that. He may have kum home to care for his großeltern, but he lived and worked in the Englisch world, traveling up and down the Mississippi River, going places she would never see, unless it was in picture books or the post-cards her cousin Rachel Miller showed her.

He lived in a completely different world.

Pressing her hand to her chest to calm her erratic heartbeat, she turned from the window and covered the kettle of simmering chicken and vegetables with a lid. Hearing a noise from the first-floor bed-room, she went to check on Viktor's grossmammi, Anna.

She opened the door a crack and peeked in. Anna sat on the edge of the bed, pulling her wheelchair closer. Esther entered and moved to stand on the other side of Anna, ready to assist her if she needed help getting into the chair.

"Danki, dear. I thought I heard voices. Did Viktor get home?" Anna peered toward the doorway.

"Jah. He went to find Reuben."

"Ach. I'd hoped he'd visit awhile first."

Esther tried not to shrug. It was better he be away, as aware of him as she'd been, lest she embarrass herself by staring at him. She needed to get her attention back on her duties rather than focus on the man who'd invaded her thoughts too many times since she'd awakened this morgen. The sooner they got back to the indifference she was used to, the better.

"Was ist letz?" Anna put her hand on Esther's arm. "Your expression shows discontentment."

Esther shook her head. "Nothing."

Anna studied her. "Nein, it's something. Tell me. Is something wrong with Viktor?"

Esther's face flamed. *Ach, nein.* As far as she could see, there was nothing wrong with Viktor. Absolutely nothing at all.

Chapter 2

Viktor tramped through the woods and emerged on the far side of the Grabers' field. Grossdaedi walked behind a plow pulled by a team of horses. He looked up as Viktor approached. "Whoa."

The horses took another step forward and then stopped. Grossdaedi held the reins in one hand. "You're home, then."

"Jah, just got back. What's this about Grossmammi being in a wheelchair? What's going on? Why didn't you let me know?"

Grossdaedi's eyes widened.

Viktor had probably sounded harsher than he'd intended to, but Esther Beachy's presence in his home…. He firmed his lips.

Grossdaedi shrugged. "I don't know. The doctor said it was probably a ministroke. A few days after you left, she complained some of dizziness and was wobbling a lot. I went home for lunch and found her sitting on the kitchen floor, not able to summon the strength to get up. The doctor sent out some therapists, but after working with her, they said she'd likely never get her strength back, so the doctor ordered a wheelchair. Therapists still kum out, but other than taking a couple of steps, she's not walking. Can't seem to stay on her feet long."

"So, this…." Viktor couldn't keep his lips from curling. "Esther Beachy is a permanent addition to the family? She isn't going home anytime soon?"

"You don't like her?" Grossdaedi tilted his head. "She's been a blessing to us. She works hard, is gut company for your grossmammi, and takes care of everything."

"I don't know her well enough to tell whether I like her or not. I just don't want someone else in my home."

"Nice having a cute girl around." Grossdaedi gave a teasing wink. "You'd like it more if it were one of the maidals you're interested in, ain't so?"

15

Viktor snorted and looked away. Judging by his unsettled reaction to finding Esther in his home, just about any female would make him edgy. His current lifestyle left nein time for socializing. There wasn't any other reason he could see. "I don't like having my home invaded."

Grossdaedi's shoulder lifted again. "She's quiet. You'll hardly notice her."

Viktor grunted, seriously doubting the truth of that. He glanced around at the other men working in various parts of the field. "What do you need me to do?"

"Guess we're pretty well done. If you want to head on back home, you could take care of some things there."

"Do you need a ramp for Grossmammi?"

Grossdaedi looked away. Then he took the reins with both hands and clicked his tongue at the horses. But his shoulders slumped slightly. "That'd be admitting defeat. Giving up on her getting better."

Viktor nodded.

"There are a couple of boards loose on the front steps, and Esther mentioned a clogged water pipe somewhere. She also said there's a problem with the washer. She's been using a scrub board to do the laundry."

Viktor's stomach flipped. On the river, he gave the directions. At home, sometimes it was a struggle to reverse the direction of his thinking and obey his elders. He raked his fingers through his hair and headed back through the woods that separated the two farms. He'd been given his orders, and they all involved close encounters with Esther Beachy.

⁓

Esther wheeled Anna to the kitchen table. "Let me get you a snack." The doctor had recommended some sort of canned milk shake, but Anna refused to drink them, so Esther had started making her homemade ones—a couple of scoops of softened ice cream with enough milk stirred in to create a thick, drinkable liquid.

The door opened as Esther placed the plastic cup in front of Anna. She didn't need to turn to know who it was—not with the way Anna's face broke into a grin. "Viktor. Kum give me a hug."

"I'll check the laundry," Esther said, heat rushing to her cheeks. She dipped her head so she wouldn't have to see him—at least, nothing more than his jeans and tennis shoes—and hurried toward the door.

"I think Viktor might like a milk shake, too," Anna said. "Make him one first."

Esther paused.

"Nein, that's alright," Viktor inserted. "She can check the—"

"Shush. It won't be any problem. I insist. Besides, the laundry will wait until after our snack. Make one for yourself, too, Esther, and sit and enjoy it with it us. We want to hear all about your travels, Viktor."

Esther obediently retrieved the ice cream and milk once more. A chair scraped behind her, then creaked as Viktor sat.

She wouldn't join them. She'd make his shake and then leave. She didn't need to listen to him talk about whatever it was he did.

Indifference was her friend. Where was it now, when she needed it? Why hadn't she realized how secure it made her feel when it was still within her grasp?

"There's nothing to tell, Grossmammi." A smile lifted his tone. "Just a lot of hard work."

"Where'd you go?"

"To the Gulf of Mexico."

Esther poured the milk shake into a cup and carried it to the table. She set it in front of him, then put away the ice cream and milk.

"You forgot to make one for yourself." Anna patted the table. "Kum join us, süße."

Sweetie. What would Viktor think of that? Esther didn't dare glance at him. "Danki, but I'll just have some tea later." She hurried outside.

Nobody followed, but then, she hadn't expected anyone to. Anna couldn't. And Viktor felt about her now the way he always had.

Indifferent.

⤴

Viktor tried not to watch Esther go. Tried not to notice the sway of her skirt above her bare feet. He failed. As soon as the door shut firmly behind her, he turned back to Grossmammi. "Why her? Why not...." He floundered for a name. "Aenti Nancy? Or what about Cousin Ruth?"

Grossmammi shook her head. "Aenti Nancy's dochter just had another boppli, and she's helping out there. And Cousin Ruth has a family. Besides, what's wrong with Esther?"

Nothing. Everything. Viktor shrugged, hoping Grossmammi wouldn't see anything he didn't want her to. Such as the attraction he fought.

It was simply because he hadn't been around women in a while. His lips twisted.

"Do you not like her?"

The same question Grossdaedi had asked. Viktor shook his head and gave the same answer: "I don't know her well enough to tell whether I like her or not."

Grossmammi smiled and patted his hand. "Then this will give you the chance to know her, jah? She's a sweet girl."

Viktor nodded and waited for the inevitable, "She'll make someone a gut frau." But Grossmammi turned her attention back to her milk shake. Gut. They wouldn't try to marry him off. A wife was something he'd like someday; but right now, with all the time he spent away from home, marriage would be a disaster. Most of his coworkers, the ones who'd married, had also divorced. Or were headed in that direction.

Besides, an Amish man wouldn't—couldn't—work on the river.

He frowned, a shudder working its way up his spine. Marriage and Amish. Why did those things seem to go hand in hand? He pulled in a deep breath.

Neither one was likely to happen for him. Not now on the first. Not ever on the second.

He finished the last bit of the delicious milk shake Esther had made, then stood. "I guess I'll get started on the chores Grossdaedi mentioned. He said something about a clogged pipe and problems with the wringer washer. Do you know what's wrong?"

Grossmammi shook her head. "Ask Esther." She grinned. "Esther is the answer to all your questions."

Viktor snorted. He opened the door, stepped out on the porch, and tested the steps as he went down. They'd be an easy fix. Just needed a few nails.

Esther stood in the side yard, taking clothes off the line and folding them. He went to her. "My grossdaedi mentioned a clogged pipe."

She kept working, placing the undershirt she'd just folded in the basket. "The kitchen sink isn't draining right, the pipe in the first-floor bathroom is leaking."

He caught a whiff of green apple as she straightened and shifted a couple of steps in his direction, reaching for the next item of clothing. He breathed in deeply, inhaling the scent, and for a second, he was tempted with the desire to nuzzle her neck.

If she were any other girl—if he were six years younger, still a teenager—he might've done it.

He mentally shook himself and stepped backward. What had they been discussing? Ah, water pipes. He turned around.

The tools he needed would probably be in the shed.

"Danki for looking into fixing them."

He glanced over his shoulder. Big mistake. She gazed at him, her green eyes showing something that might have been admiration.

His hand flexed with a sudden, inexplicable urge to run his fingertips over the curve of her cheek.

He managed a curt nod and headed toward the shed.

Too bad Grossmammi wouldn't consider hiring a different caregiver. This woman was already tying him up in knots.

Chapter 3

When she'd finished taking down the clean laundry and folding it, Esther balanced the laundry basket on her hip and headed for the haus. She wasn't sure where Viktor had gone, but he'd probably fixed the pipes already and would be out of her way. She hoped.

How would she survive his visit home?

The sooner she got it through her head that she meant nothing to him—never had, never would—the better. Then maybe they could coexist in peace, the way they had in school. He'd left her alone, never glancing her way, while he'd teased and tormented all the other girls.

Of course, she'd usually been huddled in a corner with a book, watching and praying he wouldn't notice her. And, curiously inconsistent, hoping that he would.

Esther scowled. It wasn't as if she lacked for male attention. After all, Henry Beiler was courting her. He didn't send shivers down her spine or turn her insides to mush, but sparks weren't everything. She and Henry had a relationship like a pair of old floppy slippers, ones that needed to be thrown away.

Mamm had told her that friendships made the best marriages and that love would kum. Esther shrugged, not sure if she and Henry were even friends. The floppy part bothered her. Sometimes it seemed as though the two of them rubbed against each other. It irritated both of them, and they were often miffed at the end of a date.

Esther shook her head. She was taken. So she had nein right to notice Viktor, beyond noticing him as any other member of the Petersheim family.

She opened the door and walked inside but didn't leave enough room for the laundry basket. The sharp edge of the doorframe scratched her already-sore-from-the-washboard knuckles, and she winced. She'd done this often enough that she should've known better.

In the kitchen was Viktor, still working on the leaky pipe beneath the sink. He'd taken everything out from the cabinet, and his head and upper body had disappeared into the small space.

"Could you get me a flashlight, please?"

She jumped, startled by his voice. "Jah, as soon as I deliver the laundry."

He grunted.

Why did some men communicate in grunts? At least Henry didn't. Something to be grateful for. Of course, Henry tended to ramble on about nothing in particular.

Esther entered the first-floor bedroom and put away Reuben's clothes, then Anna's, before carrying her few items upstairs. The puddle of water in the hallway still waited for her. Viktor's bag stood outside his bedroom door. She should probably ask him to gather his soiled laundry for her to wash. Maybe she could set aside a laundry basket for him.

Her face heated at the thought of handling his clothes, smelling his scent....

Ugh! She had to get over this. She dropped her clothes on the bed, not taking the time to put them away, and grabbed a flashlight. She'd give it to him and then check where Anna had gone. She hadn't been in the bedroom or the kitchen.

But then she remembered thinking she'd heard the therapist's car drive in while she was working outside. He usually parked out front, in an area not visible from the clothesline.

A peek in the living room confirmed that Anna was with the therapist. Esther hurried into the kitchen and bent, arm extended. "Here's the flashlight."

"I need you to hold it for me." His face was still buried under the sink, so she couldn't see his dark-chocolate eyes, but that didn't make it any easier being with him. She focused on the way his shirt pulled against his back muscles, and her stomach flipped.

She hesitated. Being on the floor with him, in such close quarters....

"Please?" He sounded frustrated.

Esther inhaled. "Jah." She got to her knees and clicked the flashlight on, then aimed it into the dark cupboard, trying to lean as far away from him as possible.

"Shine it here." Viktor reached over and wrapped his hand around hers. It tingled from his touch, sending goose bumps up her arm. He guided the beam of light where he wanted it.

Esther's hand wobbled when he pulled away. She hated that she missed his touch. What would it feel like when Henry touched her? He'd never held her hand, not even to help her into a buggy. A far cry from her silly schoolgirl dreams about someday being treasured by a man. Still, he talked about getting married in the fall. He planned for her to move into his family's home—a haus already filled with his three married siblings and their families. None of them had moved away. His parents still lived there, too.

She'd already escaped one overcrowded haus. Why would she want to move into another one?

She wasn't even sure she wanted to marry him. But maybe Mamm was right, and love would kum.

"Hold still." Viktor's gruff command put an end to her musings about the future.

"Sorry." Her voice didn't hold any more strength than a whisper.

He didn't respond. She watched him disassemble the pipe, and a stream of dirty water flow into the dishpan he'd placed beneath it. He reached up inside the pipe and dislodged a handful of plastic straws.

Viktor's lips lifted in a wry smile as he held out the straws to her.

She grabbed them, thankful to have a reason to move away from him, and tossed them in the trash can. "Your grossmammi uses—"

"You do the dishes. Be more careful."

So rude. Judgmental. "I don't do all the dishes. Since Anna has therapists, the home-health agency also sends aides."

"Aides?"

She nodded. "They give Anna baths and wash a few dishes. They don't use the dishpan." Esther always watered the garden with the gray water, since the soap helped kill bugs. She started to scoot away, but Viktor reached in her direction.

"I still need the light. Stay here. You do the dishes from now on."

Who did he think he was? Her boss? Der Herr? He had nein right to bark commands.

She couldn't help the irritated sniff that escaped.

One of his eyebrows shot up, but he returned to work, reassembling the pipe.

"Done," he said minutes later. He stood, then bent to retrieve the dishpan, placed it on the counter, and reached for her hand. "What happened?" He removed the flashlight from her suddenly nerveless fingers, set it next to the dishpan, and caught her hand in his. He held it up, studying it.

She shivered from the contact. She'd have to see if Henry would hold her hand on their next buggy ride. Marriage would be more exciting if—

His thumb grazed over her scratched, raw knuckles, paralyzing her thoughts. "What happened?" he repeated.

"Ach, the doorframe has a rough spot. I haven't told Reuben yet."

He dropped her hand. "When I'm home and something goes wrong, tell me. The house is mine. I'll fix it."

"The haus is yours?"

He gave a curt nod.

"But...."

❧

Viktor turned away. His heart raced as he strode to the door and ran his fingers over the edge of the doorframe. He almost relished the sharpness against his fingers, a direct contrast to the softness of Esther's palm. What had possessed him to touch her—not once but twice? Three times, if he counted when she'd run into him upstairs.

Which reminded him that his duffel bag still waited in the hall-way where he'd dropped it.

He would lose his mind being around her for a month. That was for sure.

Viktor couldn't remember experiencing sparks when he touched other girls, but then, it'd been a long time. He didn't frequent bars when the barges docked, and there was only one woman employed on his boat. She was older than he, and widowed. How long had it been since he'd gone to an Amish gathering? Not since—

He wouldn't think of that.

He glanced out the corner of his eye at Esther. She'd knelt to wipe the area under the sink and put away the things he'd removed.

Going to the meetings would be a gut idea. He obviously suffered from a deprivation of female company, and an outing would give him plenty of that. Eliminating these ridiculous feelings would go a long way toward restoring his sanity.

Esther stood, picked up the dishpan, and carefully headed for the door. He stepped out of her way but still breathed in her apple scent. Then he turned his attention back to the door, but concentration eluded him. He should put away the tools from the sink repair. But no, Grossdaedi—and Esther—had mentioned another clogged pipe.

He couldn't handle another close encounter with Esther today. He'd already had too many in the brief time he'd been home. He'd fix the steps instead. Quick, easy, and she wouldn't need to help.

Unless he nailed his finger to the steps. And the way he felt right now, that was a very real possibility.

Viktor frowned. On the other hand, he hadn't hit his finger with a hammer in years. Doing any more damage was plain foolishness. He followed her off the porch, trying not to notice the sway of her walk. But he failed.

His frown deepened as he trailed behind her to the garden. "Uh, Esther? Are there any frolics or other gatherings happening soon?"

She dumped the water on the tomato plants and turned to face him. "Jah. My brother Caleb is getting married to Miriam on Thursday. And there's a singing on Sunday nacht."

Viktor tilted his head. "The beginning of July is an odd time for a wedding."

Esther nodded. "Jah, Miriam was married before, and she's—" Her face colored. "Well, John died a couple of days after their wedding, and their boppli is due any time. The bishop approved a hurry-up wedding with Caleb. They were sweethearts before she married John."

Esther would be at her brother's wedding. He wouldn't be able to escape her there. "Who cares for Grossmammi when you're gone?"

Esther's gaze briefly met his, then lowered, coming to rest somewhere in the vicinity of his shoulder. Her face colored. "Anna wants to go to the wedding. Reuben has already hired a driver, since it'll be easier to get her in a car than a buggy."

"And the singing?"

She glanced up, then quickly looked away. "Reuben encouraged me to go to the youth functions. He said he could manage one or two evenings a week while I'm gone, if I fixed the meals in advance."

Viktor grunted.

She hurried past him, going back inside.

He went to the shed for a hammer and a few nails. Was she seeing someone? Was that why Grossdaedi had said she could go to the singing?

Of course she was. A woman as pretty as she....

Why did the thought bother him?

⌣

Esther grabbed her flashlight, as well as a rag, and headed upstairs to wipe up the water she'd sloshed earlier. She returned the light to her bedside table before returning to the hall, where she made quick work of the mess. Viktor's bag still waited in the doorway, so she picked it up and moved it into his room.

She went back into her own room and put away her clean clothes, then considered the lockless door. Her virtue was safe, for sure. Viktor didn't like her. He probably barely noticed her. But maybe it'd be best if she slept on the couch downstairs while he was home. Or go back to her parents' haus.

Nein, that wouldn't work. She needed to be available for Anna. But she didn't want to spark gossip from malicious tongues. There'd be a lot of girls upset that she'd have constant interaction with Viktor when they didn't.

She could see why they'd be miffed. But with his grunts and curtness, her infatuation would quickly fade. She hoped.

An engine started below her window, and Esther peeked outside. The therapist was leaving. Anna was usually tired after working with a therapist, although she'd already napped earlier today, in expectation of Viktor's homecoming.

Esther hurried downstairs and looked in Anna's bedroom, but she wasn't there. She followed a noise into the kitchen.

Anna sat in front of the open door that led to the porch. Esther peered over her shoulder and saw Viktor prying the old, bent nails out of the loose steps. "Wheel me outside, please." Anna glanced at her. "Sit with me awhile."

Esther dutifully pushed the older woman out on the porch. She locked the brakes of the wheelchair so that Anna wouldn't accidentally roll off.

"I need to get the dumplings on to cook."

"Then you kum right back out here, jah?"

Esther nodded. "I'll be right back." She turned to go inside but hesitated as Viktor lowered the hammer. She couldn't help but admire the ripple of his arm muscles.

He looked up and caught her staring. And winked.

Winked!

Her face flamed. She caught her breath and fled into the safety of the empty haus.

Chapter 4

Viktor glanced at Grossmammi. She looked peaceful sitting in her chair with mending in her lap. Not that she was actually sewing. Instead, her gaze was fixed on him, a dreamy smile on her face. He cringed. It didn't take too much effort to guess what she daydreamed about. She'd undoubtedly seen him wink at Esther, had noticed the quick blush that stained her cheeks a pretty shade of pink, and had done the math.

His stomach clenched. He'd have to find some way to get Esther to quit, and soon, so Grossmammi wouldn't start finding ways to push them together.

A relationship between them was impossible. And unwanted.

Something twisted in his gut. Okay, it wasn't exactly unwanted. A little female diversion during his stay would be pleasant. And Esther was conveniently located right in his home.

He was despicable. How could he even think of something like that?

He balanced a nail and took aim with the hammer, barely moving his fingers out of the way in time. One blow, and the nail lay smoothly embedded in the wood. He picked up another nail and put it in position. Lifted the hammer, and—

"She's seeing Henry Beiler."

Viktor winced. He jerked his throbbing fingers away and looked at them. He'd probably have a black-and-blue thumb.

Henry Beiler. Huh. A thin, scrawny guy. Girly-acting. Unless he'd changed a lot since they'd been in school together.

"That so?" He hoped his voice communicated that he couldn't care less. "Thought those types of things were secret."

Grossmammi shrugged. "Word gets around." She eyed him.

He waited.

"Personally, I don't think they're a gut match."

And there it was—the slight glance from him to the doorway Esther had disappeared through just minutes ago.

"Why not?" He used the claw of the hammer to pull the nail out and made another attempt at pounding it in. Better. But his fingers still throbbed.

He glanced at Grossmammi again. She frowned, her gaze set on something above her. He looked up. A spider spun a web to catch unsuspecting insects. Not unlike the web Grossmammi was carefully spinning to try to catch him.

Wouldn't happen. He didn't care one way or the other whether Esther Beachy and Henry Beiler were a gut match. He made sure the nail was level with the wood.

"I don't know," she continued. "I can't put my finger on it, but it's there."

"Hmm." He shifted to take care of the other end of the step.

"To change the name and not the letter is a change for the worse and not the better." Grossmammi's shoes thumped on the porch as she attempted to roll closer.

Viktor was glad Esther had set the brakes. Even if the action had pulled the fabric of her dress against her curves again. "That so?"

"That's what my mamm always said. Must be true."

He pounded in another nail, careful of his throbbing fingers. "So, you'd recommend her finding someone with a last name beginning with something other than *B*."

"Jah." Grossmammi picked up a sock, shoved the darning egg inside it, and reached for the needle already threaded with black yarn.

"Like maybe a *P*." Oops, he hadn't meant to say that. He shouldn't give her any more fuel. "Or an *M, S,* or *Y*," he quickly added.

Grossmammi smiled as she guided the needle, pulling yarn into the sock. "*P* sounds nice."

He was doomed.

Esther finished putting supper on the table, then slid into her chair and bowed her head for the silent prayer. When it concluded, she shot to her feet again and started ladling the chicken and dumplings into bowls.

Viktor took a sip of freshly brewed iced tea as she filled his bowl. It sloshed when she handed it to him.

She tried to control her shaking fingers. She was a big girl. She could do this. But she couldn't remember any meal she'd ever eaten around Viktor. It shouldn't be any different from eating with Henry. But it was. Somehow.

After everyone had been served, she sat once more and lifted her spoon.

Reuben glanced at Viktor. "Gut to have you home for a while."

Viktor nodded. His gaze skittered to Anna, then back to his grossdaedi. "I was thinking, maybe Grossmammi wouldn't mind a temporary, moveable ramp so she could get outside and see her garden."

Building a ramp was a gut idea. Esther wanted to back up Viktor's suggestion. It would make it easier to get Anna out of the haus for doctor's appointments, frolics, and other gatherings.

Anna shifted, the wheelchair rolling forward. "Not my garden anymore. It's Esther's. But—"

"Nein." Reuben's spoon clattered against the edge of his bowl.

Viktor pressed his lips together. Hurt shone in his eyes.

Esther sympathized. She was always getting rebuked at home.

An undefined emotion flickered in his gaze, and he frowned down at his bowl, swirling his spoon in his dinner. Then he took a bite. His glance jumped to Esther. She squirmed as his brown eyes stared into hers.

Would he find fault with her cooking? She clenched her spoon so tight, her fingernails dug into her palm.

A look of something akin to pleasure crossed his face. He liked it. Esther dared relax.

The rest of dinner was eaten in a strained silence. It seemed Reuben's harsh answer to his gross-sohn had drained all need for fellowship right out of the atmosphere, leaving only tension in its wake.

Esther peeked across the table at Viktor, uncomfortably aware of his presence. When his eyes caught hers again, her face warmed. She quickly looked away, but she couldn't resist glancing back a few moments later. How would she survive four weeks of this?

She finished her meal, then stood and started clearing dishes from the table. At least one awkward meal was out of the way. She filled the dishpan full of water as Reuben wheeled Anna into the living room.

"Gut meal." Viktor moved behind her. "You're a gut cook."

Esther shot a surprised glance at him.

"We eat like kings on the river, but they don't give us country fare."

Country fare? What did that mean, exactly? She opened her mouth to ask, then shut it, astonished that he could communicate in more than just grunts and without bossing. She stared at him, speechless.

A smile lifted one corner of his mouth. "Gut job." He turned away and headed for the door.

"Wait." Esther followed him. "Your idea for a temporary ramp—"

The smile faded. A muscle jumped in his jaw. "Grossdaedi said nein."

The screen door slammed behind him.

⌒

Viktor's shoulders slumped. Grossdaedi had already headed inside after finishing up the evening chores, but Viktor stayed, sharpening the ax for tomorrow. It hadn't taken long for him to get back into the groove on the farm. The hardest adjustment, as usual, was having Grossdaedi tell him what needed to be done, as if he were an eight-year-old bu.

Sharp pain knifed through him. His eyes burned.

Nein. He should be over it by now.

Or at least adjusted.

The ax passed inspection when he ran his thumb lightly over the edge. The thin cut wasn't deep enough to draw blood, but it stung. He relished the pain.

Viktor extinguished the lantern and closed up the barn, but instead of heading for the haus, he turned toward the man-made pond Grossdaedi and Daed had dug. Deep and long enough to swim laps in, with some parts even deeper, so that Viktor and his brothers could swing from a rope and jump in. And they kept it stocked with fish.

He sat on a boulder at the water's edge and removed his shoes. Wouldn't the community be shocked if they knew he went skinny-dipping every time he came home? He longed to get fully wet and wash the sweat and dirt away. He loved swimming.

He pulled off his shirt and tossed it on the boulder. Then he unhooked his belt buckle, unzipped his jeans, and started to slide them down.

A rock skittered behind him, followed by a weird choking noise. A dim light made a circle on the ground to his left.

He yanked his jeans up and closed the zipper as he turned.

The dark form behind the flashlight started backing away. "I didn't know you were out here." A hint of embarrassment colored Esther's voice.

"Needed to be alone." Maybe she'd go away. Though the embarrassment in her voice made him smile. It'd be nice if she stayed.

"I'm sorry." The dying light retreated further.

"Nein, Esther. Don't...don't go." Viktor hooked his belt. "Grossmammi is settled?" He studied the fading beam. "Need to replace the batteries."

"Jah." She flicked the flashlight off.

"You kum out here often?" He needed to know if she would invade his sanctuary every nacht. He stepped off the boulder into the water, only ankle deep at the edge. He'd have to swim in waterlogged denim. Somewhere in the darkness a bullfrog croaked, followed by a splash. A lightning bug blinked. Then another.

"Only when I'm stressed. I don't stay long." She sounded a bit defensive. "You didn't join your großeltern for the Bible reading."

"They'd be surprised if I did."

"Ach."

"What are you stressed about? Anything I can do to help fix it?"

A chorus of frogs began, backed up by a group of katydids.

Her silence spoke volumes. He smiled.

"Tell me about you. Why Henry Beiler?" Hopefully she wouldn't sense the derision in his voice.

She gave the whisper of a sigh. "Henry's mamm and mine are best friends. They've been planning our marriage since we were kinner." She turned the flashlight on again. "I'd best be getting back. Sorry again for intruding."

"You can stay."

The light flickered and died.

Viktor looked up at the star-studded sky. "I'll walk you back after I swim."

"Okay."

He imagined her face flaming red, and chuckled. "I'll keep my clothes on." Except for his shirt. "You'll see better after your eyes adjust to the darkness."

The water splashed as Esther apparently dipped her feet in, sending little waves in all directions. "Do you do this all the time when you're home?"

"Jah." Viktor shrugged. "Trying to decide whether you should keep your distance from now on?" He waded out until the water reached his chest.

"I should."

Jah, she should. For more reasons than one. He ticked them off in his head: out in the darkness with a man who wasn't her intended. A man with a reputation. One who'd jumped the fence. And who suffered from a severe lack of feminine attention.

He sucked in an unsteady breath and dived under the water.

Chapter 5

Esther sat on the boulder. Her hand brushed against something made of soft fabric, and she picked it up. Ach, Viktor's T-shirt. She lifted the cotton garment to her chest and hugged it close, inhaling his piney scent. Somewhere in the darkness ahead of her, he swam laps. She closed her eyes and leaned back, listening to the nacht sounds, as well as the occasional splash and intake of air as he surfaced.

She hadn't anticipated the low beam of her flashlight revealing the ripple of his muscles after he'd removed his shirt. She shouldn't have seen him like that. So different from her brothers when they removed their shirts, especially her boppli brother when she helped give him a bath. She never should've noticed the way his chest tapered down to his waist and narrow hips....

Esther pulled in a shuddering breath.

She hadn't been prepared for Viktor talking in more than just grunts, either. Hopefully, this wordier version of him would remain. Or maybe it'd be better if it didn't. She might not get over her infatuation if she got to know him. And she *had* to get over it. Otherwise, she'd always wonder what it'd be like if she'd married someone other than Henry. Someone like Viktor.

Water splattered on her face. She opened her eyes and sat up. Her eyes had adjusted enough for her to see him shake his head again, more droplets flying from his hair, as he approached. She tried not to focus on his bare chest or the movement of his muscles as he wrung out the legs of his jeans. With a chuckle, he took his T-shirt from her grasp, close to her heart, and pulled it over his head.

"Ready?" He extended his hand.

She scrambled up without help and dropped her flashlight into her apron pocket.

His hand settled on her elbow as she stepped off the boulder. She shivered from the contact.

He fell into step beside her, his hand dropping away. "You said one of your brothers is getting married on Thursday. Any of your other brothers or sisters married?"

"Jah, Aaron and Benjamin both. Benjamin and Abigail are living with my parents until they get their haus finished, maybe another month. Daed gave them a corner of the land. Caleb and Miriam will be moving in for a while, too." She drew in a breath. Viktor probably wanted to know about her sister Dorcas, since she was his age. "Dorcas's intended was killed in an accident."

Viktor made a sympathetic sound.

"Eight months ago." In case he wondered how long it'd been.

"How many younger siblings do you have?"

Maybe he wasn't interested in Dorcas. Otherwise, he would've had more questions about her. "Six. Kenan is nine months old."

"Eleven of you still at home, plus a frau, your parents, and großeltern? Sixteen people." He shook his head as if trying to imagine it.

Wow, he was still quick at math. He'd always beat the other students in competitions. Everyone knew he'd been at the top of the class, though the teachers had never broadcasted it. Might've led to pride. "Jah, sixteen people in a four-bedroom haus." She stumbled, and his hand grasped her elbow. She struggled to find her train of thought. "Ben and Abbie have the buwe's old bedroom, and Caleb and Miriam will be taking the girls' room after they finish their wedding visits, unless Ben has moved out by then. My brothers sleep in the living room now. Daed's talking about raising the roof and adding another floor."

"That's why you agreed to be a mother's helper." He moved his hand away.

She squirmed, hating how selfish it made her sound—that she was willing to do anything to escape the overcrowding of her home. But that was pretty much the truth. It was also the reason she wasn't in a big hurry to marry, especially if it would mean moving into an equally crowded home.

They slowed as they reached the haus.

"Grossmammi and Grossdaedi have had nothing but gut things to say about you." Viktor reached for the knob and pulled the door open. "After you."

"Danki." Esther stepped into the darkness and headed for the kitchen drawer where the batteries were stored. Behind her, a lantern flickered to life. She tossed the old batteries into the trash and dropped two new ones in the flashlight, then screwed the top back on. "Gut nacht." She turned toward him and stumbled, surprised to find him so near.

His gaze roamed over her face. "Gut talking with you. Sweet dreams." His hand made a move toward her, stopping mere centimeters from touching her cheek. Then he pulled back with a jerk and disappeared into the darkness. A board creaked as he went upstairs.

Esther waited until she heard his bedroom door shut before going to her room. Wet spots were scattered all the way up the stairs where he'd dripped. They'd be dry by morgen. She gathered her things and slipped back downstairs to sleep on the couch.

Hopefully she *would* sleep, not stay awake reliving his near-touch. Replaying their conversation in her mind. And reviewing the vision of his bare chest while they were alone in the darkness by the pond.

Viktor gave up on sleep long before the rooster crowed. He unpacked his things, made his bed, then decided to get an early start on the chores. He entered the living room as the bird sounded its alarm. On the couch, a figure sat up, wearing a long white nightgown. His steps slowed. *Esther.* Her brown hair was in a long braid down her back. What was she doing in here? Maybe she needed to sleep close by his großeltern, in case Grossmammi needed her.

As he watched, Esther rubbed her eyes and stretched. Then she stood, her nightgown swirling around her ankles, and took a step before her eyes met his. Color flooded her cheeks as she grabbed the quilt and wrapped it around her already-modest figure.

Wow. She looked wunderbaar in a just-woken-up state. His heart rate increased. He wanted to run his fingers the length of her long braid, feeling its thickness and softness. Maybe touch her cheek, as he'd nearly done last nacht. But nein. He averted his gaze. Something he should've done earlier. "Gut morgen." He nodded and slipped past her, going outside to begin the chores before breakfast.

Grossdaedi came into the cow stall a few minutes after Viktor. "You've got an early start."

Viktor shrugged. He never slept well his first nacht at home. Sometimes not the second one, either. The nightmares always found him. He should've adjusted by now. Should've moved on. Maybe someday, after his großeltern died and he sold the farm, he'd be able to forget....

Though last nacht, the nightmares had been tempered by pleasant thoughts of Esther. Strange how that woman had gotten under his skin.

He settled down by the first cow as Grossdaedi grabbed another three-legged stool and a bucket. Grossmammi used to make butter, cottage cheese, yogurt, cheese, buttermilk, and more with the excess milk. Probably was Esther's job now. A family of three used only so much....

She'd moved from an overcrowded home, where she probably had plenty of help, to a home where she had to do it all. Hardly seemed like a fair trade. Unless he took into account the priceless value of having a space of her own—like his pond escape. His earlier resentment about having her in his home had faded almost entirely.

"How much are you paying Esther Beachy?" he asked.

Grossdaedi's head lowered to rest against the cow's flank. "Not enough. Don't get it in your head to fire her. That girl works for nothing. And your grossmammi would be lost without her."

"Nothing?" Viktor frowned at the stream of milk pinging into the pail. He nudged a barn cat out of the way with his foot when it wandered too close.

"Her daed collects her earnings every week to help support the family. She never sees a dime of it."

A somewhat normal arrangement. As a teenager, Viktor had given his paychecks to Daed. But instead of using the money to support the family, Daed had saved the earnings toward Viktor's eventual purchase of a farm.

"What about her personal needs?"

"Dunno. Never asked. I suppose she asks Hosea for what she wants—or goes without."

That wasn't right. Should he give a little extra money to Grossdaedi to give directly to Esther? Or would she take it from Viktor, since he was Englisch? He was the one who paid for her services anyway—he sent money home to Grossdaedi for bills and everything else. Maybe he could find a way to smuggle her money if she refused.

Viktor finished milking that cow and started another. Grossdaedi moved to take care of the last one. When they were done, Viktor let the cows out to graze, then carried the buckets of fresh milk to the haus. Esther was finishing up breakfast. He inhaled the aromas of sausage, eggs, toast, and coffee.

"Gut morgen." Grossmammi rolled into the kitchen.

He set the bucket on the floor to take off his shoes, then carried the milk across the room and set it on the counter. A basket of eggs already waited there. Grossdaedi came in as Viktor leaned over to kiss Grossmammi's cheek. "Morgen."

She wrapped her arms around his neck and squeezed. "I wish you'd stay home for gut."

Not happening. He forced a smile and stepped back. His gaze went to Esther. A girl like her waiting for him would make it tempting, though.

Esther carried the plates of food to the table. His stomach rumbled.

Viktor went to the sink, washed up, then sat at his place. "Looking gut, Esther." He let his gaze skim over her. Maybe his großeltern would assume he was referring to the meal.

Color flooded her face. She dipped her head. At least she'd caught the double meaning. He smiled and bowed his head for the silent prayer.

It was his usual plea: *Why, God?* He blinked against the sudden burning in his eyes. Nein wonder he skipped prayers on the river. He wouldn't do it at home if it wasn't part of the expected routine. He might get away with missing the Bible readings, but refusing to bow his head for silent prayers would be cause for a lecture.

He set his lips against the pain in his chest and raised his head. When Grossdaedi's head came up, Viktor reached for the jar of strawberry jam and spread it liberally on his toast, then took a big bite. Nothing beat homemade bread and jam. Homemade by Esther, because Grossmammi couldn't have made them.

Nothing would beat the farm-fresh eggs, or the sausage from one of the hogs, either.

The heaviness in his chest increased. The bite of food turned into a lump in his stomach. Just like usual.

He pushed his plate away, bowed his head again for a quick, fake after-breakfast prayer, then stood. "Not hungry. Going to take care of the woodpile, Grossdaedi."

Viktor slid his feet into his shoes and went outside, letting the screen door slam behind him.

Tomorrow would be better. It had to be.

Esther watched him go, then looked back at his plate of untouched food. Well, he'd taken one bite of toast. That hardly counted. Her bread wasn't bad enough to ruin his appetite, was it? Or had she done something wrong with the butter? He'd complimented her on her cooking last nacht.

"This is normal." Anna seemed to read her thoughts. "He does this the first full day he's home, every time. He'll skip lunch and pick at supper. Doesn't sleep well the first nacht, either. He'll probably be a bear when his hunger and fatigue catch up with him."

"Don't gossip," Reuben admonished her. "It's wrong to talk about someone when he's not able to defend himself." He reached for the sugar and added a spoonful to his koffee.

"It's not gossip when it's necessary information," Anna countered. "Esther doesn't know. It's not like I'm telling her about his—"

"Anna." The warning in Reuben's voice deepened.

"Jah." Anna nodded. "Put his food in the hog bucket." She turned her attention back to her breakfast.

Esther did, as well. When she finished eating, she made quick work of cleaning the kitchen. It seemed wrong to scrape a plate of perfectly fine, untouched food into the designated pail, though. *Waste not, want not,* Mamm always said. But maybe that came from struggling to feed so many mouths on Daed's income. At least Esther's wages helped her family, in addition to giving her some much-needed elbow room.

The Petersheims seemed wealthy compared to her family. Case in point, their ability to waste perfectly gut food. But she did as told. When she finished, she carried the slop bucket outside to dump in the trough.

Viktor stood next to the woodpile, the branches and logs from fallen trees strewn about where they'd landed when Esther and Reuben had tossed them out of the wagon after the bad spring storms had gone through. Reuben had sawed the pieces into big chunks, way too big for the woodstove but easier to handle than a fallen tree for one old man and a girl. And there the wood had lain. Waiting for Viktor.

A lot around this farm waited for him. Didn't he realize that? Or didn't it matter?

Anger seemed to radiate from him as he stood a log on end, raised the ax over his head, and brought it down in a quick motion. A muscle jumped in his jaw. The log slit down the middle, and both sides fell. He grabbed one of the halves and stood it on end, then halved it in one rapid movement.

Esther slowed to a stop, fascinated by the play of his muscles as he worked. By the tight, furious moves of his body. What was he so upset about?

With a hard shake of her head, she forced herself to look away and continued to the pigpens. She emptied the bucket into the trough and then turned toward the haus, not allowing herself to look his way again.

This happens every time he comes home, she reminded herself. He must dread his return if he went through this much trauma every time. Was it the "being Amish" part that bothered him? Or were painful memories to blame? Where were his parents and brothers, anyway?

But it also meant the chances of his returning to the Amish weighed heavy on the so-not-happening side, to quote an Englisch friend.

Lily and the other single girls needed to forget their foolish dreams about Viktor Petersheim.

Esther needed to forget him.

A loud crack pulled her attention back to him. He raised the ax over his head again, arm muscles rippling.

Forget Viktor?

She pulled in a shaky breath and hurried toward the haus. A task easier said than done.

He was unforgettable.

Chapter 6

Viktor spent the morning working on the woodpile, trying not to remember the summer he was eight and tried to "help" Daed with the same job.

He barely looked up when Esther rang the dinner bell at noon. He wasn't hungry, anyway. And since nobody came to talk him into taking a break, he figured Grossmammi had spilled his secrets to Esther. His stomach twisted in knots, the same memories that haunted his sleep making him dizzy. But if he kept working without fuel, he'd be able to sleep. His penance.

By the time Grossdaedi came back outside after lunch, Viktor had finished splitting all the wood. Grossdaedi joined him in the task of stacking it neatly, kindling at one end, bigger logs at the other. The same way it had always been done, even when he was a small bu working alongside Daed. Using the same ax Daed had when....

Grossdaedi straightened slowly, his hand on his back. "Danki. Talked to your grossmammi. She feels that your idea for a temporary ramp is a gut thing. You'll make one, then, jah?"

"I need to check the fence lines today. Apparently you had some bad storms." Viktor nodded toward the woods. "If I get done in time, I'll see what materials you have and what I'll need to make one. Otherwise, I'll do it tomorrow." He relaxed as a feeling that could have almost been joy filled him. Grossmammi would be so much happier being able to get out of the haus.

"You're a gut bu, Viktor." Grossdaedi turned away. "Don't forget that leaky pipe in the bathroom, and the broken washing machine. I'm going to clean the stalls, unless you finished that."

"Nein." Viktor frowned at the ax, remembering Esther's scraped knuckles. They looked sore. He should fix the door, too, but.... He looked out at the pastures. They had to be top priority. The tornadoes that had gone through while he was gone might've damaged the fence, and he'd be liable if any of the animals got out on the road and caused an accident.

He'd check the washing machine when he finished, if it wasn't too late.

The fence was in bad shape. One portion was completely down, but since all the cows were present and accounted for, along with the few calves Grossdaedi had told him about, he didn't think they'd discovered the breach.

By the time the lines were checked and fixed, the cows were lining up to be milked. Viktor went in the barn to begin the task. Grossmammi always told him that "idle hands were the devil's playground." Nein danger of that now. When he was younger, he'd apparently had too many minutes free, though he hadn't thought so at the time.

Hearing a scuffling noise, he raised his head from a cow's flank and looked over his shoulder. Grossdaedi stood on the top step leading down into the cow barn. He nodded at Viktor, then backed out and left.

He must've been checking up on him. Viktor was glad he could do these small jobs to help Grossdaedi. He seemed to be moving slower these days.

When Viktor finished the chores, the sun was sinking below the horizon. He hurried inside the haus long enough to grab his swimming trunks. On his way outside again, he heard muted conversation between Esther and Grossmammi behind the closed door to the room shared by his großeltern. At the pond, he glanced around to make sure the coast was clear, then went behind a bush and shucked his clothes, then put on his swimming trunks...just in case.

He hoped Esther showed up. It'd seemed less lonely with her waiting on the bank yesterday evening.

Odd how her presence made his adjustment to being home happen a little quicker than usual.

Esther finished getting Anna into bed, then left the room so that Reuben could do his nightly preparations. She didn't want to go to sleep on the couch with Viktor still awake. It might be cause for gossip if anyone discovered he was in the same room while she slept.

He shouldn't have seen her this morgen, wearing only her night-gown, with her braided hair down. Hopefully, nobody would find out. From now on, she'd be more careful to get up before he did.

She hadn't seen him since that afternoon. She'd offered several times to go out and check on him, to insist that he eat something or drink some water. But whenever she'd suggested it to Anna, the older woman had said he needed to be alone. "*He's fine. Let him be.*"

Esther peeked out the window, looking for his black pickup truck. Maybe he'd left. *Nein.* It sat in the shadows of the barn. He was here. Somewhere. She glanced at the star-studded sky.

Probably at the pond.

She wasn't stressed to the point of needing the sanctuary today, but still, it was tempting to walk out and join him—to spend time in his company, maybe to talk with him on the walk home.

She'd intruded yesterday.

But he'd asked her to stay.

She hesitated as she stared out the window, listening to the quiet conversation between Anna and Reuben in the bedroom. She wouldn't be needed.

On the other hand, if word got out about her indiscretion—sneaking out to be with a man other than Henry....

Who would know? Other than the gut Lord, of course. And she didn't think He cared. After all, Viktor needed someone to reach out to him. His großeltern wanted him to kum back into the fold.

Not that he would.

Maybe it'd be okay, so long as it didn't draw her away.

She shrugged. That wouldn't happen. She had nein interest in traveling up and down a river on a barge, though her cousin Rachel did. "*So romantic,*" she'd said when they'd talked of Viktor's return during a singing last Sunday nacht. *"Able to go to all those different areas and see the country."*

Even though she was being courted by someone else, Rachel would probably spend time with Viktor whenever he joined the community gatherings. She'd love to hear his stories.

Kum right down to it, Esther wanted to hear them, too. But she didn't want to be one of the many girls flocking around him.

Esther should keep her distance.

Would.

Tomorrow.

She went to find her flip-flops and slipped out the door without her flashlight, taking a few minutes to let her eyes adjust to the moonlight before she started on her way.

She could hear the splash of the water. The croaking of the bullfrogs. The answering calls of the nacht birds and bugs. She could see the tiny flashes of fireflies.

She must've made a noise, because Viktor stopped swimming and stood chest-deep in the water. Her pulse jumped, her stomach clenching, as he waded toward her.

"You came."

It wasn't a question, but she nodded. "I…if it's okay."

"Fine. Stressed?"

"Nein." Other than her concern over his going all day without eating or drinking anything. Not to mention the angry energy with which he'd attacked the woodpile….

"Missed me, jah?"

More than she'd ever admit.

"Different going swimming at nacht from during the day." Viktor came closer.

She tried to avoid looking at his bare chest. She lowered her eyes, then dared to peek through her lashes as he held out his hand.

"Kum on in. Water's fine." He smirked.

He must know she was attracted to him. Esther drew away. "Ach, nein. I don't swim."

He dropped his hand to his side. Shrugged. "I could teach you, ain't so? Though"—he glanced down at her outfit—"it might be easier if you didn't have those skirts tangling around your legs."

Her face heated. Was he suggesting she strip down to almost nothing, as he had? Her gaze slid over him. Just a brightly colored pair of shorts, like the Englischers wore. She dipped her head again. "Nein."

She sensed his shrug more than saw it. "Suit yourself." He turned back the way he'd kum. A moment later, a splash.

The cold water would feel gut. Even now, after dark, the air temperature was still hot. Humid.

At least Viktor didn't seem angry now. He was the friendly person she'd been with last nacht. The talkative one. It was as if he had two different personalities. The curt, cold, judgmental, angry daytime version, and the warmer, friendlier, talkative nacht-time one.

She slipped off her flip-flops, held up her skirts a bit, and waded in.

The water did feel gut. She was almost tempted to sit down in it. But then she'd drip all the way back to the Petersheims' farmhaus. And all over the floor as she went upstairs to her room.

Esther returned to the boulder she'd sat on last nacht and picked up Viktor's T-shirt, catching a whiff of his pine scent. She pulled it to her chest, the closest he would ever kum to being in her arms. Then, reluctantly, she released it, folded it into a pillow, and lay back upon it, staring up at the stars. She tried to ignore the rhythmic splashing and memories of Viktor's bare chest. But that was impossible. *Ach, Lord. Why do I have to be so attracted to him?*

Sometime later, he joined her, his hand brushing against her arm as he sat. "Pretty, ain't so?"

"Jah. See that big bright star beside the moon?"

"Jupiter. It's a planet. And there's the Big Dipper." He pointed off to the side.

"Jah." She sat up and handed him his shirt.

He tugged it on. "I love it out here." His voice was only a shade louder than a whisper.

"Is that why you went to work on the river?" she asked. "So you could be outside?"

⌒

It was an invasive question. One he wasn't prepared to answer honestly.

Though, really, she should know the reasons behind his decision to leave. He was sure he'd been the topic of gossip that whole summer. In fact, he knew it. He'd seen the looks on people's faces after...after....

Viktor pulled in a deep, pain-filled breath. He looked away. "When I first started working on the river, I was outside all the time. Lot of hard, heavy work. Nowadays, I'm inside more. There's a little room on the top of a riverboat, called the wheelhouse. It's where all the controls are." Hopefully, his voice didn't wobble. Didn't reveal anything.

"Controls?" Confusion colored her voice.

"Instruments. Um, kind of like computers." He chuckled. "There's nothing to compare it to here. But it helps the boat navigate the river, day or nacht."

"My cousin Rachel uses a computer at the shop where she works."

"Not exactly the same thing." He glanced at her. How would she react if he slipped his arm around her waist and slid closer?

Nein. He wouldn't try it. Amazing how he'd changed from the adolescent he'd been when he'd left. He wouldn't have thought twice about it as a teenager.

Gut thing she couldn't read his mind. Couldn't know the temptation he struggled with.

"I saw a riverboat once, when I took the bus out to Pennsylvania with Lily." Esther turned to face him. "It was pulling these long, flat vessels."

"Barges." He looked away. Distancing himself.

"I always wondered why you left that summer."

He blinked. How could she not know?

"Lily and I were sixteen when Daed gave me permission to go to Pennsylvania to help Lily's sister for a while. She was having a boppli. We were gone maybe six months. When we came back, you'd jumped the fence."

And nobody had told her what happened?

Either she suffered from a deplorable lack of curiosity or another disaster had hit, taking the attention off him. Off his misdeeds. Off the horrible truth.

His chest tightened, closing down his airway. He pushed himself to his feet. "Best be getting back." He hated the brusqueness he heard in his voice, but he wasn't going to discuss that time. It was none of her business.

He picked up his jeans and shoved his feet into his shoes. "Kum."

Esther stood and moved to walk with him. "I think Lily will probably be staying out there. She misses her sister, and she has more cousins living in Pennsylvania than here."

"Jah." Lily was a safe conversation. "She likely has a young man there, too."

"I think so. She came back last year, talking about someone named Peter."

"There you go."

"Lily also talks about you."

There was a bit of coyness or something similar in her voice. He darted a quick glance her way. Shrugged. "I barely remember her." Mostly true. He remembered the redhead with freckles who followed him around. But he couldn't recall anything that stood out about her. She was just one more girl, like all the others. "But it sounds like you'll miss her."

It was Esther's turn to shrug. "Jah, some. She's my cousin, and we're friends. She got me in trouble sometimes when she pushed the boundaries. But I have other cousins. I'm closer friends with Rachel and Greta than with Lily. It's just that Lily did more exciting things. Rachel and Greta never went anywhere. Though Rachel wants to. She thinks your job is 'sooo romantic.'"

Viktor choked on his breath. Then a laugh roared out.

Beside him, Esther stopped and stared.

He wiped his watering eyes and gradually got his emotions under control. "Believe me, my job is hardly romantic." Sometimes, it was downright boring. Then there was the backbreaking work as they went over the same stretch of river, again and again. Kind of like milking the same cow, plowing the same field, or chopping wood to rebuild the same stack, over and over again.

"But you get to see all the places that Tom Sawyer and Huckleberry Finn saw. And cruise the river by moonlight."

Another laugh threatened to escape.

"You do know that Tom Sawyer and Huckleberry Finn are fictional characters, ain't so?"

"They are?" There was a touch of sarcasm in her voice.

He laughed again. "Esther Beachy, I think I like you."

Chapter 7

Just remembering his words from last nacht made Esther feel warm and tingly.

Jah, and she liked Viktor in return. Too much.

Esther still smiled as she fixed breakfast. All those rumors about Viktor sneaking back behind the barn with girls must've been just that. Falsehoods. Not once had he tried anything inappropriate with her. He was the perfect gentleman.

Even Lily had whispered tales about herself and Viktor behind the barn. Yet he'd said he barely remembered her. How could he possibly forget a girl if they'd kissed the way Lily had described? Esther certainly wouldn't forget anything like that.

An inexplicable desire to see Henry arose. Her brother's wedding was just a day away. Henry would be sure to claim her for the singing following and to take her home afterward. Maybe he'd be willing to hold her hand. Or when they were alone on the way home, perhaps he'd kiss her. She'd be happy just holding his hand, to see if she felt the same sparks with him as she did with Viktor.

Of course, if she didn't…. Her heart deflated.

She wouldn't go there.

She put the casserole dish of baked oatmeal with bits of banana on the back of the stove, then rang the dinner bell before heading to the first-floor bedroom. Anna had wanted to stay in bed a little longer this morgen, claiming she had a headache and felt a bit dizzy.

Esther opened the bedroom door a crack and found Anna sitting on the edge of the bed, fully dressed, except for her shoes and kapp.

"I was just going to call for you," she told Esther. "I feel a little better now."

"Ach, gut. Dizziness all gone?"

"Mostly." Anna extended her leg, and Esther crouched down to put on her sock and shoe. "The headache is worse, but maybe it's because I stayed in bed."

"I'll give you something for it." Esther tied the first shoe, then reached for the other.

"Whatever you fixed for breakfast smells wunderbaar. Like oatmeal cookies."

"It'll taste a bit like that, too. I made baked oatmeal."

Esther helped Anna into the wheelchair, then reached for her hair comb.

"Did I ever tell you about the first time I made oatmeal cookies for Reuben? We were courting, and I wanted to surprise him with cookies when we met under the old covered bridge. That was our special place. We spent hours under there, talking and dreaming. I was so proud when I presented him with those cookies." Anna sighed. "'Pride goeth before destruction, and an haughty spirit before a fall.' The Bible says that. And I sure was prideful. Reuben loved oatmeal cookies. He reached for one and took a big bite. Then the strangest expression crossed his face."

"And…?" Esther ran the comb through Anna's thinning hair, then started twisting it up the way the Ordnung required.

Anna shook her head. "I added too much salt. I'd gotten interrupted while I was mixing the dough, and I couldn't remember if I'd added salt or not. So, I measured another teaspoon and put it in. And then I got called away again, and my sister asked where I was with the recipe, and I told her I was on the salt. She added a teaspoon, too. Poor Reuben. He swallowed that bite. Truly a man in love." She grinned. "I miss that covered bridge. There used to be an old rope swing under it, and sometimes the buwe would jump from it into the river."

"Is the bridge around here? Maybe Reuben could take you on a drive."

"Ach, nein. It's in Pennsylvania. Where we used to live."

"Wunderbaar memories." Esther secured the kapp just as male voices filled the kitchen. "Sounds as if Reuben and Viktor are here. Ready?"

Anna put her hand on Esther's. "You are such a schatz. Ich liebe dich."

Esther bent to kiss Anna's cheek. "Ich liebe dich, too."

Anna's hand tightened. "Do you and your Henry have a special place?"

"Nein." Esther sighed. The only special place in her life was the pond....

And she spent time there with Viktor.

Not Henry.

"Ach, you need a special place. You need to talk with your Henry. Make plans. Dream."

It'd be a waste of time. His plans were all made. And she, being a mere woman, was expected to submit without question. She wheeled the chair into the kitchen with a little more speed than usual and parked it at the table before bringing over the food. Agitation washed over her. She should have the right to some opinion. But even at home, she was expected to obey nein matter what. And Henry expected the same. Her opinion carried nein weight.

As Viktor sat at the table, something stirred in her chest. It was so gut to see him there. *Lord, help him eat something.* He looked better rested, too, as if maybe he'd slept last nacht.

He bowed his head as Esther slid into her chair.

After the silent prayer, his dark gaze met hers.

Her heart pounded.

"I'll take a look at the washing machine after breakfast."

⌒

Viktor decided he could get used to Esther's cooking. What were the chances of talking her into giving up her Amish life and going to work as a chef on a riverboat? She'd have private sleeping quarters and everything.

If she were on his boat, they could spend a lot of time together.

Silly thoughts.

She'd be as likely to work on the river as he'd be to return to the Amish.

Viktor bowed his head for the prayer as soon as he finished his breakfast. Esther already stood by the sink, running water into the dishpan. He stood and walked over to her, then put one hand on either side of her against the sink, boxing her in.

The sudden silence at the table behind him was deafening, but he didn't glance at his großeltern. Nein need. They watched. Probably to make sure he behaved himself.

Esther caught her breath.

He leaned close, his mouth close to her ear. "Getting my toolbox. Meet me in the washroom."

She shivered.

Viktor fought a grin as he moved away, put on his shoes, and headed out to the shed.

Grossdaedi entered behind him.

Viktor tensed. Would he have something to say about his not-so-private whispers to Esther? His boldness?

"Going to town to get supplies. Did you figure what you need for the ramp?" Grossdaedi clamped a hand on Viktor's shoulder.

Viktor reached in his pocket for his smart phone. "Jah. Did it when I got up this morgen. It's all right on here." He held out the electronic device. "Take it. All you need to do is—"

Grossdaedi shied away as if it were a poisonous snake. "Can you put it on paper?"

Viktor restrained a grin and opened the toolbox for the carpenter's pencil and notepad Grossdaedi always kept there. He wrote down the measurements and the necessary supplies, then ripped out the page.

Grossdaedi took it. "Danki. Anything else you need while I'm in town?"

Viktor pursed his lips. *A half dozen long-stemmed roses, a box of chocolates....*

Maybe a verboden Englisch women's swimming suit so he could teach Esther how to swim.

Ach, the thought of that.... His blood heated.

His breath was ragged. "Nein. Danki."

Grossdaedi went to hitch up the horse, Anchor, to the buggy. Viktor slammed the lid of the portable toolbox, picked it up, and carried it to the haus. The kitchen was empty, but he could hear Esther and Grossmammi talking in a back room. He went into the small room off the kitchen where the wringer washer and two washtubs were set up.

A scrub board stood on its end in one of the tubs. He ran his fingertips over the rough metal. Nein wonder Esther's knuckles were so raw. Of course, that sharp doorjamb had contributed, as well.

The door to the room opened, and Esther slipped in, letting it swing shut behind her.

He tried to ignore his increased heart rate as he glanced up at her. "What's the problem with it?"

"The...I don't know. It just doesn't work."

He chuckled. "You're nein help."

"Seriously. It let out a puff of black smoke and quit."

Ach. That was more help. Gave him an idea where to start.

He wanted to ask her if she would be at the pond again that nacht. But maybe it'd be better if he didn't know. To keep their meetings unplanned. Just in case word got out.

He pulled in a breath. "Where can I find you if I need you?"

"The kitchen. I have baking to do."

Viktor nodded. The door swooshed shut behind her.

When Esther had finished the baking, she cleaned the kitchen, then headed outside to work in the garden. After emptying the dishpan, she leaned it up against a tree and went to the shed for a hoe to dig up potatoes.

Soon she was unearthing new potatoes and setting them in the empty dishpan.

"It's working."

She jumped, not having heard Viktor kum up behind her. She turned around. "You fixed it?"

He nodded. "Mostly. There are some problems with the engine. I need to tinker with that some more. It's running a little rough. Otherwise, it was a broken belt. There was a spare in the toolbox. I also fixed the doorjamb. You shouldn't scrape yourself anymore. Do you have time to hold a flashlight for me so I can fix the bathroom sink?"

"Let me finish gathering the potatoes, and I'll be right there."

His smile was tight. "You have dirt on your cheek."

Figured. She raised her fingers to brush it away, but they were covered in dirt, too.

"I'd help, but…." Viktor raised his hands. They were covered with something black.

Her face heated. It would've been rather inappropriate for him to touch her face, anyway. But the thought of it….

He winked and turned away. She watched him go, then went back to the potatoes.

The squeaking of the pump being primed drew her attention. He was drawing water from the well. Probably to wash his hands. Maybe he'd wipe the dirt from her cheek, after all.

Her breath hitched.

She forced her attention back to the uninteresting potatoes.

And had a series of dangerous but infinitely more interesting daydreams about being married to Viktor…having this to look forward to the rest of her life.

A shiver worked through her.

Chapter 8

Viktor set his toolbox on the bathroom floor, then moved the contents from the cabinet under the sink to the floor. Someone—either Esther or Grossdaedi—had placed a plastic dish under the drain to catch the drips. It was mostly empty, as if it'd been dumped recently.

He heard a movement and looked up as Esther slipped into the room with a flashlight.

"Reuben has a lantern flashlight, but it needs new batteries." She knelt beside him.

That'd be handy. Wouldn't take Esther away from her work, either. But…. "Then I'd miss out on the pleasure of your company."

She blushed.

"I'll pick some up next time I'm in town. Tomorrow, I guess." He added them to a running supply list. Too bad Grossdaedi hadn't taken the phone with him. He could've called him. But that would've required his walking to a phone shanty. "What time is the wedding?"

"I'll leave as soon as I get Anna up and dressed. I'll make sure breakfast is ready before I go, too. I think Reuben arranged for the driver around ten, though most guests will be there earlier. He doesn't want to tire Anna too much."

How would they manage even a day without Esther? He'd been home only three days, and it was evident how much she did. How much Grossdaedi and Grossmammi relied on her.

"She's quiet. You'll hardly notice her."

Grossdaedi's words couldn't have been farther from the truth. Even if Viktor weren't aware of her with every fiber of his being, his großeltern—and he—depended on her anticipating their needs and meeting them. She'd become the nucleus of the family.

He swallowed hard. He wouldn't whine by asking who'd do dishes or take care of Grossmammi while she was gone. That answer was obvious. Besides, Grossdaedi had already encouraged her to stay for the post-wedding singing, since she was being courted.

That fact left a sour taste in his mouth.

Had Henry changed much from their school days? He must've. Viktor certainly had.

Esther flipped the flashlight on and aimed it at the pipes, in the right position, so he wouldn't have an excuse to touch her hand.

Disappointing.

But at least the wedding tomorrow would change things back to normal between him and Esther. He'd be around a lot of girls—the same ones he used to think were exciting when he lived here. That should get him over his rapidly growing infatuation with Esther Beachy. Maybe he'd hitch up Anchor or Titan so that he could take a girl home afterward.

Esther would be with Henry.

He tried to stifle the growl deep in his throat.

The flashlight wobbled as she looked at him.

"Hold still."

"You haven't done anything except sit there and stare at the pipes."

His face warmed. "Thinking." And that would have to stop.

She started to get up. "You hold the light while you think. I have better things to do."

He frowned and put his hand on her shoulder. "Stay."

She obeyed without question. Like a gut Amish girl.

Time to get to work.

The second Viktor finished the repairs and started gathering his tools, Esther scrambled to her feet and went down the hall to peek in on Anna. She sat in the living room, quietly mending socks—an endless job.

Next, Esther went to the kitchen to make sandwiches for Thursday supper, since she'd be at the wedding and Reuben didn't cook. She made some for Viktor, as well, though she didn't know if he'd return home after the ceremony or stay for the meal. He probably wouldn't go at all.

Disappointing, in one way. In another, that'd be a relief. She wasn't sure she could stand watching him interact with every other girl but her, since she'd be with Henry. Whether or not Lily had exaggerated their behind-the-barn activities, Viktor had been a flirt.

He still was.

She wasn't sure how to respond to him half the time. *"I'd miss out on the pleasure of your company."* How would someone like Lily respond to that? Probably not by blushing and keeping quiet.

Nein. Lily would have made some sort of cooing sound and snuggled close.

Esther shoved a sandwich into a plastic baggie and folded it closed. She glanced over her shoulder to make sure she was alone, then tried to mimic Lily. "Ach, you're so sweet."

She sounded flat without Lily's honeyed coos.

She cleared her throat and tried again. "You're so sweet. I like you, too."

Better. But not perfect.

"Ach, you shouldn't say things like that." She added a giggle. "But I'll take it. You're so sweet." *Perfect.*

A masculine chuckle sounded behind her.

Great. Viktor had heard her practicing responses to his flirtatious comment. He'd think—know—she was attracted. Though maybe he'd figure she was practicing for the wedding.

Her stomach churned at the thought. She could never say things like that to Henry.

She whirled around, her face heating.

Viktor stood two steps behind her. Too close.

She drew in a shuddery breath, inhaling his piney scent.

Focus.

He raised an eyebrow. "I'd love to know what that sandwich said that was so sweet."

She opened her mouth but couldn't find any words.

He chuckled again, then walked out of the haus. His booted feet clomped down the porch steps.

Her shoulders slumped. Obviously, she wasn't Lily, and shouldn't pretend to be.

Lily would've had a snappy, suggestive comeback to his last comment, too.

And Esther couldn't begin to think what it would have been.

Probably a gut thing.

If she'd blurted out that she was developing a major crush on him, Viktor would speed back to his riverboat so fast, his tires would be spinning.

~

From the waist-deep water, Viktor glanced toward the farmhaus. Esther wasn't coming. He'd already swum the laps he'd intended. He waded toward shore, disappointment eating at him.

He shouldn't have teased her about talking sandwiches. Wouldn't have, if he'd thought it would keep her away from the pond.

He pursed his lips. Didn't matter. Tomorrow he'd be over his infatuation. He just needed to renew his acquaintance with any number of the girls who'd liked him back in the day.

Of course, he'd been Amish then. Nein longer.

They'd consider him to be in his rumspringe, since he'd never joined the church.

And any of those girls would welcome the opportunity to bring him back into the fold.

Not that they could.

A sound at the edge of the woods caught his attention, and he glanced that way. Esther emerged from the trees carrying a small plastic pail and the battery-operated lantern. Grossdaedi must've bought the needed batteries.

"Guess what I found." She headed for the boulder on the bank.

Never mind what she'd found—she'd kum. His heart swelled. He couldn't keep from grinning.

"Blueberries. I didn't know any grew here by the pond." She set both the pail and the lantern on the boulder, then lowered herself beside them. "I'll have to kum back tomorrow—I mean, Friday—and pick enough for a pie."

And there was the reminder she'd be gone all day tomorrow. Coming home with another man.

She wouldn't be meeting him at the pond tomorrow nacht.

Nein, she'd be in *Henry's* arms. Holding his hand. Maybe even kissing him.

Jealousy turned his stomach sour.

He sighed, forcing that thought to the background. He'd just enjoy the moment.

"I love blueberry pie." He waded closer. "It's my favorite."

"I know." Her voice was soft. Caressing. Warm.

Of course, she knew. Grossmammi would've told her. He climbed out of the water and sat beside her on the boulder. He inhaled, catching a scent of something he couldn't identify. Amish women didn't wear perfume, so it had to be either her soap or a natural musk.

"Want some?" She slid the pail a bit closer to him.

He hesitated, remembering the days of picking and eating blueberries right off the bushes. "Jah." He scooped up a handful, carefully, not wanting to squish any.

She took a few, too. "If any are left, I'll add them to our oatmeal in the morgen."

"You'll be gone all day, huh? You sure Grossdaedi can manage to care for Grossmammi without you?" *You think I can manage?*

"Jah, he can. It's just a day. I'll be back after the singing."

Right. With Henry. He looked away. "You ever want more excitement?"

She caught her breath. "More excitement than what?"

Than Henry. He bit the words back. "Than…this. Here. You ever want to leave?"

"Leave? The Amish? Nein." She sounded shocked. "Why would I?" Why, indeed.

He missed the quiet serenity of the Amish community. The close relationships among families. The way they were all intertwined. So unlike the Englisch. The only close relationship he had on the river was with the riverboat chef. And the pilot, though he was more of an acquaintance.

He missed his friends. All married now, with kinner, according to Grossmammi's letters. Except for Josh Yoder. And he'd left the Amish. Like Viktor.

He wouldn't allow himself to think of what might have been. He was the one who....

Nein.

He took another handful of berries. "Your cousin Rachel is thinking of leaving?"

Esther shook her head. "I don't think so. She's just curious about other places. She collects postcards and picture books from— Well, I shouldn't tell you this, but she orders them off the Internet." Esther laughed. "She has them from different parts of the country. They're interesting to look at. And she's corresponding with Amish in different regions. Some are the typical round-robin letters, but others are postcards or cards she sends to those who are sick or who have been injured in accidents. Some don't respond, but others do. She's shared some of her correspondence with me."

"Feeding her curiosity under the guise of serving the sick. Smart. The bishop couldn't find fault with her that way."

Esther fell silent.

"So, what are you curious about, Esther?"

A long hesitation. He began to think she wasn't going to answer.

"Lots of things. Too many to mention. What's your favorite song at singings?"

"Nice dodge." He nudged her shoulder with his and took another handful of blueberries. "I don't remember having a favorite. But I'll be there tomorrow nacht. Maybe one will stand out."

Her breath hitched again. "You'll be there?"

There was a note of something—fear? desperation?—in her voice.

He shrugged. "Don't worry. I'll leave you alone. Just figured it'd be nice to see everyone."

"They'll be happy to see you, too." She sounded resigned.

"But not you? You don't want me there?" He hoped she wouldn't detect his hurt.

She gave a tiny gasp. "I— Well, nein, it's not that. It's...." She gave a couple quick breaths, then scrambled to her feet. "I'd better go. I think I need to.... I...." A sob. And she disappeared into the shadows, leaving behind the lantern and the pail of blueberries.

Chapter 9

Esther let out a contented sigh after watching her brother speak his vows to his longtime sweetheart. Miriam was the only girl Caleb had ever wanted, from the time he was eighteen until now, at twenty-two. She'd married another, but he'd died six months after the wedding. Caleb had stepped in then, offering to be a daed for her soon-to-be-born boppli.

It'd be nice if someone loved her that way. If someone gazed into her eyes like Caleb did Miriam's. Watching her wherever she went.

Henry certainly didn't. It was expectations, not love, that tied them together. He stared at Sarah Hershberger with that special look in his eyes—a look Esther never received. Except from Viktor a few times. Really, she and Henry should go their separate ways so that he could court Sarah, if he wanted. And so she'd be free to be courted by....

Last nacht, Viktor had asked what she was curious about. She hadn't been able to answer.

How could she admit to him that she wanted a romance and a home of her own instead of having her life planned out for her? That she was curious to know what it'd be like for Viktor to kiss her? Curious as to what had made him leave, and what it would take to make him stay?

Ach, Gott. Please straighten out this mess. Henry...and Sarah...and me. I want.... It was a silent prayer, but she didn't dare compose the rest of it, even in her head.

She should never ask for something she couldn't have. A formerly Amish man.

If this continued, she'd have to temporarily quit her job. She didn't want to move back to her overcrowded home, forcing Daed to feed one more mouth on his already stretched income. Staying home until Viktor returned to the Mississippi River.

She loved Anna and Reuben.

She scanned the crowd of people talking and visiting outside. Inside, the wedding festivities were winding down. It was almost time for the singing, but she hadn't seen Viktor or Reuben at all in the crush of Amish who had kum for the wedding. Some had taken buses from faraway communities; others had hired drivers.

She would've figured they hadn't kum, if it weren't for the fact that she'd seen Anna earlier, in her wheelchair, a big smile on her face as she chatted with the other women. It must be so difficult to never get out, to be forced to wait for others to kum and visit with her.

Esther scanned the room again. She didn't see Anna now. Reuben had probably taken her home. Maybe—hopefully—Viktor hadn't kum. Or perhaps he had left with his großeltern. She didn't see him with the other single men.

Of course, he might be behind the barn.

Pain cut through her.

"Esther, kum." Her cousin Greta grabbed her arm and gently tugged. "We need to go back to the bedroom. It's almost time for the singing."

The tradition called for girls to wait in a bedroom for the men to kum back, one at a time, and ask the chaperone guarding the door for a certain young lady. There wouldn't be many surprises. Everyone knew Henry would ask for Esther. She darted a glance in the direction of Sarah, with her flaming red hair. *Nein.* Henry may like Sarah, but he wouldn't shake things up or cause gossip by requesting her, leaving Esther alone, unwanted.

Esther allowed Greta to pull her farther into the room.

"Did you see that man who came from Ohio? I hope he asks for me." Greta giggled. "His name is Will. He is so cute."

When all the girls had squeezed into the room, the chaperone shut the door. Several girls checked their reflections in tiny mirrors to make sure their hair was secured properly and their kapps were on straight.

The hush of expectation filled the cramped room when the first knock came.

～

Not one girl there caught Viktor's attention. And it wasn't for lack of trying. Brushing up against him, batting their eyelashes, telling him how much they'd missed him and how glad they were that he was back, along with other broad hints.

It was Esther—her quiet, calm ways; her shiny brown hair and sparkling green eyes—who drew his attention.

Viktor glanced at the single men, talking in groups, going back one by one to claim that special girl.

How much would it shake things up if he asked for one who was already taken?

Then again, he was already known as a troublemaker. Maybe he should be a rebel to-nacht and worry about toeing the line later.

His gaze sought Henry Beiler, standing in the crush of men, laughing about something. He was still slight of build. Maybe a bit stocky, or even petite—a quality that, while desirable in a woman, was just wrong when applied to a man. Esther was probably as tall as he was, if not a little taller.

Maybe she would enjoy a date with a real man to-nacht. Riding home with Viktor behind the reins of Titan. Finding a quiet place to stop and stargaze. And talk. Maybe down by the pond. Their spot.

Of course, she might be upset if he ruined her date with Henry.

She'd get over it. He could tell her he was…what? Lonely? She'd never believe that. Lost without her by his side? Overwhelmed by her beauty? Or maybe the truth—that nobody else there attracted him the way she did.

And Henry didn't seem to be in a rush to claim her. It was as if he didn't care.

Viktor turned and strode down the hallway to the bedroom. He rapped on the door, and it opened a crack. He cleared his throat.

"Esther Beachy." There would be several Esthers in there. Maybe more than one Esther Beachy. If need be, he'd clarify further.

The door shut. Then, a few heart-pounding moments later, it opened again. Esther stared at him, the look on her face changing from a polite smile to surprise to a flash of joy before settling on confusion.

"You want…me?"

Jah. Was that so hard to imagine?

"Nein one else…." The rest of the statement stalled in his throat and refused to pass through. But that should be enough. Those three words said volumes, if she chose to hear them. *Really* hear them.

As they walked through the group of men waiting in the living room, Viktor tried not to look at Henry. He didn't want to smirk or gloat that *he* had Esther for the evening. That *he* would be taking her home—and not Henry. But he caught the look of disbelief and anger that crossed the other man's face.

He may have upset a beehive by so rashly requesting Esther.

He smiled in spite of himself. She'd looked happy to see it was him.

~

Esther tried to keep her elation under control. Viktor had chosen her over all the other girls. And it wasn't because the other girls wouldn't have him. She'd heard them talking among themselves, trying to guess whom Viktor would choose. Her name hadn't kum up.

Viktor took the seat across from hers at the long table set up in the barn. He thumbed through the Ausbund, perhaps trying to refresh his memory of the Amish hymns before the singing started.

Greta sat next to Esther as a man she didn't recognize settled in beside Viktor. Esther leaned closer to her cousin. "Is that him?"

"Jah. Will from Ohio."

The tables filled rapidly. Sarah came in with Ezra. Henry hadn't taken advantage of his opportunity to pick her? Or someone else had beaten him. The last ones in were Henry and his sister. Someone picked a song, and the singing started.

Viktor had a great voice. Esther didn't remember him singing bass back when he'd lived there. But then, his voice had been the least of her concerns.

Toward the end of the evening, Esther saw Elizabeth Swartz stroll down the men's side of the table and stop beside Viktor. She put her hand on his shoulder and leaned down to whisper something in his ear.

He grinned and nodded, and then, without a glance at Esther, he got up and quietly left the barn. With Bethany Weiss, the bishop's daughter.

Esther would not think the worst. She would not. But what other reason could there be?

When it was time to go, he still hadn't returned. Bad enough to humiliate her, but to leave her without a ride? Tears burned her eyes. How could he so blatantly abandon her to go off with another girl? Sneaking behind the barn. She was half tempted to confront them, but she was afraid of what she might interrupt.

Henry approached, his sister walking submissively behind him. "Looks like you were abandoned by the runaway." A sneer curled his lips. "Want a ride home?"

Esther managed a nod and followed Henry out to his buggy. *Danki, Gott, for Henry. Help me to forgive Viktor….* Still, resentment simmered. She climbed into the buggy without help. Not that any was offered.

"Don't like you staying at the Petersheims' with him," Henry grumbled.

Esther squared her shoulders and aimed her blurry gaze out the small window toward the starry sky. "There's nothing to worry about, Henry. Obviously. He barely knows I exist." *Nein. It was all one-sided.*

Henry took his sister home first, then backtracked to the Petersheims'. Wouldn't do to take the intended home before the sister.

Esther took a deep breath, hunting for some courage. "Do you want to stop and stargaze somewhere? Spend some time together, talking? Maybe hold my hand?" It might be wrong being so bold, but she needed to know if she felt the same sparks with Henry as she did with Viktor.

After all, Anna had mentioned just yesterday that couples should have their special place. And she wanted—needed—to forget about the pond for a bit.

He jerked back, as if she'd offered to be...well, naughty.

"What's there to talk about? You know how I feel about...that. I won't lay a finger on you until our wedding nacht."

"And that's gut, jah. But holding hands? I just wanted to know if...well.... Never mind." She wouldn't change his mind about it. Why try?

"I can't believe you asked," Henry murmured. "Mamm said you weren't submissive enough. Outspoken." He shook his head. "She said I'd have to take a firm hand with you."

Esther clamped her mouth shut. Henry's mamm—Esther's mamm's best friend—didn't entirely approve of her? And she'd be living under the same roof as that woman?

Not submissive enough? Really?

What could she do to prove her wrong? Avoid ever voicing her disagreement with Henry? But she'd always agreed with everything he suggested, verbally if not mentally. Unless it was trivial stuff. She did disagree with his suggestion that she take a job in town rather than work as a caregiver. She valued privacy and hated the idea of tourists staring at her. Yet Henry wanted her to make more money. Not that she'd ever see it, anyway. It'd still go to Daed. Henry apparently ran home to his mamm with everything. Esther slumped in her seat.

It was late by the time Henry's horse drove into the Petersheims' driveway. Lightning flashed in the sky, and thunder rumbled in the distance. Esther climbed out of the buggy. "Danki for giving me a ride, Henry. I'm sorry—"

"You need to pray about your bold, unsubmissive ways, Esther. And I'll pray for your soul."

Right.

"Don't ever ask me to hold your hand again. You know better. Next thing you know, you'll be begging for a kiss."

Not likely. Not from Henry.

"Maybe I should ask the bishop to speak to you about your wanton ways. I will be taking a firm hand with you, if that's what it takes to teach you submission."

"I'm sorry, Henry. It won't happen again."

Tears escaped from the corners of her eyes. She angrily brushed them away as she watched the orange triangle on the back of the buggy disappear into the darkness. Then she turned toward the haus.

Viktor sat in the shadows on the steps of the porch. "You begged Henry to hold your hand? You *are* a bold one. Wanton." His tone was mirthful.

She pulled in a breath. "You dare to say something to *me* when *you* snuck behind the barn with Bethany?"

Chapter 10

Viktor froze, staring at her. She thought he...with Bethany? Really? She had that low an opinion of him? Well, maybe in his younger days. He expelled a breath. He'd been looking forward to giving Esther a ride home after dark, but he'd forgotten to line up a ride for her when he'd heard Bethany's urgent request. "Nein, I—"

Wait. Was that jealousy he heard? As if she wanted to be the one who spent time in his arms?

Ach, jah. He could definitely go for that.

He stood and moved closer to Esther. "Perhaps you want to go behind the barn?" His gaze skimmed over her before he forced it up to her face.

Her eyes widened. "Nein!" Color rushed to her cheeks.

He stepped nearer still and ran a finger down the side of her cheek, over her chin, then up, stopping at the corner of her mouth. "Too bad. You might've enjoyed it." His finger slid slowly across her lips.

She trembled beneath his touch.

"I'll hold you...or your hand. Anytime." He moved his fingers from her face to the back of her neck.

She seemed to lean nearer. Or maybe it was only his desire that made it appear so.

Thunder rumbled overhead, and then the clouds burst open, as if Gott Himself had turned a bucket over them.

Rain wouldn't stop him. He lowered his gaze to her lips, making his intentions clear.

Lightning flashed, followed by a sizzling sound. A burning smell. She jerked away and ran for the haus.

He spun around and watched her go. The door slammed behind her. She'd probably awakened Grossmammi and Grossdaedi.

He groaned. What had he done? Starting to kiss Grossmammi's caregiver—a girl who would be marrying another man in the fall. And his only friend right now.

"Stupid idiot." He headed for the barn.

Best to let things cool off a bit before he went inside.

⌒

Esther had climbed only a few steps when the first-floor bedroom door opened. Reuben came out, holding a lantern.

"Esther? I heard the door slam. Everything all right?"

She cringed. "Jah. Sorry. It…. I forgot it slams shut."

"I'll speak to Viktor in the morgen. Perhaps he can fix the tension."

Ach, the tension was there. Just not in the door. "Sorry I woke you."

"You or the storm. Doesn't matter. Viktor home yet?"

"Jah, he's…outside."

"Did he take anyone home?" Reuben chuckled. "None of my business, I know."

Esther shook her head. "I didn't see him leave. But he was here when I arrived."

"Ach." Reuben sighed. "I'd hoped he'd bring you home."

Jah. Me, too. "I'm seeing Henry. You know that."

Reuben turned away. "A man can hope."

And a girl could dream.

Neither would make it a reality.

She hurried upstairs and into her room. As soon as she calmed, as soon as she heard Viktor shut his door across the hall, she'd go back downstairs to sleep on the couch.

Today had been one of the worst days in her history. Abandoned by Viktor in favor of another girl. Scolded by Henry. And then Viktor overhearing the scolding and making fun of her.

Even worse, she'd almost let him kiss her. If it weren't for the lightning, she would've been in his arms this very minute.

She threw herself across the bed, allowing the tears to fall unhampered.

The next morgen, she rolled over and blinked. Still in her room. Still in full dress. Her gut dress. Even her shoes were still on her feet.

She changed clothes, released her hair, and then pinned it up again, making sure every strand was smooth, the way she'd been taught. She secured her kapp, then headed out of her bedroom. Hopefully, nobody would know she'd cried herself to sleep. But just in case, she stopped in the bathroom and washed her face with cold water.

She'd prepared a breakfast casserole before she'd left for the wedding, so that the mixture could sit in the fridge and soak up all the flavors. She slid it into the oven, then went to help Anna prepare for the day.

"You and your Henry had a tiff last nacht," the woman said by way of greeting.

And Reuben had made light of their being awake. How much had they heard?

Esther glanced at the open window, the breeze stirring the petals of Anna's violets. They'd probably heard everything. Including what Viktor had said.

Mortification ate at her. "I was just trying to do what you suggested—see if he wanted to go somewhere, to talk and to dream." Well, kind of. But the only thing physical she wanted to do with Henry at this point was to rip his face off. And that wasn't a submissive attitude.

"Henry's not gut for you, Esther. You need a man who loves you, who wants to be with you. A man who wants to hold your hand. One who doesn't parrot his mamm."

Jah, and where would she find such a man? Well, there was Viktor. A flirt.

Esther pursed her lips and helped Anna with her hair.

Anna waved her hand toward the door as Esther finished. "Go on, dear. I'll be out as soon as I do a little Bible reading and prayer."

Viktor came into the kitchen as she bent to remove the casserole from the oven. He strode over, took the pot holders from her, and effortlessly lifted the heavy dish. He carried it to the table and set it on a trivet, then came back to where she stood and turned off the stove. Finally, he laid the pot holders on the counter.

She stood there, blinking, stunned that he was acting normal after last nacht. Or maybe he was about to make fun of her again. If he did, she'd probably cry.

His fingers grazed across her waist as he turned her toward him. She caught her breath, tears brimming. He gazed down at her, his dark gaze unfathomable, then pulled in a shuddering breath and let his hands fall away. "I'm sorry, Esther. I shouldn't have said—or done—what I did last nacht. I didn't mean to hurt—or scare—you. I hope we can still be friends."

She nodded, dipping her head so he wouldn't see anything she didn't want him to. Such as maybe the fact that she'd wanted his kiss. His touch.

"You'll kum down to the pond to talk at nacht?"

Her gaze shot up. "I'd like that." Reuben and Anna wouldn't overhear, should anything be said. Or done. Which it wouldn't. But still, a girl could dream.

He grinned. "So would I." He started to turn away, then stopped and glanced back at her. "I meant what I said." The grin turned impish. "I'll hold your hand anytime."

Her face burned. She stared at him. Speechless.

He winked, then went to the sink and ran water to wash his hands as Anna rolled into the room.

Viktor stared at the water running over his hands, the cascading soap suds. He'd had bad timing. He was almost positive Grossmammi had heard his last comment to Esther. And if she had, she'd mention it to Grossdaedi, who was sure to have a talk with him.

A talk similar to the one they'd had just before Viktor had left home to work on the Mississippi.

Grossdaedi's words played through his mind: *"Fahrt nicht hoch hier."* Do not go high here. In other words, *Don't exalt yourself. Don't seek great things.*

What would he have to say about the way he'd played with Esther's emotions?

Shame burned in his throat. At least he could tell Grossdaedi he'd apologized. And assure him it wouldn't happen again.

But then, it probably would.

He'd seen the look in her eyes.

And he was just a man.

Chapter 11

Esther served Anna a slice of the breakfast casserole, then filled four glasses with orange juice.

Anna settled herself at the table. "My dochters and their families are coming over tomorrow for Independence Day. Sorry I forgot to mention it to you, Esther."

She nodded, mentally reordering her day to fit in a little extra cleaning. She wouldn't really have time to go home and help clean up after the wedding if she was needed to help Anna prepare for company. But she didn't have a choice. Expected—and needed—both places. "I'll start preparations when I get home. I mean, here. Back here."

"This is your home." Anna smiled at her. "I can peel potatoes and get them soaking for you. Maybe start some of the other things. I'll make a menu. You know the aenties will bring food. They always do."

That was a blessing. She'd have a little less work to do.

"The kinner will probably want to organize a game of baseball," Viktor said as he slid into his chair. He glanced at Reuben. "Do we have a place where they can play?"

Reuben shrugged. "Where you and your brothers played."

Viktor frowned, his tanned skin paling. A muscle ticked in his jaw. He nodded and quickly dipped his head.

Esther studied his rigid posture. Where were his brothers? All she'd heard was that they were gone. Had the whole family jumped fence and been shunned? Moved away? It was odd they'd left Anna and Reuben alone. Though maybe Reuben and Anna had refused to leave the farm. They did have other family nearby, such as their dochters, sohns-in-law, and other grosskinner. Besides, it gave Viktor a gut home base.

But then…he'd said the farm was his.

Maybe she would ask him about it to-nacht when they met at the pond.

A thrill shot through her, and she smiled, already looking forward to it.

After they finished breakfast, Esther made ham and cheese sandwiches for the Petersheims and washed the dishes. Then she hitched up Goofy to the small one-seater pony cart Daed had loaned her and started down the lane toward home.

She walked into a madhaus. Incessant talk, with Mamm and her sisters-in-law bossing the younger girls as they verbally rehashed the wedding. It seemed each one tried to outtalk the others. Such a blessing to live in a quiet home.

Esther's sisters Dorcas and Faith both wore sour expressions. She could understand Dorcas. She'd planned to marry in the fall, and it must have been hard to watch Caleb marry his Miriam—whose presence in the room was probably like an open wound, now that Dorcas had nein wedding planned. Esther gave her a sympathetic smile, but her sister only glared back.

When an argument started, Mamm sent Dorcas to start the laundry and told Faith to dry the dishes, in order to separate the two girls. Esther wished she could escape the room, but instead she rolled up her sleeves and started washing dishes for Faith.

Daed came into the haus. "You're home, Dochter. You bring money? Reuben didn't give me your wages yesterday."

Esther winced. Why couldn't Daed be happy to see her, regardless of whether she brought him money? Seemed all he thought about anymore was money—and how much value she was adding to the family.

Esther rinsed a dish and handed it to Faith, who dried it with a towel.

"Nein, he didn't pay me. He'll probably give it to you on church Sunday."

Daed shook his head. "Need the money now. Maybe I'll ask him for it when I take you back to-nacht."

Esther washed another dish very slowly as she silently counted to ten...ten times. "I came in the pony cart. I won't need a ride. But danki."

Daed grunted. "You aren't holding money back, are you?"

As if I could. Esther focused her gaze on the dish she held and repressed the disrespectful thought. Daed wouldn't hesitate to punish her. "Nein, Daed. Reuben gives you all my earnings."

"As it should be." Daed nodded. "Takes money to provide for this family. Need to add onto the haus. Maybe I'll tell him you need a raise." He stomped off.

Anna was a pleasure to work for. Esther would do it for free, just for the opportunity to live in their quiet home and care for the sweetest woman she knew. And her ehemann.

And Viktor. Esther caught her breath. Ach, how easy it would be to lapse into verboden daydreams about him...them...on the farm. Together forever.

Not that it'd happen. She needed to guard her heart.

Whether or not Henry was right for her, he'd already gone to the bishop to request permission to marry her in the fall. At this point, did she even have a say?

She frowned at the dishwater, ignoring Faith's stare. She couldn't disrespect Daed by complaining to her sister, even if she could really use more than the five dollars a month Daed grudgingly allowed her for her needs. And he usually delayed giving her the money until she was desperate.

Gut thing she didn't need much.

And that wants were strongly discouraged.

When she'd finished helping her family, she went back to the Petersheims'. They'd already eaten lunch, the few dirty dishes stacked by the sink waiting for her. She spied Viktor and Reuben working out in the field, but she couldn't tell what they were doing. Maybe getting the area ready for baseball tomorrow.

Everything was quiet inside. She found Anna sleeping in her room. Either Reuben or Viktor must've helped her into bed.

Esther fixed a pitcher of fresh lemonade, did the dishes, and went outside to fold laundry, then came inside again to work on preparations for the next day.

Anna had left a menu on the table: Potato salad. Three-bean salad. Jell-O salad. Tomatoes. Others would bring meat, baked beans, and a host of desserts.

Would Esther be wanted there, since they had so much family coming?

If only she could be a part of Anna's family, wanted and welcomed. Marrying Viktor and not Henry.

And there were those dangerous daydreams again.

⌒

Ach, such painful memories. Tears stung Viktor's eyes as he worked in the field where he and his brothers used to play ball with their friends and other youth in the community, clearing it of rocks and fallen tree limbs, branches, and twigs. He could almost hear the voices of the past, calling out to one another: the gut-natured teasing, the friendly insults, the competitive assertions—although some would say that those led to sinful pride.

Grossdaedi worked beside him, silent. Perhaps reliving his own painful memories.

After all, they were due to Viktor's decisions.

He shut his eyes, his stomach churning.

"I think we've done all we can." Grossdaedi's voice sounded gruff. As if he struggled to suppress his own tears. He cleared his throat, picked up an armful of piled wood, and started off. "I'll be back with the wheelbarrow to finish up."

"I'll get started in the barn," Viktor said, "clean out some extra stalls for tomorrow." That would help to keep his mind off the past. Maybe.

Grossdaedi nodded.

Tomorrow would be a hard day. People would understand if he wasn't around much. Ach, they'd gossip, but then Esther would know why he'd left the Amish without his having to divulge his painful past.

Maybe he'd spend the day on the pond, swimming. Or fishing, if Grossdaedi remembered to get the pond stocked.

But first, he went to check to make sure the building supplies were all on hand for the wheelchair ramp. If not, maybe he'd make a trip into town.

Grossdaedi stuck his head into the doorway. "Almost forgot to mention. When Esther gets back, you need to find her and fix the tension."

Viktor's stomach flipped, and he hitched an eyebrow. Surely, Grossdaedi didn't mean...? He turned and met Grossdaedi's gaze.

"The kitchen screen door slams." He must have read Viktor's unasked question.

Right.

"Esther could show you—"

"I can find the kitchen door. I can even find the tension bar." Did Grossdaedi think he was a dummchen? But the interruption and the comment had both been disrespectful of the elder man. He'd better apologize, and fast. "Sorry, Grossdaedi. Didn't mean to be rude."

"Jah." Grossdaedi took a step back. He didn't look at Viktor, instead directing his gaze at something on the floor. "You should know...your grossmammi and I heard the conversation last nacht. The bedroom window was open. Normally, I wouldn't interfere—"

"Then don't." And there he went, disrespecting him again. He'd thought he'd escaped this lecture, since Grossdaedi hadn't mentioned it all morgen.

Grossdaedi flinched. Straightened. Then stepped into the room, his jaw set. "If you are courting her, fine. But if you're planning on returning to the Mississippi and breaking her heart, then I will have plenty to say."

"Nein hearts will be broken." Except possibly his.

Though he couldn't begin to imagine what Esther saw in Henry.

"You're not a hormone-ruled teenager anymore. You're a man, and you need to act like it."

Ouch. "Jah." He forced the word through clenched teeth.

A slight smile lifted Grossdaedi's lips. "But it is time you settle down, join the church, and take a frau. And Esther would be a fine one."

Viktor's stomach went into a cramp severe enough to send a spasm up his back. Ach, the thought of Esther as his frau—able to kiss her, hold her.... His face heated.

His reaction didn't go unnoticed, if the widening grin on Grossdaedi's face was any indication.

But Esther would have nothing to do with him if she knew what had pulled him away from the Amish. And what kept him from returning.

⌒

Finally, evening fell. Anxious to spend time with Viktor, Esther set off for the pond, accompanied by a chorus of nacht creatures. She'd seen him slip off after he finished his evening chores, his swimming trunks grasped loosely in his hand.

She envied his freedom. What would it be like to dip into the pond water, as he did, without the constraints of heavy skirts hampering her every move? What would it be like to swim, as he did, able to go down to the depths and skim the bottom?

It must be so nice to be a man and enjoy those liberties. Even though most Amish men swam in their clothes, when they took time for such frivolity, surely their pant legs weren't as constricting as heavy skirts.

She slowed her pace, not wanting to appear too anxious. Earlier, she'd kum out and picked the blueberries she'd promised, though she wouldn't do any baking with them until all the extended family had left.

Even if Anna expected her to go back to her parents' haus in the morgen, she would return by dusk to help her with her bedtime preparations. She hated feeling uncertain, not knowing where she'd spend her hours. Her family didn't celebrate Independence Day, instead treating it as a normal day on the farm. But for Viktor's family, it seemed to be a time for celebration, for fun.

If his parents and brothers had moved away, maybe they'd kum back to join the gathering. But then, if they'd left the Amish, the parents would be shunned. Unwelkum.

She hesitated as she neared the pond. Why did she continue to meet him out here? She was only asking for trouble. He'd never return to the Amish, and he was still keeping up his old ways, sneaking behind the barn with girls.

Though not with her. He'd invited her last nacht, but he was only making fun of her. Never in a lifetime would he consider taking her behind the barn.

Not that she'd go willingly if he did suggest it.

She wasn't that kind of girl. Though she did dream about it occasionally.

Esther sighed. Henry was probably more her type than the far more dangerous Viktor.

She'd never imagined she'd be so attracted to a "bad bu."

So, why did she look forward to this time together, all the while knowing it'd lead nowhere? It didn't make sense.

Viktor tugged his shirt over his head when she arrived. Covering his beautifully toned, muscular chest. Not that she noticed. The material clung to his damp skin, so he pulled it loose and yanked the garment down. "Didn't think you were coming."

"I wrote a quick letter to Lily. She's enjoying her time with Peter. She met his parents this past week."

Viktor raised an eyebrow. "Must be getting serious, then."

She nodded. "I think so, jah."

He lowered himself onto the boulder and patted the spot next to him.

She sat, careful to keep from accidentally brushing against him. "Am I to go home tomorrow?"

"Why would you?" He shifted, his body moving a smidgen closer. "You're basically family. What if Grossmammi needs you?" He frowned. "Or maybe your family will want you home?"

She shook her head. "To them it's just a normal day."

He grinned. "Nothing wrong with a family gathering."

"Your family won't mind that I'm here?"

He chuckled. "You think any of them will want to help Grossmammi? They will if they have to, I suppose. But you're gut with her. If they wanted to help, they'd be here more often, or they'd move Grossmammi and Grossdaedi into a dawdi-haus on their property. As you can see, nobody has."

"But family takes care of family."

Viktor shrugged. "Grossdaedi left the farm to Daed, not to his dochters. Their ehemanns own land. And my aenties have their husbands' parents living with them. Since Daed died and left the land to me, my großeltern are my responsibility. Not that I mind."

His daed had died? Maybe his mamm had remarried and moved away with his brothers. Maybe he didn't get along with his step-daed, and—

"So, I'm curious." Viktor interrupted her musings. "Why are you sleeping downstairs when you have a bed in the upstairs room? Is it because Grossmammi needs care during the nacht-time hours?"

"Not usually." Heat rose in Esther's cheeks. "I was concerned what people would say about me and you sleeping upstairs alone without a chaperone." Her plan to stay on the couch for the sake of appearance had flown out the window when he'd seen her in her nightclothes—an even bigger scandal than sleeping in the room across the hall. Ever since then, she'd tried to get up earlier than he so she wouldn't be caught again.

He chuckled. "Who would know?"

She shook her head.

"The ones who would gossip about your being upstairs alone with me are the same ones who will gossip nein matter what. You haven't talked to anyone about where we're sleeping, have you?"

"Nein. But I know. And Gott knows. I guess I figured—"

"But your best friend doesn't know. Nor does the town gossip. Sleep in your bed. The door has a lock, ain't so?"

"But—"

"But nothing. You'll be safer behind a locked door than on the couch, where either Grossdaedi or I may wander into the room at any moment. And the haus doors are never locked. Anyone could kum in and see you in your nightgown with your hair down like I did...." His voice turned husky. "I wanted to see if it was as soft as it looked."

Her cheeks warmed.

His breathing became ragged. "I still do."

Chapter 12

The pond lapped just below their feet. Viktor listened, but beyond the slightest gasp at his boldness, she didn't make an audible reaction. What would she do if he dared to finger the short strands of hair that refused to stay twisted into her bun and tucked beneath the prayer kapp?

Ach, it was tempting. So very tempting.

He started to raise his hand to do just that when she shifted, scooting farther away.

"I think you've probably touched enough girls' hair." She sounded a bit strangled. "All those girls you took behind the barn...."

He couldn't remember ever touching a girl's hair. But, that aside, he heard injury in her voice, as if the thought of him kissing other girls pained her. And maybe it did. How many people had he hurt with his immature teenage actions? He apparently had quite the reputation. Enough so that Esther had brought it up twice. Grossdaedi had even referred to it.

Viktor refused to entertain a mental parade of girls he might've hurt in the process.

Esther brought it up twice.

Jealous? Maybe.

He was tempted to reach for her, to wrap his arms around her and hold her.

But that would end the evening right there.

Esther was out of his league. He'd do well to remember that.

He turned his head away, forcing his attention to the chorus of frogs somewhere in the darkness, and away from the beguiling woman next to him.

After all, according to a movie he'd once watched on the riverboat, when you let the moment pass, it's gone forever.

Gone. Forever.

Did he really want to lose the one chance he might have to kiss Esther?

On the other hand, did he want to ruin their fledgling friendship?

The answer to both questions? Nein.

She let out a nearly inaudible sigh, as if she'd been holding her breath to see if it would happen—and had relaxed when she'd realized it wouldn't.

The moment was gone.

He dared to breathe.

But if she ever mentioned his going behind the barn again, he'd be tempted to scoop her up, carry her back there, and show her what had happened.

A few stolen kisses. Mere pecks that hadn't affected him much. They were all pretty much the same. Nothing to lose sleep over. He couldn't remember who all had been on the receiving end.

But then, he'd never felt the sparks with other girls, even kissing them, that he had with Esther—whom he'd hardly touched.

Why had he been such a fool? Just because he was rebelling.

"I didn't get the blueberry pie made."

Her simple comment, so far removed from what he'd been thinking, threw him mentally off guard. Then he remembered the abandoned lantern and bucket of berries the nacht before the wedding. He'd mentioned the singing, and she'd run off crying.

He wouldn't ask. After a moment, he shrugged. "Maybe you'll have time after everyone leaves tomorrow."

"I could make it before they start arriving."

"If you do that, I won't get any. It'll be gone."

"Why not? I could hold it back until you go through the line." She glanced at him, and the white strings of her kapp fluttered in the moonlight.

Sadness washed over him. "I won't be around tomorrow. I'll take a sandwich or two to go."

"You're leaving?" Her hand reached for him, but she stopped shy of touching him. The slight movement gave him hope that maybe the moment wasn't really gone forever. Nice that she wanted him around.

"Just for the day." He forced a chuckle. "I'll be back in time for our date here at the pond."

⌒

Date. And it was just that.

She'd seen Viktor more in the past four days than she had Henry in two months. Spent more alone time with him. Nein wonder her heart strayed.

She'd fallen in love with Viktor.

And she'd have to take great pains to make sure he never found out he'd stolen her heart. To make sure nobody found out.

She struggled to control her voice so that he wouldn't hear the emotion coursing through her. "Why would you leave when your großeltern are hosting a gathering?"

He didn't answer but merely sighed and lay back on the boulder.

"Maybe you're going to your mamm's?"

He grunted. A non-answer.

"Are your brothers still at home?"

"Esther." His voice was tight. Angry. "Shh."

She blinked. He wouldn't talk about his family? Why was he so tight-lipped? It was as if anything related to him and his life was verboden.

She swallowed hard. "I guess I'll go." She moved to stand.

"Nein. Stay." He reached out and snagged her by the hand, his fingers intertwining with hers. "Sorry for snapping. I won't be with my family. Nein more questions. Please."

Tingles raced from her fingers up her arm, warming her. She'd hold his hand anytime, too. Henry couldn't possibly compare to this.

Ich liebe dich.

"I'm thinking of hanging a swing. Not on the porch—too close to the bedroom window of my großeltern and their spying. But it'd be a gut place to sit and talk, close to home when it gets too cool to swim in the pond. Can't say this boulder is all that comfortable. Maybe I should bring a blanket next time."

A blanket? Her eyes widened. *To lie on?*

He released her and sat up, reaching off into the darkness. He handed her a stiff fabric. His jeans. "Use these for a pillow. Stargaze with me."

Ach, stargazing. She folded the jeans, then lay back. His hand grasped hers again. She felt the heat from his body next to hers. Would it ever be too cool to swim in the pond? It seemed so far in the future to think of.

Wait. Did this mean he would still be around when the weather cooled? Her heart skipped a beat.

Viktor gave a contented sigh. "This is nice."

Jah. Actually, it was way beyond nice.

She was in liebe.

And not with Henry.

⌒

Viktor could get used to spending time with Esther like this. Almost as if they were a couple.

But she was being courted by Henry. What would he say if he knew his girl was out in the darkness, keeping a nightly rendezvous with another man, holding his hand?

Viktor wouldn't bring him up. Wouldn't remind her. Because that would throw a damper on their evening, and she'd go home. He wouldn't do anything to scare her off, even though he wanted to tug her into his arms and hold her close.

That day would kum, if Gott still smiled on him, forgave him, and wanted to bless him. Despite....

Ach, Gott. Why?

It was a question impossible to answer.

I am the Gott who healeth thee.

Words floated through his mind, maybe a direct message from der Herr himself. If so, it was the first time He'd ever answered Viktor.

Claiming to hear from Gott would be vanity. Must be his imagination.

Besides, he certainly didn't feel healed.

He may have obtained his independence on the Fourth of July, but in the worst possible way.

He would never be free.

Chapter 13

Esther awoke early the next morgen. It was so nice to sleep in the wide bed, and not on the narrow couch downstairs. Viktor had done her a favor, pointing out that the door had a lock. Reuben must have installed it for her in anticipation of Viktor's return.

Which spoke volumes of what his grossdaedi thought of Viktor's values. Or his desire to prevent the gossip of the neighbors on her behalf.

She tiptoed into the hallway, then paused outside Viktor's bedroom. His door was open, but the room was empty. He was gone.

The bedsheets were a tangled mess, as if he'd tossed and turned all nacht. And the laundry basket she'd set in the room was piled full.

She'd need to wash clothes tomorrow. Nein time today, not with his family coming.

She hurried downstairs and outside, hoping to find him doing chores in the barn, so she could talk some sense into him. His aenties, onkels, and cousins would expect to see him. And if he wasn't spending the day with his mamm and his brothers, where would he go? Would he celebrate with the Englisch? The downtown parade, the antique car show, the afternoon street dance, and the fireworks at nacht?

He'd said he'd be back for their date by the pond.

The barn was empty, his chores done. He must've gotten up hours ago. She peeked behind the barn, where his truck had been parked.

It was gone.

Tears burned her eyes, and she ran her hand roughly across them. *Lord, where is he? Bring him back home.*

To the Amish.

To her.

Before she married Henry and ruined two lives by refusing to make it clear that she was in love with another man.

She collected the few eggs and fed the chickens before returning to the haus. Nein dishes waited by the sink. He'd left without eating?

Maybe he'd planned to eat at the pancake breakfast hosted by a local church. She'd seen signs around town advertising it.

Pancakes. Hmm. Sounded tempting.

Maybe she'd use the fresh eggs to make pancakes for Anna and Reuben. It'd been a while since she'd last made them.

Everything was quiet in the haus. Reuben and Anna must still be sleeping. She went upstairs, made Viktor's bed, and was still straightening the room when she heard a door open downstairs.

Viktor?

She peered over the rail. It was Reuben, headed out to the barn. Her heart deflated.

Time to fix breakfast. She wasn't sure when their family would arrive, but she wanted to make sure everything was ready.

Esther mixed up the pancake batter, put some ground sausage—maple-syrup flavored—in the frying pan, and set two pans on the stove over medium heat. They should be fine for the short time she'd be gone. She hurried back to Anna's room, rapped on the door, and entered.

Anna had put on her dress, but it wasn't quite pinned together. Esther assisted her, then stood by as Anna moved from the bed to the wheelchair. "I think I'm stronger today." She smiled.

Esther nodded, but she wasn't sure. Anna had stood slowly, hesitantly, then inched her leg to the side, as if she were afraid the other one wouldn't hold her if she took a step.

"What's for breakfast? I'm really hungry." Anna reached for her shoes.

Esther picked up the comb and started fixing Anna's hair. "Pancakes and sausages. I thought about them when I realized Viktor had left without eating, and wondered if he'd decided to eat at the pancake breakfast downtown."

Anna shrugged. "He's probably not eating. He's most likely at the pond."

"Wherever he is, he drove. His truck is gone."

"Reuben told him to move it off the property for the celebration. Last year, he spent the entire day fishing. Mindless task, one that leaves him alone with his thoughts, and he came home with a mess of fish for supper the next nacht. Might this year, too. He'll clean them for you." Anna patted Esther's hand. "Did I ever tell you about the time Reuben took me fishing? My daed never took his dochters fishing. Reuben liked to fish, and he took me along once, down by the covered bridge. I loved that place. Miss it." She wiped her eyes. "Anyway, I was squeamish about putting that hook into an innocent little worm. Reuben assured me, 'It doesn't hurt them.'" She shook her head. "How does he know? He's not a worm."

Esther smiled and started twisting Anna's hair up.

"I caught my first fish. I don't remember what kind it was. Reuben told me how to take it off the hook. That fish stared me in the eyes, and when I reached for it, it started flapping. I threw the rod so high, it got caught in a tree. Closest I ever saw Reuben kum to getting upset with me while we were courting. That was his favorite rod. He went down there later with a friend and rescued it. The poor fish didn't survive the hanging, though."

Esther laughed. She secured the kapp, then leaned over to hug Anna. "Ich liebe dich."

Anna returned the hug. "Ich liebe dich, too, süße. Gott smiled on me when He brought you into our home." She released Esther. "Now, go on. Plenty to do today. I'll be out to help when I finish my morgen devotions."

Esther hurried to the kitchen but couldn't keep from glancing out the window in the direction of the pond. Maybe, if she had time, she'd see if she could find Viktor. He shouldn't be alone.

What had happened to make him withdraw like this?

Viktor stood in the middle of the pond, a wicker basket one-quarter full of fish floating, partly submerged, behind him, and his old Amish straw hat on his head. He angled it to keep the sun out of his eyes. It was amazing he hadn't scared all the fish away earlier when he'd raged—though, in a closed pond, where would they go? His eyes still burned, and his throat hurt, from the uncontrolled crying and shouting he'd done, out loud to Gott. As if der Herr had ever cared enough to listen to him.

His stomach rumbled, reminding him that he hadn't had a bite to eat all day. Judging by the position of the sun, it was nearing the supper hour, but he didn't think he'd be able to keep anything down. Maybe it'd be better if his work schedule were different, so he wouldn't be home in July. It might be easier if he stayed on the river that month and hid from his memories instead of being here, forced to relive them.

Out of the corner of his eye, he noticed a figure walking on the bank. He shaded his eyes and looked that way. Male. For a moment, he was disappointed Esther hadn't trailed him out here.

But then, he would've been embarrassed to have her witness his moments of vulnerability.

"Hallo!"

The voice sounded familiar, but Viktor couldn't quite place it. He raised his hand in a wave. Hopefully whoever it was would pass through quickly and not want to talk.

"Sorry about cutting through. Headed home."

Viktor nodded. Who was that? He did recognize the voice. "Do I know you? Viktor Petersheim."

"Hey, Vik. Josh Yoder."

Viktor froze. Josh had been his best friend. And he'd been there that horrible nacht. He'd jumped the fence about the same time Viktor had, neither of them able to handle the pain.

He swallowed. "Where've you been?"

Josh chuckled. "I've been everywhere, man...breathed the mountain air, man...travelin', I've done my share, man...."

Viktor recognized the lyrics of the trucking song he'd heard a couple times.

Josh grinned. "Gott found me. And He brought me back home. Sometime I'll tell you the story. Now, I'm anxious to see everyone.

I called the barn phone last nacht, and Daed answered. He assured me, in nein uncertain terms, that I'd be welcomed home. Kind of in a hurry to get there."

Viktor nodded, a pang hitting him in the chest—Daed would never be there to answer and welcome him home, danki to Viktor's own stupid mistakes. But he could be happy for his friend. "I'll kum by."

Josh waved and continued on. Viktor returned to his fishing.

"Vik!" Josh paused and turned around. "Hey, I just thought— did you return?"

Viktor shook his head. He opened his mouth to say something but couldn't force a sound past the lump in his throat.

"We'll talk." Josh waved again before disappearing around the bend.

It'd be nice to have his best friend back in the area. Though he'd probably treat Viktor the same way as all his other former friends had ever since joining the church. With distrust. After all, he straddled the fence: one month, almost Amish; the next month, about as far from it as he could get.

It was amazing Esther talked to him. Spent time with him, cultivating a friendship. At least he knew she didn't harbor unrealistic hopes of his returning and marrying her. Though maybe she hoped she could influence him for the sake of his großeltern. They needed him. He'd be blind not to recognize that.

But returning for gut?

The money he earned on the river went toward their care and for help. He did his part. He'd never return for gut. He couldn't.

Though, for a girl like Esther, he might consider it.

He blew out a sigh of frustration. How had his thoughts gone from the unforgiveable sins of the past to an unattainable girl of the present?

~

After Anna finished her cup of soothing chamomile tea, Esther tucked her into bed. The older woman was chatty, still overexcited about the company they'd entertained all day. The shouts of the kinner, the older cousins playing baseball, and all the aenties and young women packing the haus.

If Esther could have found a spare second, she would've looked for Viktor. But everyone knew she was there as Anna's caregiver, so they'd figured they could take advantage of her services. "Esther, please do this...." "Esther, please get that...." "Esther, please change my boppli's diaper." She'd barely had a chance to sit and eat lunch. It kind of reminded her of the constant busyness of her parents' haus.

Anna hadn't noticed, or she might've pointed out that Esther wasn't a household servant. But the Gut Book talked of the importance of being *"servant of all."* And the Petersheim family had treated her with warmth and appreciation, always saying "please" and "danki" rather than issuing direct orders. Plus, it had been nice to have Anna's dochters home.

Now, the haus was quiet. Dark. Reuben and Anna were both in bed. And still nein sign of Viktor. Maybe he waited for her at the pond.

She slipped on her shoes, filled a paper bag with a sandwich, a fresh peach, and a soda, in case Viktor was hungry, and then walked down to the pond. His truck was parked along the bank.

She didn't hear anything, other than the usual nacht sounds. Then a figure straightened beside the truck.

"You're late."

She heard the smile in his voice. "Jah, I am. Anna was reliving all her conversations with your family members."

A beat of silence. "I've been by the pond all day. Caught a mess of fish. They're cleaned and in the cooler." He caught her hand. "I brought a few blankets and two pillows. They're in the truck. Want to stargaze first? Or we could drive into one of the larger towns, find one of the twenty-four-hour fast-food restaurants, and grab a bite to eat. I'm hungry."

"I did bring you some food." She held out the bag.

"Danki." He accepted it and unfolded the top. "So, stargaze?" He took the sandwich out of the bag and bit into the bread. Basically inhaled it.

After he'd finished eating, Viktor reached behind the seat and pulled out the blankets and pillows he'd mentioned. He had them spread out in the truck bed before she could blink.

She struggled to breathe. To find some words. What would he expect? Just stargazing, like they'd done? Or would he try something more?

His hands grazed over her waist, then grasped it. She gasped as he lifted her into the truck bed. The next thing she knew, there he was next to her. "Lie down."

She sat stiffly, disregarding his directive. "Are you trying to seduce me?" She heard the tightness in her own voice. The fear that she might give in if he tried. Or maybe the fear that he would destroy all the dreams she'd been weaving about him. Maybe he heard it, too.

After a moment of silence, he rolled over on his side and looked at her. "Are you seducible?"

Chapter 14

Esther gave a horrified gasp, and Viktor cringed. He shouldn't have asked her that. But he couldn't resist. Besides, he could admit wanting to—at least to himself.

"Nein!" Esther's reply was belated, but he wouldn't fool himself into believing it was because she'd had to think about it. More likely, she had to recover from her shock enough to answer.

He rolled to his back and stared up at the sky but didn't see any stars. Odd. It had been a clear day, not a cloud in sight. But now, it appeared hazy. Smoky. "You're safe. Unless you don't want to be."

She let out a shuddery breath. He didn't figure there was any way she could answer that. At least, not truthfully. He knew better. He'd seen the attraction in her eyes. The desire she tried to hide. The verboden fascination with the bad bu.

Not to mention, she'd kum to meet him to-nacht. Even after he'd openly called it a date.

As expected, she didn't reply. Instead, she dared to lie back on the blanket and stared up at the sky. "Nein stars."

He rolled back to his side, facing her, and reached out a trembling finger, letting it trail over her check, then down to her lips. He lightly traced them, feeling her involuntary quiver.

"Just so you know, I intend to kiss you someday." He let his hand slide down her neck. "Maybe to-nacht."

"I should go." She struggled to sit up. "I'm—"

He gently held her down by the arm. "Kidding. I shouldn't tease you like that." Though it wasn't a joke. He'd meant it. He swallowed. "I know my boundaries."

In the distance came the pop, pop, pop of firecrackers, the colorful display bursting overhead. He cringed.

Five years ago to-nacht....

He tried to relax. To mask his growing unrest. To pretend he was enjoying the light show.

Somehow, the Gott-given light shows—twinkling stars, lightning bugs—were more pleasant. Not as flashy. More peaceful.

A shame he hadn't always felt that way. Maybe then—

Somewhere, something flamed into the sky.

Other than lightning, Gott's light shows weren't nearly as dangerous.

He pushed up and bolted out of the pickup, sudden tears filling his eyes.

⌣

Esther stood on the front porch of the Petersheims' haus, struggling to process what had just happened. Viktor had left her there, holding the pillows and the wadded-up blankets, before racing off to who knows where, the pickup's tires spinning gravel in the driveway.

In the distance, the emergency bell started clanging. Every Amish man knew to respond to it. She looked toward the blaze lighting the sky. Whose haus was on fire? Hopefully the family managed to escape without injury.

She opened the door and slipped inside, hoping to get upstairs before Reuben came out and caught her with the bedding from the spare room. That would be incriminating.

She should—would—stop meeting Viktor at the pond. He'd begun to push the boundaries, and at this rate, it would be only a matter of time before he kissed her. And she feared her reaction. Her skin still burned from the oh-so-casual brush of his fingers across her collarbone. She'd almost expected the fabric of her dress to incinerate beneath his touch. Her lips still tingled from his light caress.

Reuben stepped out into the hallway, yanking up his suspenders with one hand, holding the lantern in the other. He paused when he saw Esther. His gaze dropped to the load she carried, then rose to her face, his eyebrows shooting up, his mouth turning down.

Her cheeks heated. *Caught.* Hopefully, she wouldn't be fired.

This was it. Nein more meeting Viktor.

She opened her mouth to defend herself, but then she shut it. What could she say? Best to wait for the accusations and then address them.

Instead, Reuben moved past her and into the kitchen.

"Esther?" Anna called from the bedroom.

She set down her bundle on the steps and entered the room.

"What's on fire? Did you see?" There was panic in Anna's voice.

Esther shook her head. "I don't know. It was off to the east."

"Five years ago today, I lost my home, my only sohn, and most of his family in a fire. We need to pray."

Viktor tore into a driveway and parked off to the side. The roof and the top lofts of a barn were on fire, probably the result of some foolish kids setting off firecrackers in the back field. Or, even worse, teens who should've known better. Teens like he had been.

Two Amish men exited the barn, leading horses. He could hear more animal screams coming from inside the burning structure.

Saving the animals would be the first step, followed by trying to save the haus.

He jumped from the vehicle and ran, passing the older Amish men as he entered the barn. He opened the back doors and let out the cows.

Other men, Amish and Englisch alike, had arrived by the time he emerged from the barn, and the women had begun a bucket brigade, passing pails of water from the well all the way up a ladder, on which a man stood dumping water over the roof of the haus.

The barn would be a total loss. Nein hope for that. The haus...?

Viktor took over pumping water from the well while someone else went to find more pails.

Sirens sounded from down the road. He saw flashing red lights. Someone had called the local volunteer fire department. Not him. He hadn't even thought of it.

His cell phone was probably dead by now, anyway.

He stepped away as the professionals took over.

Bishop Joe—short for Josiah—came toward him. "Danki for your gut work, Viktor. Can I expect to see you at services on Sunday?"

Viktor frowned. "We'll see."

He couldn't lie to the bishop, but he probably wouldn't be there.

He started to turn away when he noticed Grossdaedi striding toward him, an angry expression on his face. "Excuse me, Bishop Joe. Need to talk to the bu, here, a moment."

The bishop nodded and went to speak to someone else.

Grossdaedi grasped Viktor by the arm and steered him away from the crowd. Once they were alone, his grip tightened. "What. Have. You. Done?" Each word was punctuated with a slight shake.

Viktor frowned. "What did I do?"

"I saw Esther coming in with blankets and pillows. If you defiled her in any way—"

"Hold it." Viktor raised his free hand. "I haven't even kissed Esther, on the cheek or anywhere else. I certainly haven't…. Wow. You have a really low opinion of me." That hurt. Almost as much as the memories this day awakened.

Grossdaedi frowned. "It wasn't you? I suppose it might've been Henry. But I've seen her expression when she ends a date with him. And I've also seen her expression after she's spent time with you. She wore the one she always wears after an outing with you."

He wouldn't ask what the difference might be, though maybe he'd think about it later. He shook his head. "She was with me. But we were only stargazing and talking, until the fireworks started." Not quite true. "And then…. Then…." His throat swelled shut, and he spluttered to a stop with a sobbing cough.

Grossdaedi pulled him into a hug. "It will get better. It will. But you need to give it to Gott instead of trying to carry it alone." He patted his shoulder before releasing him. "Sorry I misunderstood. But this would not look gut if anyone else discovered it. You don't want to ruin her reputation."

"I don't want to give up her friendship, either." Viktor scuffed his shoes in the dirt. "She can't marry Henry. She doesn't love him. He's not gut for her."

Grossdaedi turned away. "I'm not sure *you* are gut for her. But she would be gut for you, I know."

If only he could be gut enough for her. Gut enough for Gott's love and forgiveness.

Gut enough.

Maybe someday.

Chapter 15

Esther didn't know how long she knelt on the floor beside Anna's wheelchair. She'd moved the chair to the front room and placed it in front of the big window where they could see the orange glow in the sky. They also could see their barn, so they would know when Viktor or Reuben returned. The fire trucks had wailed by over an hour ago.

Esther and Anna took turns praying out loud. Esther wasn't used to praying that way, but Anna wanted to hear the prayers, not just think them. Maybe it comforted her to know what Esther was praying, too.

Admittedly, Esther had never put much thought into her prayers. Speaking them aloud forced her to think, to concentrate, to really voice her concerns. It made Gott seem more real, more likely to answer, than did the impersonal prayers she usually formed in her head.

Anna tightened her grip on Esther's hands. "And, Lord, we pray for Viktor. Please help him to find a way to forgive himself and to be at peace. You know he needs You. Please do whatever it takes to bring him to his knees. Draw him to Yourself, Lord—even if he doesn't return to the Amish, at least bring him to faith. But if You see clear to bringing him back to the Amish community, I would be grateful. But not my will...."

Esther had callously mentioned his family. They were the ones who'd died five years ago. Anna's only sohn. Viktor's daed. And most of his family. Was Viktor the sole survivor? Was that what had happened to pull Viktor away?

Tires crunched on the gravel driveway. Esther opened her eyes and peeked through the window. Viktor drove the truck around to the back of the barn.

Anna leaned forward. They both watched as he opened the barn door, lit a lantern, and stood there, waiting. A few minutes later, Reuben drove his buggy in. Viktor unhitched the horse, then disappeared with it inside the barn.

Reuben came toward the haus. The kitchen screen door squeaked but didn't slam. He entered the room, his shoulders slumped.

Anna squeezed Esther's hand, almost painfully. "What happened?"

Reuben raised his head. "Bishop Joe lost his barn. We saved the haus. Viktor thought maybe fireworks caused the fire, or someone's carelessness with them. But apparently, the bishop's oldest sohn and some of his friends were smoking in the barn loft, watching the Englisch display. Someone dropped his cigarette. But nein lives were lost. This time. Bishop Joe is very upset. I'm thinking he'll be speaking about this on Sunday." He started for the hall. "I'm going to shower before Viktor finishes with the horse and comes in. Then, I'd love a mug of that nighttime tea, Esther." He stopped and looked over his shoulder. "Viktor explained. Sorry for jumping to conclusions."

A mixture of relief and embarrassment washed over Esther, and she glanced at the blankets and pillows still piled on the steps.

"I'll get the water heating." Esther stood and looked at Anna, who released her hands. "Would you like some, too?"

"Jah. Danki. And fix some for Viktor. I think we all need to relax."

Esther nodded. She left the room and carried the blankets and pillows upstairs, then went down to the kitchen and filled the teakettle with water. Anna joined her shortly.

The kettle had just started whistling when the door opened and Viktor walked in. He smelled smoky, as if he'd been downwind from the blaze. Or even in it, rescuing the animals.

Gut thing she and Anna had prayed. Going into a burning barn was dangerous.

His gaze met hers, and he hesitated, then looked at the clock hanging on the wall. "You're still up?"

"Anna and I were praying. Then Reuben suggested we might benefit from some tea."

Viktor nodded. "And a hug."

Esther's pulse accelerated.

But he walked past her and fell to his knees in front of Anna.

⁓

Grossmammi's arms closed around Viktor, and he buried his head in her lap, as if he were a small bu. He resisted the urge to sob.

Grossmammi's hands ran over his back, alternatively rubbing and patting. "There, there. It'll be all right."

Really?

Viktor pulled in a shaky breath and sat back. "Danki, Grossmammi." He pushed to his feet and turned. Esther stood by the stove, staring at him.

Was it disappointment he saw in her eyes?

She dipped her head before he could tell for sure. She lowered a tea bag into each of four mugs, then filled them with boiling water.

His heart ached for what could've been. If he hadn't left town, if he hadn't done the things he had, he might've had the opportunity to be gut enough for Esther. To court her. They might've been married by now.

Of course, she might've chosen Henry over him, anyway. As she apparently had.

She might be fascinated by the bad bu, but she wasn't crazy enough to toss Henry by the wayside. Viktor scowled just as Esther glanced his way. She immediately averted her eyes.

Way to go, Petersheim. He blew out a frustrated breath, wanting to tell her to forget the tea; that he'd go find something to do to vent. But maybe that wasn't the answer. Maybe staying there, being forced to calmly, quietly drink some sort of herbal refreshment, was just what he needed. After a hot shower. "I'll be back before the tea's finished steeping," he said, then took the stairs two at a time.

When he returned, the other three were seated at the kitchen table. Grossdaedi methodically dunked the tea bag in his mug. Up, down. Up, down. Up, down. Then he pressed his spoon against the bag to drain it, removed it from the mug, and set it on a small ceramic dish.

This scene was peaceful. Unlike most of Viktor's day. Even though he'd been alone, he'd wrestled with his memories—until more pleasant thoughts of Esther had broken in. Viktor pulled out his chair, sat, and peeked at her from under lowered lashes. She met his gaze, blushed, and dipped her head.

He glanced at his großeltern and, seeing that their attention centered on their steaming cups of tea, smiled and leveled his gaze at Esther. When she darted another glance his way, he winked.

The color deepened in her cheeks.

His smile widened. And then, regardless of the possibility that his großeltern watched, he extended his stockinged foot and nudged hers.

Every fiber of Esther's body seemed tuned to Viktor's movements. He lifted the tea bag from his mug, mimicking Reuben's actions, and took a sip. His foot rested comfortably, warmly, against hers. And she didn't pull away. Instead, she wished there was some way they could "hold feet" instead of hands.

Why, why, why couldn't she feel for Henry the attraction she felt toward Viktor? It didn't seem right or fair that she was promised to a man she didn't love. A man she felt nothing for. She really hadn't been given a choice. Their mamms had arranged it, Henry approached the bishop, and Daed had agreed. Not fair.

Granted, she could have refused when Henry had asked to drive her home after singings and frolics. And she hadn't. She'd known that by accepting, she was giving him permission to court her. She could've said "nein" at any time. But she hadn't. That wouldn't have been submitting to Mamm's wishes. Or Daed's arrangement.

And Henry's mamm thought she wasn't submissive enough.

Really? Mindlessly obeying every wish as if it were a command?

She should've refused.

And now, her mistake stared her in the face.

In love…with another man.

If she felt this way now, during courtship, how much farther would her thoughts stray after marriage? It wasn't fair to Henry. Or to herself.

Besides, she'd seen him give that "special look" to Sarah Hershberger. Never to her.

She needed to part ways with Henry, even though she wouldn't fool herself into believing she had a chance with Viktor.

She didn't. Their relationship consisted of friendship. Sort of.

And even that was ending, since she had decided to stop meeting him at the pond.

Her heart was breaking.

Should she quit her job and head home, freeing some other girl to work here?

Her parents needed the money. Not the extra mouth to feed. She had to stay.

And she needed to master her emotions.

Anna pushed her wheelchair back from the table. "The dishes will wait for morgen, Esther. I'm ready to get back to bed."

Esther carried the dishes over to the sink while Anna wheeled herself from the room. Then she followed the older woman down the hall.

Anna put her hands on the armrests and stood, then took a step toward the bed without assistance. She sat on the edge, scooted back, then lifted her legs in.

"You're in love with Viktor. Time to let Henry go."

Esther's jaw dropped. Were her emotions really that easy to read? She wanted to deny it, but that'd be a lie.

Instead, her eyes filled with tears. An admission, albeit a silent one.

Anna reached for her hand and squeezed. "Trust, Esther. Trust and pray."

Chapter 16

The hot shower and herbal tea relaxed Viktor enough to give him the best nacht's sleep since he'd been home. In the morgen he stretched and sat up, glancing at the clock. *Wow.* He'd overslept. He opened the bedroom door and headed for the stairs but stopped when he saw that Esther's door stood open.

Something had shifted in their relationship. In his favor. He couldn't pinpoint what it was.

Or maybe he could.

The shy glances. The frequent blushes.

Warmth spread through him.

Henry needed to be worried. Very worried.

Viktor crossed the hall and peeked in her room, though what'd he say to her beyond "Gut morgen," he wasn't sure. He couldn't ask her on a walk or a buggy ride. Their dates needed to be kept unplanned. At least until she realized what had happened and decided to break up with Henry.

If she chose Viktor, would she jump the fence, too? More likely, he'd return. She'd make staying around an easier thing.

The room was vacant.

Well, not completely. She hadn't moved out. Viktor glanced around, making sure the coast was clear. He listened for sounds downstairs and heard muted conversation. Esther and Grossmammi. He stepped into the room and ran a finger over the cover of her well-worn Bible, then slipped a few dollars in between the pages. He smoothed her pillow and tugged on the string of her black bonnet, hanging on a peg.

A plain room. For a plain girl.

What was she curious about? Did she wonder, as he did, what it'd be like when they kissed?

Would it be something special, or would she eventually end up another nameless, faceless girl from his past?

If only he hadn't kissed so many girls before. If only he hadn't been such a reckless teen, driven to live dangerously after the deaths of his parents and brothers. Driven to control his life instead of letting Gott take the reins.

Esther was the complete opposite. A gut Amish girl. Submissive. Quiet. A blessing.

The man who married her would be blessed, indeed.

If only *he* could be that man.

He left her room and strode downstairs. Esther wasn't in the kitchen, but a delicious smell was coming from the oven. His stomach rumbled.

The soft voices echoed from down the hall. She was probably in the bedroom with Grossmammi.

Viktor headed out to the barn and started on the before-breakfast chores, such as milking, letting the cows out, and feeding the horses. Grossdaedi was in the cow barn. Viktor must've really slept soundly to not have heard the family get up and start the day.

Grossdaedi winced with every move he made. Had he hurt himself while fighting the fire? Or was it simply a sign of age after unusual exertion? These painful back episodes seemed to be occurring more frequently these days, and after less effort.

Another clear indicator of how much Viktor was needed. He went on by, going up the ladder to the loft for some oats for the horses.

But how could he move back for gut? How could he face his memories, day in and day out?

Or would they go away in time?

Probably not.

Starting a relationship with Esther would be opening them both up to hurt. He probably should back off and spare her that pain. But the potential loss of Esther hit him hard. Too late for him. He'd already started to fall in love.

He finished his work, then went to check on Grossdaedi. He found him hunched over, a hand to his back, the milking pail by his feet.

"Go inside, Grossdaedi. Take a hot shower. I'll finish up the milking and let the cows out."

Grossdaedi shook his head, slowly forcing his spine straighter. "Don't coddle me. I just strained my back a little. I'll be fine. I'll finish the milking and let them out."

Right. Viktor would call a chiropractor that afternoon and see if he could schedule an appointment for Grossdaedi.

It looked like Grossdaedi had only one cow left to milk. "Just let me take this full pail inside for you," Viktor offered.

Grossdaedi nodded his agreement, which spoke volumes about his pain level. "I'll be right in."

Viktor lifted the pail and carried it inside, mentally adjusting the day's schedule. He'd need to stay close to Grossdaedi and help however he could.

Esther placed a platter of sweet rolls on the counter. Homemade, of course, and filled with fruit, from the looks of it. An empty package of cream cheese lay at the top of the trash can.

His stomach rumbled again. He washed his hands and sat at the table.

"You can't marry Henry." He spoke the words as soon as they passed through his mind—for the hundredth time. "You're making a mistake."

Esther blinked. "Freeing me up to make an even bigger mistake with you?"

Ouch.

"He may not love me, but at least he hasn't cheated on me. You, on the other hand...."

Careful, Esther. Don't say it.

"You haven't been faithful since the day you were born. You went behind the barn with how many girls? You were with Bethany at my brother's wedding—*after* asking me to accompany you to the singing. With the implication that you'd drive me home, not Henry."

He blinked, remembering the polite look she'd worn when she'd kum to the door at the wedding. Polite, for Henry. Her expression had transformed into a flash of joy when she'd seen it was him.

His heart pounded.

Jealous. Definitely jealous.

He stood and started walking around the table toward Esther. "I didn't go behind the barn with Bethany."

Grossmammi rolled into the room. He hesitated a moment, then nodded at her and went to push her wheelchair to the table. "Morgen." He helped Grossmammi settle at her place.

Esther approached the table, and he glanced at her. "Bethany told me that their generator had stopped, and they needed me to take a look. That's what I did. Fixed the generator." He leaned over, kissed Grossmammi's cheek, then straightened. "Be right back. I need to kiss the girl."

Grossmammi beamed and looked up expectantly, as if she thought it'd happen there. In the kitchen. In public.

The joy of approval washed over him. She welcomed the idea of Esther as her gross-dochter-in-law.

Esther stared at him, wide-eyed. "What? Nein. You can't."

"Here or behind the barn. You choose." He moved toward her.

She backed away.

"I'm not picky, süße." He used Grossmammi's pet name for her. *Sweetie.* "Here or behind the barn." He'd prefer the privacy of behind the barn. He didn't need Grossmammi's opinion on his technique.

Esther cast a frantic glance toward Grossmammi, then apparently realized nein help would kum from that direction, and a look of resignation crossed her face. Fear shone in her eyes. Was she afraid of him? "Behind the barn," she whispered.

He couldn't quite identify the expression on her face. Not repulsion. It was more positive than the fear that still shone in her eyes. Expectation, perhaps? Curiosity?

"Gut choice." Grinning, he turned to Grossmammi. "We'll be back." Then he reached for Esther's hand.

She avoided his touch.

Grossmammi looked disappointed. "I'll have your grossdaedi call you if you aren't back by the time he comes in and washes up."

A limited time frame. Too limited. Not a second to waste.

He scooped up Esther in his arms, ignoring her gasp as her body came into contact with his, and strode from the room.

Thankfully, she didn't resist him. Maybe he'd shocked the fight right out of her. And thankfully, Grossdaedi wasn't in sight when Viktor came out of the haus, down the porch steps, and headed behind the barn. Because that would've been the end right there.

He lowered Esther to her feet in the tall grass behind the barn. Tears had made tracks down her cheeks.

"Ach, süße. Don't cry. I won't hurt you." He flattened his left hand against the barn wall. As he had with the girls in the past.

He raised his right hand and gently brushed the tears from her face.

His fingers trembled. He'd never done that before.

"Relax. Take a deep breath."

She obeyed, sucking in air as if she'd never get enough.

Viktor waited for the exhalation before leaning forward and brushing his lips against hers. She tasted sweet, like a mixture of blueberries and cream cheese. *Delicious*. And there was a tentative response. Or so he thought.

He pulled back. Looked into her wide eyes. A remnant of fear remained. Possibly mixed with a bit of longing.

He moved his hand from the barn wall and cupped her face with both palms—another thing he'd never done. He leaned in again, gauging her reaction. One kiss morphed into two, three, a continuous stream.

She matched him, kiss for kiss, her lips softening, parting. Responding with a passion that surprised him.

Ach, Esther.

Why had he waited so long?

More important, how would he walk the straight and narrow after this?

〜

Esther trembled in his arms as his body pressed her against the barn wall. She wanted to hold him, so she wrapped her arms around his neck and squirmed closer.

Desire rose within her like sweet, thick maple syrup. Her heart pounded so quickly, he probably could feel it. Hear it.

His lips firmed, his hands sliding away from her face to cup the back of her neck. His kisses deepened. She pressed herself closer, her stomach clenching, toes curling, knees weakening. *Wow. Wow. Wow.* Her fingers tangled in his hair.

His lips roamed, kissing her nose, her eyelids, her mouth....

It felt so *gut* to be wanted.

She tightened her embrace, kissing him with all the desire she hadn't known she possessed.

He pulled away, slowly, reluctantly, long before she wanted it to end.

"Grossdaedi's calling." His voice was ragged. He trailed a finger over her cheek, down to her lips. Took a shuddering breath. "You're a wild one, ain't so?" His hand slid down her neck. "Take a moment before you follow." He pulled in another shaky breath and turned away.

Wow. Oh, wow.

Esther leaned back against the barn, raising her fingers to her lips.

Nein wonder Lily nearly swooned whenever she talked about going behind the barn with Viktor.

Lily...and all those other girls....

Tears burned Esther's eyes.

She was one of many.

It meant nothing to him.

She fell to her knees.

Ach, Gott. What have I done?

〜

Kissing Esther was nothing like Viktor had ever experienced. Now he feared he wouldn't be able to get enough. He struggled to pull himself together as he rounded the barn.

Grossdaedi had started down the porch steps. He paused when he saw Viktor.

"I thought you'd be in before me. Your grossmammi told me to call you."

Viktor managed a nod and trailed Grossdaedi up the steps. He hoped that was all Grossmammi had told him. He didn't want a lecture. And he didn't think he'd be able to carry on a normal conversation anytime soon.

At least not without a cold shower first.

He certainly hadn't expected that response from Esther. Maybe it would've been better to kiss her in the kitchen with a chaperone. It would've been a much shorter, much less passionate, kiss, for sure.

He followed Grossdaedi into the kitchen, knowing he'd have to be very careful now. Because one of them was bound to have a broken heart. Maybe both of them, if his reading of all the signals she'd been sending proved right.

Grossmammi looked up expectantly, as if she wanted to hear a play-by-play.

"Need. Shower." He walked past her, ignoring the disappointment in her gaze, and went upstairs.

Chapter 17

Esther needed to stop at the outside water pump on the way to the haus to splash cold water on her face so that nobody would suspect anything. Though Anna would, she realized. Viktor had explicitly spelled out his intentions.

They would both know she'd just been thoroughly kissed.

And humiliated. Though maybe they didn't know about his reputation with other girls. Anna's hopeful, excited look flashed in her mind. Did her employer really have her best interests in mind in her apparent encouragement of her attraction to Viktor?

How could she face them?

How could she face *him*?

She needed to leave. Right now. She couldn't stay here.

But where would she go? She'd have to kum up with quite a story to talk Daed out of the necessity of the extra income.

She had to pull herself together. She took a step and caught her bare foot on something. She looked down and saw her white kapp, one of its strings stuck between her toes.

Her kapp? Esther leaned over to pick it up, and her hair fell over her shoulders. She fingered a long section of brown curls.

She knelt, looking for her hairpins. But she couldn't feel any in the tall weeds surrounding her. What had he done? Flung them off? Taken them with him, leaving her to face his großeltern with her hair down? Looking like a loose, worldly woman?

How could he shame her like this?

She wouldn't need to worry about quitting her job. Reuben would fire her. Her transgressions would be brought before the bishop and reported to the church. She'd have to kneel and confess. And Henry....

Well, at least she'd be free. One benefit.

Or maybe she was overreacting.

How had past girls handled this situation? She couldn't remember seeing any with mussed hair after going behind the barn with Viktor. Lily had certainly never mentioned it.

Maybe he'd been as out of his mind as she had been and hadn't realized what he was doing.

Esther ran her hands through her hair, remembering the feel of Viktor's fingers against her scalp. She shivered, her stomach clenching again. Why hadn't she realized what that meant at the time?

She found a few pins caught in her hair and used those to loosely pin it back up. She secured her kapp, trying to summon her "gut Amish girl" demeanor. Not the type who allowed a man to lure— make that *carry*—her behind the barn.

She turned toward the haus, but her attention was caught by Viktor's truck. A silent, nonhuman witness to their kisses.

Why couldn't Gott have laid on the horn and interrupted them?

At least she could check the mirror to see if she looked like the gut Amish girl she needed to be. She opened the unlocked door and scrambled into the driver's seat, feeling naughty. Inhaled Viktor's piney scent, probably made stronger by the sweltering heat inside the vehicle. His seat curved against her back, warming her.

Ach, Viktor.

Esther lowered the sun visor and peered at her reflection in the small mirror. Her face appeared red and blotchy from her tears, and several loose strands of hair had escaped her kapp. She tucked them into place. Better.

Her lips were swollen. She lightly touched them again, remembering his kisses, his touch.

Wow. Oh, wow.

Maybe it wasn't such a bad thing. She'd have a memory to warm her at nacht if she was forced to marry Henry.

The passenger door opened.

She jerked her fingers away from her lips, her face burning.

"Planning on learning to drive?"

Reuben.

Esther bowed her head, tears threatening again. This was it. She'd be fired.

⌒

Viktor went back downstairs after his cold shower. The frigid water had done little to erase his memories of the too-brief time with Esther.

She absolutely could *not* marry Henry. He'd kill all the passion in her. Viktor frowned, remembering Henry's unkind criticism of Esther.

Not submissive enough. Need to take a firm hand....

Would Henry be physically abusive? What else could he have meant by "take a firm hand"?

If Viktor were Esther, he would have ended the relationship right there.

Besides, if her response to his kisses were any indication, she didn't love Henry. It'd be an unhappy marriage from the start.

Viktor rounded the corner into the kitchen. Grossmammi sat alone, a cup of koffee in her hand, a plate of one of Esther's sweet rolls in front of her. Odd that nobody else was in there. Where were Grossdaedi and Esther?

Had she returned from behind the barn?

Or had Grossdaedi found out what had happened and gone looking for her?

His blood chilled.

He cleared his throat. "Where's Grossdaedi?"

"He went to see where Esther disappeared to." Grossmammi set down the cup. "Well?" The expectant look was back in her eyes. "You're in love with her, ain't so?"

Jah. Big time. He didn't know how he could possibly continue to live without her. But it was too soon to declare his feelings to anyone. Viktor forced a smile and shook his head. "I'll be back."

He hurried outside, descended the porch steps, and almost ran around the barn. Grossdaedi sat in the passenger seat of Viktor's truck. Esther was in the driver's seat, her head on the steering wheel, her shoulders shaking.

Crying.

Ach, dear Gott. How can I fix this?

The prayer slipped out, almost unnoticed.

He yanked open the driver's side door of the pickup with a glance at Grossdaedi. He sat there, hands clasped, his brows wrinkled in confusion.

Remembering the fear in her eyes from earlier, Viktor stopped short of pulling Esther into his arms. He'd probably scared her. That would be adding fuel to the fire. She wouldn't welcome it. He needed to move very slowly now.

He pulled in a calming breath. "If you're going to take driving lessons, shouldn't your instructor be someone who actually knows how to handle something other than a horse and buggy?"

Nobody laughed.

But he hadn't expected them to.

He touched Esther's shoulder. "Scoot over, süße."

She stiffened but slid closer to Grossdaedi without looking up.

Viktor squeezed in next to her and shut the door, trying to ignore the way his leg pressed against hers. He inserted the key in the ignition and twisted it toward him, then pressed the power buttons to lower the windows. "Hot in here, ain't so?" He looked past her to Grossdaedi. Took in another breath. "I'm the one who picked her up and carried her back here. I'm sorry. It won't happen again." Not because he didn't want it to. "Don't fire her. She's the best thing to ever happen to this family."

Grossdaedi frowned. "I warned you not to hurt her."

And her hurt was obvious, based on all the tears.

Viktor glanced away. As much as he hated being scolded, it was worse with Esther there, her face buried in her hands, sniffling.

He turned back to her, caught her chin in his hand, and gently lifted her head to face him. Then he glanced from her tear-filled green eyes to Grossdaedi's angry brown glare. "I'm sorry, Grossdaedi. I'm really sorry, süße. I didn't mean to hurt you." He swallowed. Hard. "It won't happen again." Though he might be subjecting himself to a lifetime of cold showers to make it true.

He couldn't keep his gaze from lowering to her oh-so-kissable lips.

⌒

Esther found nein comfort in his words. She pulled away from Viktor, took the handkerchief Reuben pressed into her hand, and wiped her eyes, trying to staunch the flow of tears.

She wanted it to happen again. She wanted Viktor to pledge his undying love for her and make things right. Starting by asking her to allow him exclusive courting rights. Followed by asking Bishop Joe if he could marry her.

And she'd confessed as much to Reuben when he'd climbed into the pickup cab with her and made that wisecrack about her learning to drive.

She hadn't given Reuben a chance to talk, let alone fire her. Instead, she'd confessed her every sinful thought, as if he were Gott himself. Or Bishop Joe.

She'd confessed that she was in love with Viktor. That she was jealous of all the other girls he'd kissed. That she didn't want to be the "gut girl" who mindlessly obeyed her parents' every wish. That she wanted to make her own decisions.

She'd admitted that she wasn't as submissive as she should be.

After all that, she hadn't been able to bear looking at Reuben, not wanting to see the inevitable pity and judgment in his eyes. Instead, she'd buried her face in her arms on the steering wheel and cried, leaving Reuben sitting in stunned silence, probably wondering how to handle her "total meltdown," as Lily would call it.

The next time she saw Henry, she'd try to end their relationship. But he hadn't made arrangements for another date. He seemed content to simply bring her home from the singings and frolics.

Probably because he shared her lack of feelings. Both of them planning to marry against their will.

But she didn't know how to break up with him. When she told Henry, would it end there? Or did she also need to talk to the bishop? Could it even be broken off once Bishop Joe had given his approval? She didn't know of anyone who'd tried that.

She'd be the first.

Esther shifted, suddenly remembering the two men still sitting in the truck with her. Viktor's leg pressed against hers, his arm loosely resting on the seat behind her. A light, comforting touch. Nonintrusive.

Apparently he'd been talking with his grossdaedi, because he nodded. "That's wise. I'll do that," he told the older man. Then he winked at Esther.

Reuben patted her shoulder. "Everything has a way of working out, Esther. Kum on in as soon as you've calmed down."

"I'm not fired?" Did she sound as shocked as she felt?

Reuben chuckled. "Nein."

"I'll drive you over to talk to Henry later." Viktor pulled his arm away. Crazy that she immediately missed the comforting touch. He opened the truck door and climbed out.

"What?" Esther straightened and looked from Viktor to Reuben.

Reuben nodded. "Already decided that'd be best." He opened his door and slowly turned sideways to get out.

Already decided"? Had Reuben spilled her secrets while she'd been lost in her thoughts?

Ach, nein. Nein. Nein. Nein. What would she say to Henry? Especially with Viktor standing there listening?

"But first, I'll walk down to the phone shanty and look up the number for the chiropractor," Viktor said. "Then I'll be back for breakfast. Grossdaedi, you take it easy. Just tell me what you need, and I'll do it." He backed up a step.

Esther scooted toward him.

"Maybe we should work on that ramp for your grossmammi," Reuben said. "I'm guessing she's chomping at the bit, wondering what drama she's missing."

Esther slid out of the truck. Viktor's hand briefly gripped her elbow. Long enough to steady her. Long enough to send fire shooting through her arm.

The passenger door shut.

Esther dared glance up at Viktor.

His lips quirked, and he raised his hand, as if he wanted to touch her cheek. Then he glanced over her shoulder at Reuben and let his hand drop to his side. "Want to kum with me to the phone shanty?"

Jah. It'd mean more time to regroup before going on with life.

But then, *nein.* It'd be time alone with Viktor—something she didn't need more of right now.

"Nein." She shook her head. "And don't take me to see Henry."

She'd go alone, without witnesses.

Hurt shone in Viktor's eyes, and he leaned forward. "Don't delay, süße. You're not going to marry him. You're gonna marry—" He shook his head, then turned and strode away.

Chapter 18

After talking with the receptionist at the chiropractor's office, Viktor jogged back to the haus, hoping everything would be back to normal. Even though he had nein idea what could've transpired during his brief absence.

He went into the kitchen. Grossdaedi sat at the table finishing up his breakfast, but Grossmammi was gone. He heard voices coming from the other room. The therapists. He'd seen a car parked on the side of the road, but he'd thought maybe it was tourists, prowling around and snapping pictures of "Amish" cows. And freshly laundered clothes. They seemed to favor clotheslines, for some reason. He rolled his eyes.

Esther.... He looked around. Nein sign of her. He looked back at his grossdaedi.

"She went to start laundry."

Viktor nodded and went to the sink to wash. "They were able to fit you in at the chiropractor's. Your appointment's at two."

Grossdaedi grunted. "Waste of time and money."

"You'll feel better afterward. Always do." Viktor headed to the table, swung a chair around backward, and straddled it. He reached for a pastry and took a bite. "Mmmm."

"Back always hurts again in a few days," Grossdaedi grumbled.

"That's because you never take it easy. This time, I'll make sure you do."

"You and Esther." Grossdaedi shook his head. "The girl's like a mother hen."

Viktor smiled. He finished the pastry and stood up. "Want some more koffee?"

"Jah, danki."

Viktor topped off Grossdaedi's mug and filled one for himself, then straddled the chair again. "We need to talk about the ramp. Where do you want it?"

"Off the side of the back porch, at the end opposite from the steps."

"I'll get started, then. You rest."

"Feel worthless." Grossdaedi looked away. "I'll supervise."

Viktor pressed his lips together to keep himself from saying he didn't need a supervisor. Then he gave a tight smile. "Okay." He downed his koffee and stood. "I'll get the supplies."

He headed out to the workroom and collected the toolbox, then started gathering supplies to haul across the yard.

The door opened, and Esther appeared, a full laundry basket propped against her hip. It pulled the fabric of her dress taut across her chest. He looked away, his blood heating. Then he glanced back again. "Need some help?" He didn't wait for a reply but moved toward her, reaching out to take the basket.

"Danki." She avoided his gaze.

He grasped both ends of the rectangular basket and stepped backward. "After you."

She went out the door, descended the porch steps, and headed for the clothesline, the dusty purple material of her skirt swaying against her bare calves. He slowly raised his gaze to where the dress flared out over her hips, then narrowed around her waist. *Beautiful, so beautiful.*

"Down here. Danki." She pointed to a place on the ground, near the tree where the pulley that operated the clothesline was mounted. He'd installed it a few summers ago to make life a bit easier for Grossmammi, so she wouldn't have to carry clothes the length of a long line of rope. It benefited Esther, as well.

There was so much he wanted to say. And nothing he could. Everything waited on her. On her decision.

Well, there was also that pesky matter about whether he would return to the Amish.

He set the basket on the ground, then reached out with a trembling hand and brushed her cheek.

Her breath hitched. Her gaze shot to his.

His eyes stung as he stared into hers for a long, silent moment.

Choose me, Esther. Choose me.

Then he pulled away, turned around, and walked off.

The ramp waited.

⌒

Esther's hands shook as she watched him go, his stride sure, his back straight.

Everything had changed. Her formerly well-ordered world was nein longer calm and peaceful but reminded her of the snow globes she'd seen in thrift stores and yard sales, overturned and shaken up. She seemed trapped in the "bubble" with Viktor, everything all topsy-turvy and unsettled.

When he disappeared around the corner of the haus, she started hanging clothes on the line. Anna's dresses, mostly. She always wore some shade of blue. Reuben said it matched her eyes.

It'd be so nice to love and be loved like Anna. Daed never said nice things to Mamm. Or if he did, they were private, and Mamm didn't talk about them. They'd never shared a special, loving look that Esther was aware of.

But they must love each other some, or they wouldn't have such a large family.

What would it be like to have kinner with—

Time to stop that line of thought. She shook a dress out until it snapped, then pinned it to the line.

The next article was a pair of work pants. Reuben's. Kind of a light denim color, but not actually jean material.

"There you are."

Esther looked up to see her cousin Rachel kum around the haus.

"I'm going grocery shopping, since I didn't have a chance when I got off work yesterday, and I thought I'd stop to see if you wanted to kum."

"Jah, I need a few things," Esther said. "Just let me finish hanging up these clothes, and then I'll get the list and tell Anna where I'm going." She reached down for the next item. One of Viktor's T-shirts.

She was grateful for the presence of her cousin, preventing her from hugging it close to see if his piney scent had survived the washing.

Rachel picked up a towel, shook it out, and hung it up. She peered over her shoulder. "How's it going with Viktor home? Lily is so jealous. I don't think it's going so well with Peter, because she's talking about coming home early so she can see Viktor." She reached down and grabbed another item from the basket.

"She...she is?" Pain shot through Esther, spearing her heart, at the thought of Lily and Viktor.

"Jah. She called the phone shanty a couple of days ago. Daed heard it ring and took the message." Rachel pinned up one of Anna's dresses and looked at Esther. "Is Viktor as wild as Lily says?"

"I...I don't know." How could she answer that? "He hasn't been, at least around me. Maybe it depends on who he's with."

"It really caused a stir when Viktor picked you at the singing after Caleb and Miriam's wedding. A few days ago, Henry was shopping at the store where I work, and someone teased him about it. Something about the 'river rat' stealing you away." Rachel shook her head. "I've never seen Henry so angry. He slammed down a bag of flour, and it exploded everywhere. I was still sweeping up white dust the next day."

Esther hung up another shirt, followed by several pairs of black socks, while she tried to think of what to say. There seemed to be nothing suitable. Henry's temper was quick and volatile. She really did need to break up with him.

Rachel shook out a pair of pants. "Henry says he's going to talk to your daed about getting you removed from this job. Something about ruining your reputation, staying in the same haus, unchaperoned, with...." She hesitated. "Um, a lady-killer. Isn't that cute? That's what Henry called Viktor. As well as a few other things that I won't repeat. But 'lady-killer' stood out. After Henry left, I asked my boss what that meant. She said it's a man who takes advantage of women's attraction to him."

"He doesn't, though. Or he hasn't with me." He hadn't, had he? Esther lifted the last item from the basket and shook it a little too hard. How dare Henry say something like that! And wanting her to quit her job…? Being married to him would be a continuous trial. But Daed would say that Henry had the right. "Besides, I am chaperoned," she added, whether for her cousin or herself, she couldn't say. "Anna and Reuben are here. I won't quit, Rachel. Daed needs my income, and I'm safe here. Perfectly safe."

All except for her heart.

⌇

Viktor removed the porch railings where Grossdaedi indicated he wanted the ramp, then started building the support base. After a few minutes, a girl came around the corner of the haus and leaned against one of the porch posts. He looked at her. Dark blonde hair, an aqua green dress…. He recognized her from school and from singings but couldn't recall her name. It'd been a while.

"I'm Rachel."

She must've seen his confused expression.

He frowned. *Rachel…Rachel….* Where had he heard that name? *Oh, yeah. Esther's cousin.* He smiled.

"Ah, the one who has wanderlust and thinks my job is 'sooo romantic.'"

Rachel giggled. "Esther has been talking, jah?"

"She has." He laid out another length of lumber. "And my job isn't that romantic."

"My wanderlust is fed by books and postcards right now. But I don't think I'll forgive Lily for going to Pennsylvania and not taking me along. I've never been there."

"Why has she taken Esther and not you?"

Rachel shrugged. "Technically, Lily isn't my cousin. She's on Esther's daed's side of the family. I'm on Esther's mamm's side. And my parents don't entirely approve of Lily." She hesitated. "I'm sure you know why."

Viktor reached for his hammer and some nails. "Can't say that I do."

Rachel crossed her ankles. "Really? Lily has some stories...about you."

He held a nail in place, then tapped it with the hammer. "Esther said that, too. But it's been a while since I was a teen."

"Not that long."

"Long enough. Things changed. I really don't remember her." He aimed the hammer. And swung.

"I'm ready to go." Esther came out the kitchen door.

He looked up. She'd put on black stockings and tennis shoes. He missed the view of her bare calves.

The hammer smashed into his thumb. The same one he'd hit a few days earlier. While thinking of her.

He grunted, his gaze shooting from Esther to his throbbing thumb.

She was dangerous to have around during construction projects.

"Shall I kiss it to make it better?" Rachel asked.

"It's fine." Viktor couldn't keep his glance from straying to Esther. To her lips. They were parted, as if in shock at Rachel's bold offer. Or maybe she was preparing to kiss his thumb instead.

His stomach clenched as he imagined her mouth against his skin.

"It's fine," he said again, his voice husky.

Maybe if he caught her alone, he'd ask her to kiss it and make it better.

Maybe.

Chapter 19

Esther giggled as she followed Rachel out to the buggy. "I cannot believe you said that to Viktor."

Rachel laughed and climbed in. "Did you see how he looked at you? Like he could just eat you up. I about melted. Are you sure nothing happened? Because if nothing has, something sure will. Soooo romantic. Maybe you'll be the one who brings him home. Then again, I don't want you hurt—either by him or by the angry flour-smasher. Henry should be worried."

"Henry has nothing to worry about." A lie. But Esther didn't want to gossip about kissing Viktor, not even to Rachel. She looked away and noticed an envelope resting on the seat. Gut—an easy way to change the subject before her feelings were revealed. "You got a letter?"

"Jah. You know I told you I sent cards and encouraging notes to a man in Seymour, Missouri? I asked him to send me a postcard sometime so I could get a sense of that part of the state. I didn't really expect him to, though. Most men never write me back. I guess that borders on improper…I don't know. But he did. Write back, I mean." She reached inside the envelope and pulled out the contents. "You can read the letter if you want."

Esther unfolded the piece of paper and glanced at the picture inside—the skyline of Springfield, Missouri—then turned it over.

A view from my room.

—David

"Wow. I can't imagine living in a place like that. I thought you got the names and addresses from the *Budget*. He's not Amish?"

Rachel laughed. "He is Amish. He doesn't live there. That's the view from his hospital room. Go on, read the letter." She flicked the reins. "Ach, and don't think you've fooled me. You're avoiding the Viktor conversation, jah?"

Caught! Esther squirmed, her face heating. She snapped the letter open and began to read.

Rachel,

Thank you for sending me cards and telling me you're praying. It appears the recovery will be long and hard, so I appreciate your continued prayers. I asked someone to pick up a postcard of Seymour, but he couldn't find any. He said Springfield had several different ones, though. This is the view from my hospital room.

Please keep writing. I look forward to reading the encouraging words in future cards and letters from you.

Sincerely,
David Lapp

Esther looked up. "Is this the first letter he wrote you?"

"Jah." Rachel nodded. "I hope he writes again. If he can't send postcards, maybe he could just describe the area. He might get the hint if I describe ours."

Esther refolded the letter and slid it back inside the envelope as Rachel pulled the reins and the horse turned onto the road leading to town.

As they lapsed into comfortable silence, Esther smiled, thinking of Viktor—thoughtful and industrious. How much of the ramp would he get built while she was gone? It was gut that Reuben had agreed to let him build one. Then she frowned, thinking of Viktor striking his thumb with the hammer. Had something distracted him? Maybe Rachel told him Lily was coming home. He might've been thinking about her. He'd claimed he didn't really remember her, but.... "When is Lily arriving? Did your daed say?"

How long would she have before Lily stole Viktor's attention away?

Rachel frowned. "Nein. He told me that she'd call you, to-nacht, at seven. I forgot to tell you. It's another reason I came by today. Is that all right? I know you have to get Anna to bed. If it's okay, I'll meet you at the phone shanty."

"I can probably slip out for a minute."

Soon they neared the big haus where Henry lived with his family. Since she was in the area, Esther figured she'd get this unpleasant task over with. Otherwise, Viktor might insist on bringing her over himself. "Wait. Stop here a minute. I need to say something to Henry."

If she could find her courage.

Rachel grimaced as she pulled into the driveway. "I'll wait in the buggy."

"This won't take long." Esther climbed out, walked to the front door, and opened it. "Hallo?" Nein answer. And nobody came out from the barn. She went back to the buggy, shrugging as she climbed in. "Not sure where they went, but I guess I'll talk to him after the singing Sunday nacht."

"Don't tell him I told you about the flour incident." Rachel snorted. "I probably won't forget that as long as I live. I didn't know bags of flour could do that. I mean, 'Whack!' And then, 'Poof!' And...." She laughed. "Poor Greta was covered in flour from head to toe."

"I won't say a word." Esther squirmed. Maybe she should tell Rachel about kissing Viktor and her plans to break things off with Henry. She could hold her accountable and maybe act as a source of encouragement. "I was actually thinking about breaking up with Henry," she said without further deliberation. "Returning all the gifts he's given me, not that there's much. Just a windup clock in some ugly mustard color, and a set of flatware."

Rachel grinned. "Personally, gut. I don't like him at all. But what will your parents say? I know you've been virtually promised to Henry since the day you were born. His mamm and yours talk all the time about when you two join the families...."

"I know." Esther groaned. "And I don't even know if they'll let me change my mind. But I see how Reuben treats Anna, and I want that. It's like she's his greatest treasure."

"It might also have something to do with the handsome man living there with you, ain't so?"

"It might…." Oops. Esther hadn't meant to say that. "I mean…."

Rachel laughed again. "So, does Viktor treat you that way? Like you're his greatest treasure?"

⌒

As soon as Grossmammi's therapists left, Grossdaedi rolled the wheelchair outside so that she could check the progress of the ramp. Two unneeded supervisors, in Viktor's eyes. And Grossdaedi wasn't content to merely sit and watch. He kept coming down off the porch and giving Viktor directions for things he already knew how to do.

At least it made Grossdaedi feel needed.

Viktor's stomach rumbled, and he looked up from the almost finished ramp, expecting Esther to step outside and tell them lunch was ready.

How long would it be before she returned from town? He wasn't even sure what she and Rachel had gone there to do. Nobody had said.

He wouldn't ask.

Hearing the clip-clop of a horse's hooves on the road, he glanced that way, stopping work to study the buggy.

Turn in, turn in, turn in….

The buggy passed by. He returned to work but caught the knowing glance Grossmammi shared with Grossdaedi. They probably thought that these previously foreign feelings toward a woman would lead him to return to the faith.

It'd happened before, to other men. Lured back home by some woman they couldn't live without.

If he were a praying man…. But he wasn't, so why even think about praying? Probably because he'd prayed once since coming home and reuniting with the lovely Esther. And Gott had seemed to hear that prayer. He'd kept Esther from being fired. Kept her in his life.

Or maybe it wasn't Gott, because Grossdaedi hadn't seemed all that intent on firing her in the first place. Instead, he'd stared at Esther with a mixture of amusement and concern when Viktor had burst in on them sitting in the pickup. And then Grossdaedi had told Viktor, calmly, quietly, that she needed to break up with Henry. Immediately, if not sooner.

Viktor couldn't have agreed more. And he'd offered to take her to do so that very day.

It hurt to think that she might have been crying over the thought of losing Henry. It hurt worse to recall her refusal to end the relationship.

Or maybe her tears had been more related to her worries about being fired, since that was the only question she'd asked: *"I'm not fired?"*

Heavens, no. He'd elope with her first.

His stomach flipped.

Pain shot through him. He blinked and stared down at his bruised hand. He'd hit his thumb with the blasted hammer again.

Apparently, even just thinking of Esther while doing construction was dangerous.

He'd *need* a kiss—maybe two—to make this better.

"Looks like they finished the ramp," Rachel observed as she pulled the buggy to a stop in the Petersheims' driveway. "You'll have dinner outside to celebrate, ain't so?"

"Nein. Supposed to be a chance of thunderstorms. Besides, I never did fry the fish that Viktor caught. We were out of cornmeal. So, that's what I'm fixing to-nacht. Want to kum in awhile?" She looked over her shoulder at Rachel.

Hands closed around her waist. She swallowed a scream as shock waves raced through her. *Viktor.* He lifted her down, then held her while she got her balance.

His hands moved to grip her upper arms. "Where'd you go?" He sounded harsh, angry. It reminded her of Henry. She jerked away.

"Grocery shopping. I have some packages to unload." Had something happened to Anna? Was Reuben worse?

Viktor released her, raised his hand, and let his finger trail over her cheek. Her cheeks flamed. Then he seemed to remember that they weren't alone. His gaze shot to Rachel, then back to Esther. "In the future, clear it with me—where you're going and how long you'll be away." His voice had gentled, thankfully.

Still, Esther blinked in disbelief. "What? Why? I asked Anna."

"I had to fix sandwiches."

Seriously? He was that big of a boppli about fixing a simple sandwich?

"If you need groceries, I'll take you to the store in my truck," he told her. "Or I'll do the shopping for you. What if Grossmammi needed you?"

"Reuben said—" Esther stopped. She didn't need to explain herself. Clear it with him? Really? She worked for Anna and Reuben—not Viktor.

"I don't care what Grossdaedi said."

"Sounds like somebody missed you," Rachel quipped from inside the buggy.

Viktor froze, his cheeks turning red. After a moment, he grabbed a few of the plastic grocery bags. "These yours?" He turned to carry them inside without waiting for an answer.

Esther looked at Rachel.

Rachel rolled her eyes. "Men."

They both giggled.

"I'll see you at seven." Esther grabbed the rest of her purchases and carried them inside. She found Viktor standing in the kitchen, digging through the bags and emptying their contents on the table.

"Grocery shopping?" He lifted a bottle of body spray in the air. "Nein wonder you smell so delicious."

Her face heated. She hadn't expected him to unload the groceries. Now to confess her vanity…her verboden use of scent….

She caught a glimpse of his blackened thumbnail. "Is that from the hammer?"

He frowned at his hand. "Jah." He looked up, met her gaze, and held out his thumb. "Kiss it and make it better?"

Chapter 20

I don't think that's a gut idea." Esther sounded strangled again.

Viktor's frown deepened. "It might help." He wiggled his thumb, then winced. Moving it was painful.

With a sigh, Esther snatched up the body spray and folded her arms across her chest, as if protecting herself. "I'm okay with being your friend, Viktor. But a relationship between us won't work."

A relationship? He talked about his thumb and right away she thought relationship?

"I'm Amish. I'm finishing baptism classes next month—with Henry—and joining the church. You already left the Amish." Pain darkened her eyes.

He blinked. For a moment, he was tempted to deny any interest in a relationship. But he'd be lying. And honestly, Esther had him thinking about the future. Things he'd never thought much of before. Thoughts of a frau and kinner, and....

He reached out and cupped her face with his hand. "I might return." *Someday.*

A flash of something that might've been hope lit her gaze but immediately dimmed. Jah, she wanted a relationship with him...same as he did with her. She held his gaze and leaned slightly into his touch, probably unaware that she was even doing that. "Really, Viktor? Really? Because I don't think you will return. And unless you do, I just can't risk—"

"Risk what?" *Your heart? It's mine already, my love.* He swallowed the words. Too soon to declare his feelings—or his knowledge of hers. It wouldn't help his case. "You haven't joined the church yet. You just admitted that. So, you won't be shunned. A relationship between us would be okay." He winked, letting his finger trail across her cheek to her lips. He traced their outline. "You might enjoy it."

She gulped and backed up a step, dislodging his hand. So much for helping his case. "You're a flirt. A...a...lady-killer. And...and I'm not a flirt. I'm wanting…I want someone who'll be faithful to me. Not someone I can't trust."

Ouch. But then, his track record to date gave her nein reason to believe him. Never mind that he hadn't pursued any girls—except for Esther—since he'd been home. That he hadn't, really, since he'd left the Amish. "And you trust *Henry?* I've seen him gazing at another girl."

She winced but didn't comment. She didn't need to. He saw the truth of that statement in her eyes.

"That aside, think about it, Esther. *Think!* I heard Henry say you aren't submissive enough. That he needs to take a firm hand with you. He might be abusive. Sounds that way to me."

She looked down. "He's right. I'm not submissive enough. I voice my opinion entirely too often. And you know, as well as I do, that's not allowed. I was raised to do as I'm told. To keep quiet. To accept orders without question."

He raised one eyebrow. "Then do as you're told. Dump Henry. Give me a chance."

She backed up again. He saw the refusal forming on her lips.

He held up his hand. "Men like a happy-ever-after ending, too, Esther. It's possible for a man to be faithful to one woman for life."

She frowned. "For you?"

"For me. Just a chance—that's all I'm asking. I'll keep my word. I won't…I won't kiss you again." Though he would be sorely tempted.

"I can only offer friendship."

He held her gaze. "I'll take friendship." And he'd run with it.

"Nein kisses. Nein touches."

She might as well ask for the moon. It'd be just as impossible. "Not until you beg for them, süße."

She looked relieved and disappointed, all at once. But she'd accepted that. Her smile flickered.

He resisted the urge to touch her cheek again. "I missed you today. Haus was empty with you gone."

She turned away. "So, it wasn't about the sandwiches."

He chuckled. "I can make sandwiches. It was about you, süße."

"I won't beg." She left the room.

He watched her go, remembering her unrestrained response to his kisses. *Jah, you will, süße. You will.*

⁓

Esther hugged herself tighter, then forced her arms to release their grip. It was a wonder she hadn't shattered the plastic bottle of body spray. And a gut thing nobody saw it—other than Viktor and Rachel. They wouldn't tell.

Besides, she wasn't the only Amish girl to use scented products. Not that it made it right. *Vanity, vanity. All vanity.* The preacher's words from last church Sunday rumbled through her memory. It was vanity. She wanted to be pretty—smell pretty—for Viktor.

She should be stronger when it came to him, not virtual putty in his hands. She wasn't even sure who'd "won" the exchange in the kitchen. She had the feeling he had—and that he knew it.

Esther took the bottle upstairs, then came back down and checked on Anna. She sat in the bedroom doorway, her Bible in hand. As Esther approached, she looked up with a troubled expression.

"Was ist letz?" Esther asked.

"Conversations are sometimes not so private, süße." Anna fingered the edges of the Book.

Esther's face flamed.

"I can't take sides. But I agree that Henry isn't right for you, and I want you to give Viktor a chance. I want you to be my gross-dochter-in-law. I think Viktor would be a gut ehmann. They say the way a bu treats his mamm is how he'll treat his frau. Viktor is respectful, caring, and will almost move mountains to do what I want, and I'm his grossmammi. But with Viktor's heart toward Gott the way it is…. You are wise."

Esther couldn't think of what to say. She dug her fingernails into her palms.

Anna closed the Bible and rolled backward to put it on her pillow. "Viktor, he lives for himself. He has to be in control. He wants what he wants."

Esther nodded.

"I know you've fallen in love with him. It's plain to see. Besides, Reuben told me what you said, out in the cab of Viktor's truck. He said he didn't tell Viktor anything, other than that you need to end things with Henry. But I think Viktor knows your feelings. Your eyes are so expressive. And so we pray, both of us, for Viktor. And you prepare the way for Gott's answer."

She was talking in riddles. Esther blinked, trying to decipher the meaning behind her words. Prepare the way for Gott's answer—how? She might end up trying to work things out the way she wanted them.

She was so confused. So disoriented. So uncertain.

She didn't know how to act.

How was life supposed to go on as normal when everything was so topsy-turvy and unsettled?

⌒

With Esther safely home, Viktor went outside and got to work. He needed to check the eaves on the haus, make sure they were clear. He might not be home when hurricane season started, though it was rare for a Gulf Coast hurricane to reach all the way to northern Missouri. More likely, it'd be a tornado coming in from the West, across Kansas and Iowa. Or straight-line winds. Those did a lot of damage, as well.

The driver parked his van in the driveway, and Grossdaedi climbed out of the back. Viktor had planned to take him to the chiropractor's, but knowing Grossmammi needed a caregiver, and with Esther gone, he'd called for a driver for Grossdaedi. During his absence, Viktor had hovered around Grossmammi, feeling antsy, until Esther had gotten home. Close to suppertime.

Grossdaedi moved stiffly toward the stairs, then about-faced and headed to the opposite end of the porch to the new ramp. He wouldn't have to climb, and it had handrails, which he made use of. Viktor frowned as he watched the scene from his perch on the roof. He needed to pick up supplies to build handrails for the porch steps.

He needed to quit his job on the river. Return home. And fulfill his duty to his großeltern.

Needed to relinquish horsepower for an actual horse and join the church.

A frown settled on his face.

It was time. Almost time. Maybe a matter of months.

He wasn't ready.

He'd never be ready.

He lay back on the hot roof and pulled his straw hat over his face to shield his eyes from the blazing sun. His stomach roiled.

Down below, someone rang the dinner bell. Probably Esther. The smell of fried fish drifted past his nose.

He didn't move.

Gott, why? Why, why, why?

Tears leaked out from the corners of his eyes, down into his ears.

He swallowed, imagining Daed coming out of the barn, swinging Daniel up into his arms, and carrying him into the haus. Mamm ringing the dinner bell. Joel and Hezekiah running along beside Daed. Isaiah coming in from the fields. Deborah would be setting the table as they all tracked in, washed up, and took their places. He could almost hear the creak of the chairs, the lively conversation. Could see them bowing their heads for silent prayer.

His nose and throat plugged. He couldn't breathe. Against his will, he sat up. It helped him not to feel so smothered. His hat fell to his lap.

With a flick of his wrist, he sent it flying like a Frisbee. Then he pushed to his feet and wiped his arm across his eyes.

He'd stay away as long as he could.

When he had nein other option, he'd do what he had to do.

Esther would be undoubtedly married by then. If not to Henry, then to someone else. But he couldn't expect her to wait.

Not for a man who didn't want to return.

Chapter 21

Esther was putting away the cleaned, dried supper dishes when a low moan sounded from the living room.

"Are you hurting?" Anna asked her ehemann, her voice soft, compassionate.

"Chiropractors are a waste of time and money," Reuben grumbled.

Esther hung the dish towel on the edge of the sink and left the dishwater sitting while she went into the other room. She felt a stab of conviction that she'd forgotten about his appointment. Nein wonder Viktor had been upset about her absence that afternoon. Shirking her duties.

Reuben flinched as he shifted on the chair and shook out the issue of the *Budget* he was reading. Esther cringed as she watched him. Had Viktor ever seen his grossdaedi immediately following a session? And speaking of Viktor, where had he disappeared to after their confrontation in the kitchen? She'd fried up the fish he'd caught, and he hadn't bothered to kum in and eat it.

Reuben moaned again.

"Do you want a pain pill?" Esther asked. She'd thought going to the chiropractor was supposed to make him feel better. Maybe it was really just a waste of time and money.

"I'll wait until bedtime. Might get some sleep then, jah?" Reuben almost snapped.

Esther blinked and stepped back. "All right. I'm supposed to get a phone call from my cousin at seven." She looked at the clock. Quarter till. She needed to hurry. "Rachel is meeting me at the phone shanty. Do you need anything before I go?" She glanced from Reuben to Anna and back again.

Reuben shook his head, then grimaced. "We'll be all right for a few minutes. Hurry back."

"I will." She slipped her shoes on and darted down the porch steps and around the side of the haus toward the road. A pounding sound came from behind her. She paused and turned around. Viktor ran toward her.

"Where are you off to?" He sounded nonchalant, but there was a dark look in his eyes. "Meeting your beau for an evening tryst?"

Ouch. As if Henry would ever arrange one of those. Besides, the only beau she wanted to meet was him.

"Lily's supposed to call."

"Will Grossmammi be okay, with Grossdaedi's back issues?"

"They said they'd be fine for a few minutes." She started walking, and he fell into step beside her.

The dark look faded, replaced with something akin to wariness. He frowned.

Esther's shoe snagged something hard in the road. Her arms flailed as she tried to keep her balance. The next second, Viktor's arm curled around her waist, holding her tight against his side. "This doesn't count." He winked as he released her, then slid his hand across her back to grasp her hand, the one closest to him. "You needed the support."

Jah, and she loved his touch. She resisted the urge to hold on tight.

But she didn't need the gossip from any Amish neighbors who might see them. She glanced around, checking front windows and side gardens. She didn't see anyone. Not even a buggy coming down the road. Ach, wait—there was Angie Yoder, taking laundry off the clothesline while her kinner played nearby. But maybe they wouldn't recognize Viktor, with his straw hat hiding his face. He wore suspenders, too, but with blue jeans. They looked gut on him. Too gut.

"Why are you dressed like that?" She belatedly pulled her hand away, immediately missing the contact, and gestured at his attire.

"Trying them out, süße."

Why? To see if some of his Amish clothes still fit? Maybe part of a tentative plan to return? Her hopes mounted, and she moved a little closer to him. "I fried the fish you caught for supper. Where were you?"

"On the roof, checking the eaves. I heard the bell." A muscle worked in his jaw. "Grossdaedi doesn't look so gut. Though he's usually in some pain for a day or two after a session with the chiropractor."

So, he'd noticed. Esther nodded. "He told us that the doctor treated him, but he may need some sort of surgery, or he'll end up bedridden."

Viktor's jaw tightened, the only indication that he'd heard her.

What was going through his mind? Nein time to ask. They were nearly at the phone shanty, set beside a crossroads right by Rachel's haus. The phone rang once, loudly, followed by silence. Rachel must already be in there and had answered. Onkel Samuel stood out in front of the barn, holding the reins of two Belgian draft horses, while he talked to Bishop Joe.

Viktor veered sharply to the left, putting distance between him and Esther. She looked at him. His gaze centered on the men talking by the barn. Maybe he worried about why the bishop was speaking with her onkel. Or maybe his concern was Esther's reputation.

"Onkel Samuel is a preacher now," she told him quietly. "They're probably discussing the fire, and when the barn raising will be." At least she hoped they hadn't gotten wind of her behavior with Viktor.

They approached the phone shanty, and Esther hurried toward the open door.

"Ach, Esther just arrived," Rachel spoke into the receiver. "And she brought Viktor with her." She raised her eyebrows. "Nein, they weren't holding hands. Not everyone is as bold as you, Lily."

Esther's face heated. She and Viktor had been holding hands… and they'd gotten rather "bold" behind the barn. She cringed at the reminder of times Lily had spent there with him.

Now Lily would want to talk to Viktor—and Esther wouldn't be privy to their conversation. If only she could listen in. Or maybe she shouldn't be so curious. She might get hurt. As expected, Rachel held out the phone to Viktor.

He frowned, then glanced at Esther. "I have business with the bishop." He pivoted and strode away.

They watched him go. Still silent, Rachel extended the phone to Esther and stepped out of the shanty, shaking her head.

Esther took the phone, entered the shanty, and sank down on the stool set in there. She hated talking on the phone. She twirled the cord as she held the receiver to her ear. "Hallo?"

"Ach, Esther. I was just going to tell you something, but, listen. I just had the most wunderbaar idea ever. How about if I move into the Petersheims' haus with you? They have room, and it'd be so much easier for me to spend more time with Viktor."

Esther's heart nearly shattered. It'd kill her if she lost him to Lily. But then, was there really a danger? He'd declined talking to her just now.

As Lily rambled on, Esther's heart became battered and discouraged. She slumped as her hopeless dreams slipped through her fingers. Somehow she'd have to keep Lily out of the haus, and maintain some semblance of control, even if she couldn't control what Viktor did with his time.

"I could help with Anna," Lily offered. "Maybe more with cooking or gardening, because it creeps me out to even think about helping someone bathe, dress, and do other such things."

Esther stifled a gasp. To her, helping Anna with "other such things" was a labor of love and not something to get "creeped out" over.

"I'll clear it with my parents, but it won't be a problem, jah?" Lily went on. "I'll tell them you need the help, and I was hired on. You could share a little of your earnings, ain't so? I'm so excited. I'll travel out there by bus on Monday, and I'll stop at home long enough to tell my parents where I'll be. Then I'll kum right over."

Esther swallowed. "I think the Petersheims might have something to say about this." Not to mention she didn't make any money. Daed did.

"Ach." She could almost picture Lily waving her hand dismissively. "They'll need me there to draw Viktor back into the fold. As soon as we explain that, they'll be all for it. We don't need to mention that I haven't made up my mind yet."

"*As soon as we explain*"? Esther frowned, getting to her feet. "Nein, I don't think it's a gut idea. There've been some more health concerns, and—"

"You're just being mean. I need a chance at happiness, ain't so?"

Anger washed over Esther. "What happened with the man you saw in Pennsylvania?" She probably sounded catty.

"I'm exploring my options." Lily laughed. "Danki for saying jah. I've got to go. See you Monday." The phone clicked.

"Lily? Wait. Lily!" Nein answer. "Nein!" Esther shouted into the receiver, as if that would make Lily hear and understand. Still silence. She reluctantly hung up and stepped outside the small shanty. All three men and Rachel stared at her, frowns on their faces, probably because of her loud show of temper. She belatedly dipped her head. "Sorry. Lily has decided she wants to move into the Petersheims' haus as a second caregiver." She probably shouldn't have worded it like that. Lily might get into trouble for doing things outside the proper order, but Esther couldn't think of a different way to put it. And if Lily got into trouble, so be it.

Rachel gasped and grabbed Esther's hand. There were a few masculine grunts. Probably some nonverbal communication, considering all the different sounds. She didn't glance up to see the men's expressions.

"Nein. Out of the question," Viktor said. "We have one caregiver; we don't need two. And you don't need the extra stress. I mean, work."

⌒

Viktor didn't need the stress. Nor did he want to see the pain in Esther's eyes when Lily came on to him. It was bad enough to see the hurt in her eyes, to hear the anguish in her voice, when she came out of the shanty and relayed Lily's message. Would he ever earn

Esther's trust? It'd be difficult to do while Lily tried to flirt with him, as she undoubtedly would. Just like some of the girls had at Caleb and Miriam's wedding—brushing against him, touching him…. *Nein.* What he needed was—

"I need to go," Esther said. "I told Anna and Reuben I'd be gone only a few minutes." She backed away.

Viktor glanced at the two men. "That reminds me. Grossdaedi might need some sort of surgery. Don't have the details yet, but…."

"Just let us know." Bishop Joe nodded. "He'll have help. You will be at the barn raising, ain't so?" He peered at Viktor over the top of his glasses.

"I'll be there." Viktor turned away. This July had already turned out rougher than most. He'd expected the first day home—and the Fourth of July—to rear their ugly heads, as always. But he hadn't been prepared for a barn fire, for Grossmammi and Grossdaedi's health issues, or for Esther. He couldn't resist a quick glance at her. Nor had he expected the sharp longing for things he could never have.

"You need to make plans for your return, jah?" Bishop Joe said. "We'll talk."

Viktor stiffened. Gave a noncommittal grunt. And strode down the road. Esther trailed behind him, not quite able to keep up with his fast clip. As soon as they'd turned the corner, he slowed.

Esther caught up with him. "What was it like when you left the Amish?"

He glanced at her. "You breathe. Just breathe deeply, over and over. Eventually, your mind clears, and you realize what breathing is, and that you were suffocating all along. You discover freedom from someone holding the Ordnung in your face. All the rules…."

Esther looked more than a little alarmed. As if maybe he'd been too adamant. That wouldn't stop him from being honest, though.

"But it's like a fence around a yard where small kinner play," Esther countered. "The boundaries are there to keep them safe."

"And to keep them naive, ignorant, sheltered. Wouldn't you like to be free to speak your mind without getting into trouble? To make your own choices? Not be told what to do, every moment of every day?"

"But the rules are for our benefit. To promote community, family, unity. To help us go to heaven when we die."

He snorted. "And driving a tractor instead of a team of Belgian draft horses will keep you out of heaven."

"Nein, but maybe it'll make you slow down and listen to Gott's voice instead of a noisy piece of machinery. Maybe you'll be able to hear your grossdaedi calling for you, instead of having to wear protective earphones to keep from going deaf. Maybe you'll know what messages are being silently communicated at your haus, day in and day out, instead of ignoring the—"

"I know what messages are communicated, süße. I hear them loud and clear." He stopped and faced her. "Grossdaedi needs me. Soon I'll need to quit working the river and put my hand to the plow. On the other hand, they may need the money I earn on the river to pay for Grossdaedi's surgery. Can't have both. One or the other. Which is more important? The money or the help? Tell me." He started walking again. "Grossmammi needs you. I need to join the church, marry you, and start producing kinner." He chuckled as a red blush stained Esther's cheeks. "Little too graphic for your innocent ears, jah?" He shook his head. "Neither of us is ready for that." He smirked. "You need to break up with Henry."

Conflicting emotions crossed her face. Embarrassment and anger? He wasn't sure.

"You need to make peace with your past."

He couldn't argue with that.

"So, Grossmammi told you. Or was it one of the aenties?"

"Nobody's told me anything. All I know is, five years ago, Anna lost her only sohn and almost his entire family." She looked down. "I assume you were the only survivor."

He blinked. "Grossmammi and Grossdaedi, too. They were on the first floor. I got them out in time."

Esther reached for his hand. Viktor gripped her softer, smaller one as if it were a lifeline.

"Daniel would've been six this year. He'd barely started walking." His voice broke. That information had slipped out without warning. He swallowed, surprised, and yet relieved to have shared it with someone who cared.

"What happened? If you want to talk about it." Her voice was filled with compassion.

He shook his head and aimed his burning gaze at the sky, painted in streaks of red, orange, and lavender by the setting sun. Swallowed the lump forming in his throat. "Maybe I'll tell you if you meet me at the pond later."

It might be easier in the darkness.

⁓

Maybe. Maybe not.

Hours after he'd extended the offer, Esther still struggled with whether to meet Viktor.

After she'd gotten Anna settled, Reuben had made his way to bed. He moved a little better now, not quite as slowly or painfully. Maybe he'd feel better yet in the morgen.

She went to the kitchen and peered out the window into the darkness. Viktor would've finished with the evening chores. He'd probably be finishing his swim by the time she arrived at the pond.

If she went.

She had resolved not to go anymore. Not after their passionate moments behind the barn. The less time she spent alone with him, in a setting conducive to romance, the better.

Yet there didn't seem to be any setting that wasn't conducive to romance. She'd never thought of the road as a particularly romantic place, but walking together to-nacht, holding hands, had made it so.

Or the kitchen—who would've thought more things than the oven and stove could heat up the room?

There weren't any safe places.

One last time. To-nacht. And that would be it.

Though that would make it seem that she'd gone only to hear his story, nothing more. And what would that say about her character? Nothing complimentary.

Besides, she looked forward to their time alone at the pond.

If he didn't try to kiss her. He'd said he wouldn't.

If only she didn't want him to.

But she did. Being in his arms felt right. As if she belonged there.

With a soft sigh, she stepped into her flip-flops and headed out the door.

She heard the splashing of the water before the pond came into view, and her stomach quivered at the thought of possibly seeing Viktor's bare chest again.

If only they were free to have a relationship. She, free from Henry and expectations. Viktor, free from the Englisch world and his past. Whatever it might entail.

But they weren't. She, by her own lack of doing—by her fears of being rejected by her family for wanting to be free from Henry. For wanting a chance to choose for herself. It seemed better to not even try than to risk failure. To just accept it as her lot in life, and—

"You came." He stood waist-deep in the water, his chest bare. "Kum on out, Esther. Play. Live. Breathe."

Suddenly she wanted to. She wanted to feel the freedom he'd spoken of. She kicked off her shoes and waded in, the chilly water reaching her knees, hips, waist, then higher. She hesitated. Her dress rose around her, floating on the water, tangling around her hips. She tried to push it down.

"Kum on. It doesn't get any deeper here." There was a smile in his voice.

Who would know?

Besides, she was already in deep enough to drown. In more ways than one.

Chapter 22

Viktor couldn't believe she'd joined him in the water. But he was glad. Her dress must be pretty heavy and cumbersome when it was soaked through. Not much he could do about that. He wouldn't suggest she take off her clothes, even though it would be easier for her—and, well, more enjoyable for him.

It'd also be a sin. And even though he'd rebelled, there was nein point in encouraging her to. It was enough that she'd decided to test the waters.

She squealed, and he jumped, startled. "What?"

"Something bit me." She pushed at her skirts again and backed away.

He chuckled. "It's a fish, probably a minnow. Don't worry. They won't hurt you. Just nibble a little." Kind of what he'd like to do.... He looked away.

She splashed at the water. "So, what do you do out here if you don't know how to swim?"

Learn to swim. He couldn't suggest that. Her dress would weigh her down. "Uh...." Maybe he should've thought this through before inviting her in. *Nacht-time water volleyball?* He smirked. That'd be something for the teenagers to consider. *Water basketball?* He'd need to buy a hoop or rig up a makeshift one. Not a bad idea, actually. *Water fight? Hmmm.* He looked back at her, just in time to end up with a face full of water. She giggled.

With his arm, he sent a wave of water back at her. She squealed again and wiped her face, then gave him another splash. He retaliated. She took a moment to recover, then used both hands to push water at him. Still giggling.

He was glad the pond was so secluded, away from the prying eyes of neighbors.

Viktor moved a little closer to Esther, sending her another spray.

146

She shoved water back at him, then lost her balance and disappeared beneath the surface.

Viktor felt for her. He found her thrashing arms and hauled her against him. She came up coughing hard, with one hand covering her mouth—the dictate of gut manners. With the other hand, she clutched his shoulder. He patted her back, still holding her against him.

Finally, she stopped sputtering, but her chest still heaved.

"You okay?" His pats turned into gentle rubs, up and down, over her back.

She wiped her eyes. "I think I swallowed half the pond." She started to giggle, then stilled, as if just remembering where she was.

He loosened his grip, allowing her the opportunity to move away. She stayed.

It would be easy...so easy....

Her hand slipped around his neck, fingering the wet strands of his hair. Her other hand slowly slid up his chest. She sighed, then whispered his name.

He trembled, his stomach clenching. *So easy....*

He couldn't.

He made a halfhearted effort to push her away. She didn't go far. Her hands didn't move.

"I think...we'd better go, süße." His voice cracked. "Because I am going to kiss you if we don't."

Even if you don't beg me to.

Esther clung to him, her other arm going around his neck. She didn't want to let go. For more reasons than one. "What if I fall again?" Slipping under the dark water, gulping mouthfuls of water—and maybe a minnow or a tadpole or who knew what else?—and not knowing which end was up had been scary. She didn't want it to happen again.

"You'll be fine. Kum on, I'll help you." Viktor shifted against her, his hands closing on her waist. Tightening, in preparation to shove her away. He sounded firm. Determined. Unmoved.

"Nein." She wanted him to carry her. Nein way would she walk on her own. "I could've drowned." She pressed herself closer.

He made an odd choking sound. "Süße, trust me." He lifted her and set her a little further away, keeping a hand on her elbow.

She squirmed back into his arms. And held on. "Nein. I'll drown."

"You won't drown. I'll be right here."

She couldn't keep the whimper from escaping. Silly of her, considering that they'd been playing and having fun until…ugh. What if she'd swallowed a water bug or a crawdad? Her stomach churned. Who knew what was swimming down there? She grasped a handful of his hair again, her other hand flattening against him.

His chest rose and fell. "I'm not going to be responsible for my actions if you keep this up, süße." A touch of humor lightened his voice. He bent a little, an arm sliding behind her knees, and scooped her into his arms.

She looped her arms around his neck and snuggled close.

His breathing roughened. He carried her to shore, and lowered her to the ground. Something soft pillowed around her feet.

"Get your shoes on. We'll go for a walk to dry off." He removed her arms from around his neck and stepped back.

"You saved my life." Her legs turned into some sort of boneless gel that was unable to support her, and she collapsed onto the soft thing—a quilt. He'd brought the bedding again? For stargazing? She gave a kind of choking laugh.

Viktor shook his head. "You were never in any danger…from the water." He reached for her hand and tugged. "Kum on."

Nein way would she be able to walk home. Not on these rubbery legs. At least not yet. "I think I ate a bug or something." She rolled away.

He sighed and sat beside her, resting his hand on her back. His fingers made some gentle circular movements that turned her insides to mush. "I'll teach you how to swim."

"I'm not getting back in there. Ever."

"Jah, you are. I'll buy you a bikini." His fingers moved to her ribs. Tickling her.

Esther's face heated. She'd never be brave enough to bare her body that way. "What?" She twisted around, dislodging his hand. He lay on his side, facing her, propped up on his elbow.

"Just kidding. How about a nice, modest T-shirt and a pair of shorts, like the Englisch wear?"

She blinked. "That'd be *im*modest." Not as immodest as a bikini, but still....

"Just try them out. We'll buy some at a garage sale. Then, if you don't like them, not much money will be wasted."

She couldn't afford to waste any money.

"Or we'll get back in the water now and work through your fear if it takes all nacht. One or the other. You choose." His fingers found their way back to her ribs, gently exploring.

She tensed, caught between knowing she ought to slap his hand away and wanting to allow him that seemingly innocent liberty. "I'll give them a try." She tried to relax under his touch. He wasn't doing anything wrong, really. Just making her long for more…making her want his kisses....

"Gut girl." He leaned a little closer. "Now, are you ready to walk until we're done dripping, or—"

"Or." *Jah. Definitely.* Her belly clenched. Somewhere in her head, alarm bells went off, but she pushed the snooze button.

He chuckled. "Or what?" His fingers roamed, tickling, and she squirmed closer to him, knocking him off balance. His upper body came to rest against hers. His fingers stilled.

She wrapped her arms around him, holding him close, her hands pressed on his bare back. She liked touching him as much as she liked looking. Maybe even more.

"Süße." There was a boatload of warning in his voice. His hands left her, flattening on either side of him as he started to push himself up.

Nein. Don't leave me. Her heart pounded. She slid her fingers a little. Exploring. Pressing on his firm muscles, pulling him to her. He groaned as his head lowered, his breaths feathering her face. Teasing, not touching. She leaned closer, finding his lips. His response to her kiss was gentle, letting her take the lead. It wasn't enough. Wasn't near enough.

"Viktor, kiss me." So much for not begging.

The mental self-reproach faded to nothingness as he pressed her deeper into the softness of the blanket, taking control. Deepening the kisses.

Passion ignited. She poured herself into his kiss, his touch, mentally slapping the blaring alarms to silence them.

Ach, Viktor.…

⌒

Viktor pulled her closer, cradling her in his arms. He didn't want to leave the haven of her embrace. Didn't want to pull away. Especially when she leaned into his kisses, opening up to them. Jah, he'd stay there all nacht. And all the next day. Forever.

Ach, Esther.…

An Englisch vehicle slowly crunched over the gravel road by the pond, the bright headlights flashing over them as it passed by. Loud rock music blared from the open windows, interrupting their solitude. The music faded as the vehicle continued down the road.

What if a buggy had also gone by but they hadn't heard it? He doubted anyone would see them, but he needed to protect Esther's reputation. To protect her from herself. And from him.

Viktor forced himself to roll away. "We should probably go, süße." Nein "probably" about it. They were out of control. Or close to it.

She made a whimpering sound and turned in the opposite direction. "I'm so…so sorry. I…I don't want…." Her voice broke. And then a sob escaped.

He sat up and grabbed her hand as she started to scramble to her feet. She fell back in his arms, her shoulders heaving.

"Hey, don't cry." He crossed his arms around her chest and nuzzled her neck.

"I don't want to be one of them."

He blinked. "One of who?"

"Them. The girls who went behind the barn with you."

Ach. *Them.* Whoever they were.

"They never meant anything to me, süße." He kissed her ear.

Her chest rose and fell. "Exactly. And...and I don't. Because you're going to return to the river, and you aren't coming back. Not for gut, anyway. I'm just like them. Lured into your arms, a temporary diversion, and...and you'll love me and leave me. You don't even know my name. I'm just...süße."

"Esther." He kissed her ear again. "Your name is Esther. 'Süße' is an endearment." He trailed his lips down her neck. "I've never called any other girl 'süße.' Ever."

"Really?" She sounded needy. Insecure.

"Really. Just you." There wasn't much else he could say. At least not yet.

He wasn't ready to return for gut. But when he did, he wanted her.

And she still technically belonged to another man.

He released her. "Break up with him, my love."

Oops. He hadn't meant to use that endearment. Though he'd meant it.

Why wouldn't she commit to that simple directive? It'd make it easy for him to court her openly. To declare his intentions...whatever they were.

He couldn't ask her to wait until he was ready to return. That might be as soon as next month. Or it might be later.

Probably closer to later. Unless Grossdaedi needed surgery.

Esther sniffed. "You promised to tell me what happened."

Ach. He shut his eyes. Tried to ignore the pain that stabbed his heart.

He should step away from this relationship now. Let her start getting over him.

Because he'd be leaving at the end of the month.

Maybe it was time to destroy her trust in him. Tell her the truth about what had happened. It was guaranteed to drive her away.

For what woman wanted to be loved by a murderer?

Chapter 23

Esther smiled. This was the first time anyone had ever called her "my love." To be honest, she'd never thought she'd hear those words. And hearing them from Viktor...they made life gut.

"Maybe we should talk on the way home." Viktor's voice was flat, emotionless. He stood and reached for his shirt, tugging it over his head. He shoved his feet into his shoes.

Esther started to gather the quilts, but Viktor shook his head. "Leave 'em. Camping out here."

She hesitated. "Really? Why?"

He gave her a long, silent look.

"Then you don't need to see me home. I'll go after we've talked." She let the quilt fall back to the ground.

"I'm taking you anyway."

Why was he talking in short, choppy sentences, like he had when he'd first returned home? She much preferred the wordier, friendlier version of Viktor to the curt, quiet one.

She slid her feet into her flip-flops. "Okay. I'm ready."

He nodded and started walking. He didn't reach for her hand. She swallowed her disappointment.

What had happened? Maybe begging him to kiss her had been the last straw, and he'd decided they were done. Finished. The relationship over before it even began, all because she'd been bold, depriving him of the thrill of the chase. She should've been stronger. From now on, she would be. Regardless of her previous track record.

She pulled in a breath. "So...what happened?" Hopefully, he didn't hear the hurt in her voice.

Or maybe it was her insistence on knowing his past that was causing him to withdraw.

"The short version." Viktor looked away, and the distance between them seemed to grow. "Some friends and I were having a party in the back field. We had a keg. We got drunk."

Esther winced. She'd heard rumors about his drinking but had hoped they weren't true. Apparently, they were.

"Someone had bought firecrackers, and we were shooting them off. I'm not really sure…." His voice broke, and he cleared his throat. "Far as we could tell, one went through an open window and ignited a mattress in my brothers' room."

She caught her breath. *Ach, nein.*

"The haus wasn't on fire when I got home—or if it was, I didn't notice. I fell asleep in the living room. I woke up choking on thick smoke. It was everywhere. And it was hot…so hot." He gave a bitter laugh. "I'd thought I'd gone to hell there for a bit, before I realized…. I woke Grossmammi and Grossdaedi, and they got out and rang the emergency bell. But my parents…they never had a chance."

Tears burned Esther's eyes. "Ach, Viktor."

"They died trying to save my siblings. Mamm had my sister in her arms. Daed's body was in my brothers' room. I killed my family. I stayed around long enough to make sure Grossmammi and Grossdaedi had a home, and then I took off."

She caught her breath. "How awful." She reached for his hand—inadequate comfort, she knew. His was cold and clammy. "You might not have been to blame."

"Ach, I'm to blame, süße. I'm basically a murderer. And now you know why coming home is so hard for me." He freed his hand from hers.

"But maybe your brother had been smoking in bed. Or maybe a bolt of lightning—"

"A firecracker caused it. The fire marshal issued his report before I left."

"Were you the only one shooting off the firecrackers? You said you were with friends."

"I was with friends. But you know, it doesn't matter who shot that particular one. I was there. I was as guilty as the rest, ain't so?"

Her heart broke at the pain in his voice. "Ach, Viktor," she whispered again. She searched for something else to say, but mere platitudes were all that came to mind. Words that wouldn't help.

He turned to face her, grasped her shoulders, and gave her a gentle kiss. Then he pulled away. "Don't bother, süße. I've heard them all before."

Different words came to mind. "You were guilty of being drunk and stupid, not of intending to harm or kill others."

Viktor sighed. "I just wish…." He fell silent.

⌣

"You wish what?" Esther reached for his hand again. He let her catch it. To be honest, he needed the contact. If only he could lose himself in her arms forever. Forget reality.

"I wish I could do that day over," he finished. "I wish I'd never started drinking. I wish I could've died with my family so I wouldn't have to face the guilt." The words poured out, unstoppable. His eyes stung.

She gasped. "Don't say that."

"I wish…." *I wish I knew for certain that Gott forgave me.*

And that was the plain and simple truth.

But how could he possibly know for sure? He wasn't Gott. And to claim to know the mind of Gott would be a sin. He only hoped to work hard enough to somehow atone for his wrongdoings. To make amends for the lives lost due to his own foolishness.

Beside him, Esther gave a soft sigh. Her hand tightened on his. They walked the final few yards to the farmhaus in silence.

He released her hand, glanced at the open window to the bedroom of his großeltern, then silently trailed his fingers over her face. He leaned forward and gave her a gentle kiss, first on one cheek, then on the other. "Gut nacht." He whispered the words in her ear, then brushed his lips over hers before pulling away.

He turned back the way he'd kum. To the pond.

Where painful memories of the past would war with pleasurable thoughts of Esther in his arms.

⌒

Esther watched him until he disappeared into the nacht. Then she slipped around the corner of the haus, opened the back door, and stepped into the kitchen. Except it wasn't as empty or as dark as she'd expected. A kerosene lantern glowed brightly in the center of the table, and sitting there, with a full glass of the lemonade she'd made earlier, was Henry.

Henry! The one who never made unexpected calls on her. Or expected calls, for that matter. The one who seemed happy just to take her home from singings and frolics. He must've felt free to enter the Petersheims' haus and make himself at home after they had gone to bed. Had he checked upstairs to see if she was in her room? If so, he would have seen that Viktor was out, as well. Her stomach hurt. Henry must've tossed pebbles at her window first. Not a courting practice she'd ever experienced, but she remembered Dorcas slipping out of their room when her beau had done just that.

Henry's dark eyes fastened on her. He didn't smile; he just stared at her as if she were some sort of unusual creature. Such as a pond monster. Esther froze on the spot and ran her hand over her still-damp dress. At least it wasn't dripping, but the material clung to her chest, hips, and legs, probably making her look disheveled. Trashy. She resisted the urge to check her kapp and hair to see if they were in order. Unlikely, after her dunking, and then lying on the blankets with Viktor, kissing.

Henry's mouth settled into a disapproving line. Still silent.

She blinked. Maybe—hopefully—he was a figment of her guilty imagination, and he'd go away, vanish into nothingness, if she ignored him. She started to scoot past.

He cleared his throat.

Esther sucked in a gulp of air, changed course, and poured herself a glass of lemonade. Then she sat across from him at the table.

"Where've you been?" Henry hissed.

Like a snake. Was it wrong of her to compare the sound of his whisper to a reptile? The beadiness of his eyes? How could she think such a thing about the man she was promised to? It wasn't right.

Break up with him. She heard the echo of Viktor's command. Jah, she needed to. And now would be a gut time.

"Look at you—you're a mess!" Henry sneered, pointing a finger in her face. "It looks like you took a bath with your clothes on. And *where* is your kapp?"

It was gone? Instinctively she raised her hand and felt the loose tendrils of her hair. While not down, it was definitely disheveled. And kapp-less.

Where had it fallen off? In the water? On Viktor's blanket? Probably not on the road.

He shook his head. "Disgusting." His lips curled back in repugnance.

And that made his thoughts more than clear.

Nein matter what others expected, she couldn't live with this treatment for the rest of her life.

Esther straightened her shoulders, stood, and grabbed the lantern. "I'll be right back." She hurried to the stairs and went up to her room, found another kapp, and put it on. Then she gathered the few gifts Henry had given her.

It was time.

She went back downstairs and dropped the items on the table in front of Henry.

He looked at them, then raised his gaze to her, his brow furrowing. "What's this?" His tone still sounded judgmental, but his expression was confused. Hurt.

"I can't marry you." She forced the words past the lump of fear in her throat. *Please, Gott, set me free.*

"Nonsense. We've already made plans."

They hadn't made any plans. Their mamms had.

"I've already talked to the bishop. We're approved."

"I know, but...." *I don't love you.* She couldn't say that, even if it was true—and becoming truer by the minute. "You don't love me," she said instead. "I'd ruin your life. You know as well as I do that you're interested in Sarah Hershberger."

Twin spots of color appeared in his checks, and he looked away.

"You'd be free to court her if it weren't for me."

His gaze narrowed as he seemed to consider that possibility. But then he shook his head. "What about the *river rat?*"

She sucked in a breath, preparing to reassure him again that there was nothing between her and Viktor. But that'd be a lie. There was something. Everything. She frowned. "He hasn't asked to court me." But he had mentioned marrying her and making kinner....

"Word has it that you two have been seeing each other."

She rolled her eyes. Oops—not a show of submission. But then again, neither was breaking up with Henry or returning his gifts. "Well, of course we see each other. I work for him." She laughed, hoping to sound nonchalant, as if his comment was of nein consequence.

She instantly regretted her levity. It wouldn't reflect well on her when he told his mamm, as he was sure to do.

Henry stood. "That river rat has a reputation. If he has made any inappropriate moves toward you, you need to get out. Immediately. And since he usurped my rights at your brother's wedding, I'm saying you need to be removed from this haus anyway, especially in light of these rumors."

"Nein." Her throat closed further. "Ach, Henry. Nein. Anna needs me. Besides, people always talk, and it doesn't mean anything."

"There's a remnant of truth behind all gossip."

She had nothing to say to that. In her case, it was true.

Henry shoved the gifts across the table toward her. "Keep these. The wedding is still on. I'll talk to my mamm. And to Bishop Joe. We'll move it up. Besides, I think both of them will agree that you need to leave here sooner rather than later. And since you won't go willingly, you'll have to be physically removed. I expect Bishop Joe will ask you to kneel and confess for your willful attitude."

"I can't…." She swallowed. She opened her mouth, then shut it again, pressing her lips together. Repressing the urge to scream "Nein" like she had earlier at the phone shanty. She didn't want to wake Anna and Reuben. Besides, Henry wouldn't hear her message any better than Lily had.

"You can and you will. We're not calling it quits. I *will* marry you."

"I think she has some say." The voice came from the shadows behind Henry, startling them both. Reuben stepped into the light. "And if you're implying that things are happening under my roof, I will vouch for Esther's character. Take your things and go."

Henry scowled but gathered the gifts and stormed out the door, slamming it behind him.

Esther's eyes brimmed with tears. Reuben walked over to the window and looked outside for a few moments. Finally, he turned. "He's gone."

"It's not over." Her voice broke.

"Of course not. I don't think he's a man who likes to lose. And if you break up with him, he loses. Right now, he sees you as a spirited filly that needs breaking." Reuben shuffled to the table, picked up Henry's lemonade, and dumped it in the sink.

"He's going to talk to the bishop about moving up the wedding." She could barely keep from wailing. She wasn't free. She'd never be free. It almost seemed as if she was drowning in the pond again, but instead of finding freedom and safety in Viktor's arms, she choked on a water bug.

Reuben didn't comment. After several moments of silence, he turned to her. "So, where were you to-nacht, Esther? And where is my gross-sohn?" He leaned against the sink and speared her with a penetrating look.

One that surely took note of her soggy appearance.

Chapter 24

Viktor smoothed out the quilt again. It had large wet spots where he and Esther had lain, but they would dry. The least of his concerns right now. He shed his swimming trunks, slipped into his jeans, and lowered himself to the soft bedding. Hugged the pillow against his chest, a poor substitute for Esther.

It was a beautiful nacht to camp under the open sky. A gentle breeze cooled the air. The stars twinkled as if all were right with the world. As if Gott were still on His throne, still in control.

If He was in control, why had He allowed the fire to kill Viktor's family? Why hadn't He let them get out alive?

He pictured Daed, big and strong, reaching for his youngest sohn with his fingerless left hand—a reminder of yet another of Viktor's mistakes. At the age of eight, he'd grabbed Daed's hand by the fingers while he was cutting wood. Everything changed after that accident. Grossdaedi had taken over the majority of the farm work, relying heavily on Viktor and his brother Isaiah to pick up the slack while Daed recovered.

Daed had forgiven him, meanwhile blaming himself for being careless.

He had never fully regained the use of that hand. How could he, when he'd lost all his fingers?

Wasn't it enough that Viktor had taken Daed's fingers? But no, he'd had to finish the job, ten years later, and take his life.

And here he was now, in love with an Amish woman. Gott must be laughing.

Or maybe not. Maybe it was another attempt to break Viktor. Taking away his family, his life, his faith, and then the woman he loved.

A horse clip-clopped down the road, then stopped and whinnied.

Minutes later, a branch snapped.

"Grossdaedi?"

Nein answer.

He sat up and peered into the darkness. All he could see was the outline of a figure. Male, judging by the hat and trousers.

"Who's there?" His voice was sharper than intended.

"Figured you were here." The man chuckled harshly. "Bet her kapp is, too."

It took a few seconds for Viktor to place the voice. *Henry Beiler?* He rose, frowning. *Her kapp?* He hadn't noticed it on the quilt, but then, he hadn't been looking for it. Might be in the water. Wherever it was, it would have to wait until tomorrow morgen to be found.

But how did Henry know Esther was without her kapp—unless he'd been at the farmhaus and talked to her? He would have seen her all wet.

Viktor's mind whirled, trying to catch up with the implications. How to defend Esther's reputation? How to protect her from this scum?

"And your grossdaedi said he'd vouch for her character." Henry scoffed.

Ach, Grossdaedi had been there. Relief washed through him. But then, that meant Grossdaedi knew he'd broken the promise he'd made in the cab of his truck.

"Nein need for him to lie," Henry said. "I think we both know.... I didn't realize she'd be so easy."

Viktor stiffened. "What are you implying, Beiler?" He clenched his fists.

"I'm not implying anything. I'm accusing."

Viktor silently counted to ten—once, then a second time. A third. He started on the fourth.

"She's not going to be a virgin when she marries me, ain't so?"

Viktor sucked in a sharp breath, grabbed Henry by the suspenders, and yanked. Some things are worth fighting for. Esther's honor was one of them. "That's right, Beiler. She won't be."

Too late, he realized that Henry could twist those words around to destroy Esther's reputation—or blackmail her into a hasty marriage.

"Because *you* aren't marrying her." Viktor released the suspenders with a snap. "She's marrying me." And that solidified his resolve.

Henry stumbled backward. When he found his footing, he let out a howl of outrage and charged Viktor with his head, hitting him in the stomach. Viktor doubled over, his breath leaving him with a whoosh. Recovering, he shoved Henry, who shoved right back.

They tumbled to the ground, rolling around, bucking for the high position. They rained punches on each other—blows that would probably cause pain well after the fight ended. A fist connected with Viktor's eye, then with his jaw. The metallic taste of blood filled his mouth. He hit Henry in the nose. Blood gushed.

Finally, Viktor pinned Henry. After sitting on his chest a few moments, both breathing heavily, Viktor rolled to his feet and backed away. "Get outta here."

Henry rolled in the other direction and stood. He made a few threatening movements toward Viktor, then apparently changed his mind. "This isn't over." He turned and half stumbled, half ran toward the road. A few minutes later, the clip-clops of his horse resumed, fading into the distance.

⌒

"Well?"

Esther had never heard Reuben use such a firm tone of voice. As if he was going to get answers—or else.

She collapsed onto a kitchen chair. Her hands shook. She stared up at him. "I was at the pond. We…we were talking."

Reuben's gaze skimmed over her, probably not missing an inch of the damp, clinging dress. Probably not even the slightest wrinkle. She gulped. Why hadn't she taken the time to change clothes instead of just adding a kapp? Loose tendrils of hair still tickled her neck. She picked at her skirt.

"Talking." It wasn't a question. And yet it carried a buggy load of doubt.

"We had a water fight." She felt like a child, having to explain her actions.

He hitched an eyebrow.

"Um…I slipped. Almost drowned. I think I swallowed half the pond. Viktor rescued me." Hopefully that would eliminate further questions.

"Which, of course, resulted in mouth-to-mouth resuscitation, jah?"

Esther's face heated.

"You're playing with fire, young lady. I'll have a talk with my gross-sohn. Who is…where?"

She couldn't bear to let Viktor get into trouble for her imprudent actions. Even if it meant losing her job. "I started it," she rushed to say. "I splashed him first." *I clung to him, asked him to kiss me….*

Reuben's other eyebrow shot up.

Esther sighed. "He's still at the pond. Said he was camping out."

"It's been a gut many years since I had a courting teenager in my home. Not that you and Viktor are teens." Reuben straightened. "And never should a courting couple share the same haus. I'm not sure whether to send you home at nacht, to hire someone else, or to tell Viktor to find somewhere else to stay."

Esther dipped her head, shame weighing on her.

"Look at me." He waited until she lifted her gaze. "Your daed left me in charge of you. If something happens while you're under this roof, he's going to blame me. With Viktor's reputation…and with Henry seeing you like this…." He waved his hand, indicating her clothes. "There will be trouble, Esther."

Esther slumped. "I'm sorry. I didn't mean to cause problems." She had only been trying to be a friend to Viktor, and it had escalated. Big time. "I'll quit." Her heart broke. "My cousin Lily is coming home. She—"

"Nein, I'll not hire Lily. Anna needs *you*. I can't think of another girl in the district I'd trust with the care of my frau. And…. But…. However…." Reuben frowned. "I need to pray. *We* need to pray. And we must figure it out before Bishop Joe gets here—likely Monday, since tomorrow is a church Sunday—and tells us how it is."

"Monday is the barn raising."

Reuben smiled. "Gut. With my back problems, Viktor won't let me participate, so that gives us another day."

"I won't meet Viktor at the pond anymore."

"Don't make promises you can't keep." Reuben's lips twitched, as if he fought a smile. "You won't be able to stay away. But you do need to resolve things with Henry before you allow Viktor to court you anymore…which appeared to be what you were trying to do when I came in and sent him packing."

"*Anymore*"? Esther's heart warmed. Had Viktor been courting her? What a wunderbaar thought. She smiled as she ran her fingers along the rim of her glass.

"But I don't think Henry will be in a hurry to let you go. And so, I suggest…. I suggest—"

The kitchen door opened.

Reuben straightened. Esther twisted around in the chair, then shot to her feet.

Viktor stood there, the bedding clasped loosely under one arm, his clothes spattered with blood, one eye swollen shut.

"Need a shower."

⁓

Viktor needed more than a shower. He also needed an ice pack. Judging by the way it throbbed, his eye was probably already starting to bruise. He walked over to the laundry room and put the blanket and pillow in an empty basket. He hated to cause Esther more work, but….

"What happened?" Grossdaedi studied him when he came back in the room. Esther's mouth parted, forming an o.

Viktor grimaced. "Henry. But don't worry. I think he got the worse end of the deal. I broke his nose."

"Henry attacked you?" Grossdaedi frowned, adjusted the belt on his bathrobe, and stepped away from the sink.

"I attacked him first. He accused me of...." Viktor glanced at Esther, then looked back at Grossdaedi. His face warmed. "Of anticipating our wedding vows." He raised his chin. "Give me a few minutes, jah?" He turned and jogged up the steps.

"Esther?" Grossmammi's voice quavered from the back bedroom. Viktor heard a chair scrape across the kitchen floor, followed by the soft sound of conversation. Blocking out the sounds, he grabbed some clean clothes, shut the bathroom door, and turned on the shower. Cold.

When he went back downstairs, Grossmammi was seated in her wheelchair at the kitchen table. Steaming cups of tea steeped in front of her and Grossdaedi. Esther poured Viktor a mug of hot water and handed him a packet of herbal tea. He went to the freezer and took out an ice pack, then sat at the table and looked at her. "I'll give you a ride home from the singing tomorrow, süße. I don't want you alone with him."

"I think I'll not go." Esther's voice shook.

"Nein, you'll go," Grossdaedi said, "and you'll hold your head high. You aren't going to let the rumors beat you before they start." He removed his tea bag from his cup and placed it on the saucer beside it. "You always go."

As if there wouldn't be enough rumors when her former beau had a broken nose and the man who took her home had a black eye.

Silence fell.

Grossdaedi stared at his tea, his brow furrowed.

Viktor rubbed his jaw. It hurt, probably from clenching his teeth so much. Of course, it didn't help that Henry had struck him there.

He glanced at Esther, then studied his tea. He needed to solve this. But how?

The only thing he could think of was to elope with her now—which would imply guilt on their part, and would quite possibly result in her being shunned. Or not, since she hadn't joined the church yet. But people would suspect her of indecency just the same. He could tell her that he wanted to marry her, but that she'd need to wait for his return. Or he could release her to some Amish man in gut standing and get out of the picture completely.

That was probably the best option.

Maybe his old friend Josh Yoder would be a gut choice, since he'd returned home. From wherever he'd been.

He'd talk to him tomorrow after church.

He must really love Esther to put himself through this much pain for the sake of her well-being. But it was about time he started putting others first. Benefitting their lives. Instead of ending them.

Chapter 25

Esther put on her nicest dress and pinned it shut. She used to enjoy Sundays—spending hours with family and friends, attending the singing at nacht, and being in a courting relationship.

But now, she didn't want to go. Viktor's return had shaken her world, and she nein longer knew how to behave. It'd caused the problems she'd had with Henry from the beginning to escalate. Viktor had somehow highlighted them in bright neon yellow, so that she couldn't miss them. Couldn't overlook them. Even if she wanted to.

She didn't want to.

She twisted her hair up in a bun and secured it, then pinned on her kapp.

It was sweet of Viktor to offer her a ride home. Especially if Henry had implied what Viktor had said he had. But that didn't seem possible. Henry—the one who wouldn't even hold her hand, the one who had told her she was wanton for even suggesting it—saying she'd "anticipated her wedding vows." With Viktor. A man she wasn't promised to.

Henry must have a terrible opinion of her.

Though being promised to another hadn't stopped her from kissing Viktor. From "making out" behind the barn and on the quilt beside the pond.

Maybe, according to Henry, those actions qualified as anticipating one's wedding vows. But, by *her* definition, he shouldn't have insinuated any such thing. If only she were allowed to demand an apology. But Daed would say that she must've done something to prompt that accusation from Henry. Bishop Joe might say the same. It went beyond horrible. Even worse was having her reputation torn to shreds by someone who planned to marry her.

And since Henry still insisted on a wedding, what would he do to her every day of their married life? Heap loads of shame and guilt on her until she broke?

She shook her head and went downstairs to warm the sweet rolls she'd prepared the day before.

Scuffling noises came from the first-floor bedroom, so after she slid the pan into the oven, she went to investigate. Anna sat on the edge of the bed, her hands braced on either side of her, as she struggled to stand. She seemed much weaker than the day before, perhaps due to having stayed up so late last nacht.

Esther helped Anna dress, then checked the cinnamon rolls. She set the pan on the counter as the door opened. Viktor and Reuben strode in.

Viktor looked bad. His lower lip was busted, his jaw bruised, and his eye was still swollen shut. That must really hurt.

She handed him an ice pack as he passed on the way to the table. He nodded his thanks, his dark eyes unfathomable.

Was Henry truly in worse shape? That was what Viktor had said.

If that was the case, maybe Henry would stay home from church today. Esther almost smiled.

But maybe he'd be there anyway, showing off his battle scars and garnering sympathy for his imminent fatal attack on Viktor's reputation. And her honor.

Tears stung her eyes.

Esther glanced at the table, making sure everything was ready, before sliding into her seat and bowing her head for the silent prayer.

Ach, Gott. She'd lain awake all nacht, staring at the dark ceiling praying and worrying about how things would go. Mostly worrying. She'd gotten up once and tried reading her Bible. Tucked inside, she'd found twenty one-dollar bills, which would kum in handy. She must've put them in there and forgotten about them.

Scripture-wise, she must not have turned to the right passages, because all she'd found were messages about the wrath of God and

His plan to cut down, wipe out, and otherwise obliterate a people. Not exactly words of comfort.

She'd shut the Bible and cried, begging forgiveness for falling in love with Viktor.

And yet nein peace had kum. Her world was still in turmoil.

Did Gott have any control over this? Or maybe she was supposed to confess to Bishop Joe before Gott forgave her.

Maybe, as the preachers said, it was all about joining the church and serving the community.

The thought left an empty feeling inside.

Maybe it was all about obeying the rules, so that Gott wouldn't rain down judgment on her. The preachers had said that, too, citing incident after incident in which various Amish communities had been wiped out by a natural disaster due to the abundance of unconfessed sins of the people.

Reuben cleared his throat, and she raised her head, her face heating. She grabbed the plate of cinnamon rolls and started passing them around.

If unconfessed sins incurred the wrath of God, then why were some Amish so happy? Like Anna—even now, amid so much turmoil, she wore an expression of contentment. Maybe being loved by Reuben made all the difference. Would Esther be happy all the time if she married Viktor?

She glanced his way. Met his gaze. Her face warmed even more, and she quickly averted her eyes.

Nein. As pleasant as the thought was, something else was missing.

She'd figure it out later. Her head began to hurt. Right now, she had more immediate problems. And she couldn't think of a single solution to any of them. She slumped in her seat.

By Reuben's own words, Henry would be reluctant to let her go. Yet Reuben had encouraged her to break things off with him. He'd stood up for her when Henry had confronted her the nacht before. And now what? Should she just give up? Accept her lot in life as a gut, submissive, Amish girl? Accepting her fate as the unhappy frau of Henry for the rest of her life?

Or should she fight it and end up in trouble with her parents, the community, the preachers, the bishop, and the church? Everything was at risk.

Well, maybe not everything. If Reuben was right, and Viktor had been courting her this whole time, then she could "jump the fence" to be with him. She dared glance at him again. He smiled and winked.

She straightened a bit, hope flaring. Maybe he'd marry her, and she could stay here and take care of Anna and Reuben as Viktor's frau, living an Amish life, on an Amish farm, but being "not quite Amish."

But how could she ask?

Even with an "unsubmissive attitude," going up to Viktor and demanding to know his intentions—or even proposing to him— would be wrong.

Which left her with nein answers. Still.

A natural disaster might be a blessing in disguise, solving everything.

Maybe she should pray for a tornado.

⌒

Viktor stretched, glad that the seemingly endless preaching service had finally reached its conclusion. He stood, smiled, and nodded his greetings to the men around him. He'd been out of church for so long, he'd struggled to translate much of what the preachers had said, speaking as they did in High German. If one of them would've preached in Englisch, and had something of value to say, he might've felt it worthwhile to sit on a hard bench in a dusty, smelly barn for hours upon endless hours.

It'd been especially uncomfortable with Henry, still looking like he'd gotten in a losing argument with a semitruck, glaring at him the whole time. He'd even thrown in an obscene gesture or two. During church services. At least one of the men near Viktor had smothered a gasp upon seeing it. And more than one eyebrow had arched.

Beside Viktor, Josh Yoder got to his feet. He hadn't fidgeted at all during the service. At least, not that Viktor had noticed. Josh wore a contented smile. Maybe having received his daed's forgiveness and welkum home was enough, because he'd missed as many church Sundays as Viktor.

Viktor grimaced. He'd never receive forgiveness or a father's welkum. If only he could.

He looked at Josh. "Can we talk awhile?"

Josh nodded. "Let's go through the line and get food first. I have things to tell you, too."

"I could drive out to another town so we could go to a restaurant," Viktor offered. His stomach rumbled.

"Nein, let's just eat here. Honestly, it's been a while since breakfast, I don't want to sit in a vehicle for the twenty minutes or so it'd take to drive somewhere. And then to stand in line?" Josh chuckled. "I don't think so."

Viktor nodded. It had been a while since breakfast. And Esther's cinnamon rolls had worn off a long time ago.

"Do you want to take our plates down by the pond?" Viktor asked him.

Josh nodded. "Be there in a bit. Need to talk to the bishop about joining baptism classes." He grinned. "I hope he doesn't ask too many questions. I may have some ulterior motives."

Henry walked past, making another obscene gesture at Viktor. Josh raised one of his eyebrows. "What's that about?"

"I'll explain later." Which reminded Viktor—he needed to look for Esther's kapp while he was at the pond. Top priority, so that Josh, or anyone else, wouldn't see it and ask questions.

Viktor joined the line of men exiting the barn and approaching the food tables.

"Gut to see you here, Viktor." Bishop Joe was all smiles. Henry must not have talked to him. Yet. "What happened to you? Caught on the wrong side of a horse's hoof?" He chuckled. "We need to talk about your return, jah? Maybe Tuesday?"

Viktor felt a lump in his stomach. The bishop was right—they needed to talk. Just not about his return. Not yet. He pulled in a breath. "Jah. Tuesday is gut."

"I'll kum by then. Sometime between breakfast and the noon meal. Will that work?"

The only thing going on was Grossmammi's session with the therapists, and Viktor still hadn't figured out their schedule. So far, it didn't seem to follow any pattern. They came sometimes early, sometimes late. "Jah. Should be fine."

"Gut, gut. Glad to hear it." The bishop's smile widened, and he turned to speak to the next person. That grin would undoubtedly fade and die when Viktor had his say—or Henry spilled his poison.

Viktor went through the line and filled his plate with food, taking a couple of Esther's roast beef sandwiches. Then he headed to the pond. Alone. He sat on the boulder, staring out at the blue expanse of water, wishing he'd brought his pole and tackle box. He didn't see Esther's kapp anywhere. Not on the ground, not floating on the water. It might be tangled in the quilts he'd brought home the nacht before.

Or Henry might've kum by earlier to collect it as evidence of her wrongdoing.

Viktor's insides churned. He eyed the sandwiches with distaste. Maybe he'd eat later.

A twig snapped, and he glanced over his shoulder to see Josh approaching.

A mixture of relief and anxiety filled him. The last time they'd had any real conversation had been the nacht everything had changed. And he wouldn't venture a guess at how meaningful their discussion had been, with everyone inebriated. Amazing how the same thing had precipitated their departure, almost simultaneously, and they'd returned about the same time.

Josh sat next to him on the boulder. "Sure is peaceful here. Don't think there's another place quite like Amish country."

"Agreed."

Josh picked up a sandwich. "When I left here, I went to St. Louis awhile. Wow. Talk about culture shock. After that, I just went wherever I wanted. Saw whatever I wanted, including some of the places we learned about in school. Got a job whenever I ran out of money. Then I met a guy who'd walked the Appalachian Trail. I bought some gear and went to Georgia. Figured I'd hike it just to say I had." He took a bite.

"Nice." Viktor reached for the bottle of water he'd snagged and took a sip. "I still had to support my großeltern, so I went to Iowa. Signed on to work on a barge on the Mississippi. Started at the bottom and worked my way up."

"Think you'll ever kum back for gut?"

Viktor shook his head. Then shrugged. "Someday. It's getting nearer. The health of my großeltern is in decline. But…." He swallowed. "There's this girl. She makes me want to return." He looked down.

"You wouldn't be the first to return for a girl." There was a smile in Josh's voice.

Viktor sighed. "I love her, but I can't ask her to wait. Problem is, she's promised to someone else. I think he's abusive. I want her to break up with him, but she won't."

"You love her, you fight for her."

Viktor shifted. Time to change the subject.

"So, you hiked the Appalachian Trail." He picked up his sandwich and forced himself to take a bite. He still wasn't hungry. Well, maybe he was—there went his stomach, rumbling again. Only his taste buds weren't interested. Or maybe they were. Esther had added horseradish sauce to the roast beef. *Nice.*

"Changed my life." Josh grinned.

"You were pretty angry when you left."

Josh looked away. "Jah. Being involved in the death of his best friend's family does that to a man."

Viktor took a deep breath. He knew what guilt felt like. But he'd never meant for Josh to waste years wandering the country. "It wasn't your fault." And there he went, spouting the platitudes he'd silenced from Esther, in a desire to reassure his friend. "I don't blame you." Not much better.

Josh shook his head. "Lost a lot of jobs due to my out-of-control drinking and my horrible temper. Not very proud of who I became."

"So, what happened?" How had Josh let it go? If only Viktor could find the answers—and the same peace he saw in Josh's eyes.

"Long story short, I was hiking one day, not even sure what state I was in at the time. I hiked most of it so drunk, it's amazing I didn't fall over a cliff. But there'd been a heavy snowmelt, causing mudslides in the mountains. I witnessed a man being washed away. His trail name was 'Broom Man.' I reached out and grabbed him out of the raging river of mud, and saved his life."

Viktor reached for a dill pickle. "And…that changed you, how?" He took a bite, savoring the sour tang and crunchy consistency.

Josh shook his head. "Broom Man was out of his mind. At least I thought so at first. He fell to his face, started crying and confessing and praising, all mixed up together. But then he started saying something about…. Well, I know we were raised in a gut Amish church, but, Viktor, I have never heard the preachers say this stuff before. Ever."

Something inside Viktor shifted. Came alive. He set the pickle down and turned to Josh. "What kind of stuff?"

"He talked about how Gott loved us so much that He sent His only Son to die for us. About how, if you admit you're a sinner, believe in your heart that Jesus Christ is Lord, and confess your sins, then you can be saved. You can *know* you're saved, Vik. Not just hope that you're somehow gut enough, because you're not. You'll never be. Even your gut works are nothing but filthy rags. This is what really got to me—a verse Broom Man quoted from Ephesians. *'For by grace are ye saved through faith; and that not of yourselves: it is the gift of God: not of works, lest any man should boast.' Through* faith, Vik. Not of works. Did you get that?"

Viktor opened his mouth but said nothing. He'd never heard that teaching, either. What he'd been taught all through childhood had to do with obeying the rules, about works.

"I'm nein preacher, and neither was he; but when I heard that, I was on my face before Gott, too. And then, it was amazing—that was it. I cried out to Gott, confessing my sins, and the next thing...I can't explain it. Something washed over me. Into me. Changed me. All the anger and the guilt was gone. The urge to drown it with drinking was gone. All gone. And suddenly, all I wanted was to live, completely and totally, for Gott. It could happen to you, too, Vik."

A strange yearning filled him. Tears burned his eyes. "It can't be that simple." His voice broke. *If only it could be.*

Josh leaned away, reached into a back pocket of his black trousers, and pulled out a small book. The Englisch New Testament. "Let me show you."

✑

Viktor didn't show up at singing, to Esther's dismay. Even more disheartening, Henry claimed the spot across from her. His gaze raked her over, making her feel dirty. Cheap. She shuddered. Why hadn't Viktor kum, especially after stating so vehemently that he'd take her home afterward?

Wait. He'd said he'd take her home. Not sit across from her. Not attend. So maybe he would still show up.

And her earlier belief that Viktor might have misunderstood Henry? Nein way. The looks Henry gave her more than confirmed the truth of his words.

She sighed. The snacks she'd nibbled on—cheese and crackers, homemade summer sausages, and cookies—congealed in her stomach, making her nauseated.

She couldn't sing. Not with this lump in her throat.

Esther pushed to her feet, ignored the questioning looks of her cousins sitting on either side of her, and left the barn. She walked toward the field where the buggies were parked in rows, like an Englisch car lot.

"Where are you headed?"

She jumped at the male voice, then grinned when she recognized it. She turned around and smiled at Viktor. "I don't know. But I'm glad you came." Then she noticed the other man standing slightly behind him. She studied him for a moment before recognition dawned. Viktor's best friend. And the former beau of her cousin Greta. She wouldn't be happy. "Hi, Joshua. I didn't know you were back."

Joshua's smile lit his whole face. "Gut to see you, Esther."

"We were talking all afternoon. Didn't mean to keep you waiting. Singing isn't over yet, is it?" There was something different about Viktor. He seemed more relaxed. Happier. There was a light in his eyes she'd never seen before, despite one of them still being puffy and bruised. Just spending an afternoon catching up with his friend must have worked miracles.

If only she could feel as relaxed and happy. Her afternoon had been spent deflecting questions from her cousins and friends about Henry's face and Viktor's eye.

But then, Joshua was known to be just as much of a "bad bu" as Viktor. A drunk, a troublemaker, a flirt.

Had they been drinking this afternoon? Or worse? She hadn't seen Viktor drinking at all during the time he'd been home, but…

She eyed Josh and then Viktor. "You're not…drunk, are you?" Her voice squeaked.

"Haven't had anything stronger than water." Viktor chuckled. "Are you ready to go, süße?"

Esther glanced over her shoulder at the barn. Nobody had kum looking for her. It was only a matter of time. "Jah." She didn't want to spend one more minute in Henry's company.

Viktor turned to his friend. "See you later, Josh. Danki for everything."

Joshua nodded. "Gut talking to you, Vik. I'll be praying. Nice seeing you again, Esther." He continued toward the barn, where Greta was. Unwarned.

Viktor didn't reach for her hand. Probably wise, with the chaperones standing just inside the barn doors. Instead he led the way down the long row of buggies. "I stopped at home so I'd have a ride for you. Hope you don't mind the truck." He looked over his shoulder and grinned, then opened the passenger door for her. She climbed in, drawing a big breath of the piney scent that filled the cab.

"Buckle up, süße. I'm going to take you into town. I'm in the mood for a Cherry Berry Chiller. Ever had one?"

She pulled the seat belt across her front and snapped it into place. "Nein." But then, she never left Jamesport, except for rare trips to Pennsylvania with Lily. "You don't mean Jamesport, jah? Because I never heard of a Cherry Berry Chiller."

"You'll like it." He shut her door, then jogged around to the driver side and climbed in next to her. With a twist of his hand on the key, the engine roared to life.

"Stay tuned for news and weather at the top of the hour," a male voice said, making Esther jump. "Coming up next—"

Viktor pushed a button and silenced the voice. He backed out of the field and drove past the barn just as Henry exited. He raised his arms in frustration as they drove past. Viktor leaned over and waved jubilantly.

Esther turned to Viktor. "How are your eye and jaw?"

He raised his hand and lightly touched his jawbone. "Still hurts here, but I think the swelling around my eye has gone down some. At least I can see again." He pulled onto the road, the truck tires spinning gravel as they picked up speed.

"Well, that's gut, since we're barreling down the road at a rate at least twice the speed of a buggy." Esther giggled, then sobered. "When did Joshua get back? I hadn't seen him—or heard." Odd, considering how fast news usually traveled through the grapevine.

Viktor shrugged. "He's been home about a week, I think. Maybe a little longer. Today was the first chance we had to talk."

Would it be too nosy to ask what they had talked about? She studied his expression. It still seemed relaxed. Happy. Open. Which was unusual, in a gut way. But it confused her. What had happened? "I'm glad you had a chance to talk."

"Me too, süße. I'm still trying to process it all."

That comment increased her curiosity a hundredfold. Yet he seemed content to leave it at that. He turned the radio on again and started singing along with the song that played.

She sighed. He'd shut her out. In favor of a song. With instrumental accompaniment. On the radio.

About as far from Amish as he could get.

Chapter 26

Viktor glanced at Esther out of the corner of his eye. Her right hand grasped the door handle; her left clutched the seat belt, as if holding on would help protect her if something happened. She'd apparently never ridden in the front seat of a vehicle before. She'd get used to it, though, hanging around with him. Or maybe she'd be happy to stick to a slow-moving horse and buggy.

He stopped at a red light in town. "You okay?"

"Fine." She didn't release her grip.

He laughed. "You seem a bit tense, süße."

"The truck…goes so fast. It's…faster than a runaway horse." She turned to him with wide eyes. "You buwe seem to have a need for speed, ain't so?"

He shrugged. But she was right. Most Amish buwe loved racing, whether horses, buggies, or motor vehicles.

"Does Henry? Or did he?"

It was her turn to shrug. "I don't know. He never mentioned it."

Viktor frowned. "What do you and Henry talk about, süße?" He stepped on the gas when the light turned green.

She rolled her eyes. "He mostly talks about how wunderbaar it'll be when we marry. I stay quiet. He talks about how he and his mamm will train me right."

Viktor tightened his grip on the steering wheel. He wanted the punches he'd landed yesterday to hurt worse.

"Sometimes, it's hard to believe my mamm and his are best friends. His mamm has always spoken ill of me and how I was raised." She sighed. "I tried to break up with Henry. Did Reuben tell you? I gave back his gifts. There weren't many."

Viktor grinned, his hope growing. So, she had tried to break things off with the scum. Gut to know her heart was inclined toward him. "Tried?"

"Reuben made Henry take the gifts and go, but Henry made it clear he wouldn't release me."

"Grossdaedi didn't tell me any of that." Grossdaedi hadn't told him anything. Probably didn't see the point. If Viktor were Henry, he wouldn't want to give Esther up, either. She was one of a kind.

"Reuben said we needed to figure out how to solve this before Bishop Joe hands us his verdict. Because what he says stands." She looked over at him as if she expected him to have the answers to her problems.

There was nein way the bishop would choose the "bad bu" over the one who'd apparently toed the line.

Viktor sucked in a breath. Might as well lay all his cards on the table in the biggest gamble of his life. "I told Henry you were marrying me," he said quietly.

Maybe too quietly, because she didn't answer.

He dared a glance at her.

She stared at him, her eyes wide, lips parted.

"Was ist letz, süße?" Maybe he shouldn't have sprung that announcement on her.

Tears glistened on her lower lashes. Her bottom lip quivered.

He whipped the truck into a parking spot at McDonald's. He'd planned to place his order at the drive-through window, but he'd changed his mind.

He unbuckled his seat belt, then reached across the cab, unfastened Esther's, and tugged her toward him. He wrapped her in his arms and held her close. "Wait for me," he whispered. He kissed her forehead, her eyes, and the tip of her nose, then brushed his lips over hers. "Wait for me, süße."

⌒

Wait for me? *For what?* Esther opened her mouth to ask, but his lips came back to claim hers, and her passion flared. She snuggled closer, hating the confines of the truck cab and how she kept bumping things with her elbows. She didn't know what, nor did she care. She wrapped her arms around his neck and pulled herself nearer.

After too few minutes of bliss, Viktor untangled himself, turned off the engine, and took the keys out of the ignition.

"You want to marry me?" Her voice squeaked. She waited for his reply, hardly daring to breathe. *Jah, jah, jah....*

"I'm not proposing, just…wait for me until I return to the Amish." He inhaled a shuddery breath. "It'll be soon. This year or next."

Hold it. He sounded like Henry, telling her the way things would be. *Wait? Up to two years?* He didn't want her to jump the fence? He didn't want her enough to kum back now? He wouldn't even commit by asking her to marry him? Just "Wait"?

Not even an "Ich liebe dich"?

Her eyes burned with tears. This was not how she'd envisioned her marriage proposal. Not that it was a marriage proposal. *"I'm not proposing."* Of course, she'd never dared to dream much of proposals, since her marriage was basically arranged. Even so, there were occasional thoughts of some man loving her enough to....

She swallowed.

Her dreams didn't matter. They weren't reality.

But she couldn't commit herself to someone who wouldn't commit to her. She blinked back her tears. "Nein." It hurt to say.

He pulled back, opened the truck door, and got out. His eyes were dark, unreadable. A muscle jumped in his jaw. "I guess that's all there is to say, then." His chest rose and fell. "I'll get your drink. Be right back. Unless you want to kum inside?"

She shook her head, not daring to answer. Afraid the sob she barely held back would escape.

The door shut. She watched as he strode off.

A tear ran down her cheek. Then another. And another. Followed by a whole flood. She buried her face in her apron and struggled to get herself under control before Viktor returned. Washing her face with cold water would probably help. And there would be a bathroom inside. She lowered the apron, slipped out of the truck, and headed into the building, to the back, where the restrooms were. She held her head high, not looking at anyone. She didn't want to see the pity or the open gawking at an Amish girl. Bad enough in Jamesport with all the tourists.

She washed her face in the sink and used her apron to dry it, since there weren't any paper towels—just a contraption that blew out air when she walked past it.

Esther left the bathroom and started for the door when she thought she heard someone—Viktor?—call her name. She turned around.

He approached, holding two pinkish-red drinks in clear cups. He handed her one. "Hope you like it." His jaw was still tense, and he avoided her eyes. His voice held the false cheerfulness she heard on Sundays, especially from the preachers' wives.

She imagined the unspoken "süße." And barely held back another sob.

How would she handle Anna calling her that without breaking down?

It wasn't fair. She loved him. She would wait…if he asked her to marry him. If he told her he loved her.

If she could get free from Henry.

Had Viktor expected her to swoon over his offhand remark? *"I told Henry you were marrying me."*

Besides, he'd probably said it in the heat of the fight.

She sighed.

But then…wait. He'd also said, *"You're not going to marry him. You're gonna marry—"*

Marry? With an unspoken "me"?

That didn't exactly count as a proposal, either. More a statement of fact. A decree. Just like Henry.

Was it so wrong to want to be asked? To have him pledge his undying love before she promised to wait?

The rejection had stung, stabbing deep inside and plunging into parts of him that he hadn't known existed. It had stunned him, stealing his breath for a long moment. His eyes still burned. He hadn't expected the answer she'd given. He'd anticipated something along the lines of a joyful "jah" and maybe a few more heated kisses, because she loved him. Or so he'd thought. After all, he'd almost asked her to marry him. He'd indicated his desire strongly. But actually asking? Not yet. He'd had in mind a more romantic location. Beautiful, heartfelt words. A bended knee. And….

Well, it didn't matter.

Because "not yet" had turned into "not ever."

His jaw hurt from clenching. Especially in light of the blow from the fight. He blinked, swallowed the painful lump in his throat, and followed her out to the truck. He forced himself to be a gentleman, opening her door for her, though he couldn't bring himself to meet her eyes. It took all his energy to keep standing and not crumple in a dejected heap on the ground. He stared at the asphalt as she buckled up.

"Nein," she'd said.

There wasn't a more painful word.

His eyes watered. He blinked. He refused to cry.

He swallowed the stubborn lump once more and opened his door, spying his cell phone on the dashboard. The cord of the charger dangled from the cigarette lighter. He grabbed his phone and plugged it in.

Esther stared out her window.

He shut his eyes against the burn, then opened them again. He inserted the key in the ignition, started the engine, and drove home. Silently. The whole trip.

"*Nein.*"

There was nothing else to be said. It ended everything. Because there was nein way he could be friends with her after this.

He pulled into the driveway and stopped the truck in front of the haus to let her out.

As she exited, he swallowed that pesky lump in his throat. Again.

He started to drive away when he saw Grossdaedi shove the screen door open and rush out on the porch, waving his arms.

Viktor stopped the truck and pushed the button to lower the passenger window.

Grossdaedi's face was an unusual shade of gray. "Anna has fallen," he said to Esther. "I can't get her up. She's crying. I…I was about to go to the phone to call for an Englisch driver to take her to the hospital."

Esther disappeared inside.

Grossmammi! Viktor slammed the gearshift into park, then left the ignition running as he jumped from the vehicle and raced toward the haus.

Chapter 27

Esther knelt beside Anna and smoothed her hair back. She must've fallen while getting ready for bed, since her kapp had been removed and her hair was loose, flowing over her shoulders. "Are you okay?"

"My hip...I think." She half sat, leaning in the corner of the dresser and the bed. She touched her upper leg, but not on the thigh. "I tried to transfer from the chair to the bed. My hip gave out, and I went down. Ach, Esther. It hurts." The last word was drawn out on a whine.

Viktor burst into the bedroom, not even pausing to knock. He dropped down beside them. "What happened, Grossmammi?" Reuben followed him into the room.

Anna repeated what she'd told Esther.

Why didn't he pick her up and put her either in bed or in the wheelchair? Admittedly, Anna might be stunned when he scooped her up. Esther could identify, remembering how surprised she'd been when Viktor had lifted her without warning. How nice it'd been to have him hold her close, to feel his heartbeat....

Nein. She couldn't allow herself to go there.

Viktor asked Anna some questions, and when she'd finished telling him what had happened and showing him where it hurt, he sat back on his haunches and looked up, his gaze skittering from Reuben to Esther.

"We need to call for an ambulance. I don't want to risk further injury by attempting to move her. Esther, my cell phone is in the truck. It's not fully charged, but you can call from out there. It'll be faster than running to the shanty."

She stared at him. She wouldn't have the first idea how to turn on the phone, much less use it. It was gut that he was done with his silent treatment, but he was back to barking orders.

His dark gaze moved from her to Reuben, then back, and he stood. "I'll do it, then. Don't try to move, Grossmammi. But if there's something Esther can do to make you more comfortable, let her know."

"I'm not going anywhere with my hair down," Anna said. "Or in my nightgown."

Viktor grunted but motioned for Esther to take over. He backed out of the room. "I'll be right back." The door shut behind him.

Esther twisted Anna's hair up the best she could, given the awkward position she was in. She pinned it into a bun and secured a kapp over it. Then she reached for Anna's black bonnet. She wouldn't want be caught without it.

"My clothes, süße."

Esther's breath caught at the endearment. But she didn't cry. She tilted her head, studying Anna. She seemed pale and shaky. Esther swallowed. "I don't think I can get the nightgown off." She summoned a smile. "You'll have to go in that. At least it's more modest than the gowns the hospitals make you wear, from what I've heard."

"I won't wear them." Anna shook her head. "I won't."

Esther forced her smile to stay in place. "Would you like a pillow under your head? Or a blanket to cover you?"

"It's hot. Nein blanket."

Viktor reappeared. "There's an ambulance out on the highway. It'll be here in a few minutes. Esther, get together whatever things she might need, like a comb and a toothbrush. You know."

At least he was thinking clearly. The whole situation scared her. Was Anna in danger? Would this setback destroy her sweet spirit? Esther didn't have any idea how to help in this current situation.

It seemed like forever, but was probably only minutes, before the ambulance skidded into the drive, siren wailing. The EMTs secured Anna on a gurney and carried her out. Then the ambulance took off.

"I'll take you to the hospital, Grossdaedi." Viktor motioned to the truck. "Get in."

Esther followed, but Reuben stopped her. "You stay here. Go to bed. Tomorrow, if we haven't returned with Anna, start cooking. Many meals. I don't know how long she might be in the hospital, but you won't be allowed to stay with Viktor and me. Not without Anna here. You'll need to go home until she's back."

She wouldn't be allowed to stay? Esther blinked back tears, for Anna and for herself. She'd have to move back home and lose the income Daed depended on. Being there would also mean she'd be pressured by, and about, Henry, and she'd be surrounded by chaos yet again. The worst part would be having to leave this precious couple just to keep up appearances. She didn't even want to leave Viktor, despite his not loving her enough to ask her to marry him.

And Anna...how could Esther handle not being there for her? The woman depended on her.

She stepped out on the porch and watched as Reuben climbed in the truck, slowly, due to his back issues.

Viktor got behind the wheel, pulled the seat belt across his chest, and hooked it, then shut the door. The tires spun and gravel flew as the truck sped out of the circular drive to the road. At least they'd get to the hospital soon after Anna arrived. The truck disappeared into the darkness. Nothing but a pair of red lights racing away.

The sudden silence felt oppressive. Esther could almost feel the weight of it crushing her chest. Why wasn't she allowed to go? Nein room in the cab? Not family? She'd be too worried to sleep, not knowing what was going on.

"Go to bed?" Esther said to the emptiness around her. "He's joking, ain't so?"

She went into the haus, cleaned up the few dishes Reuben and Anna had left from the simple meal she'd prepared for them, then swept the floor. How many meals would she need to fix to make sure they were fed while she was gone? "Many meals." So vague. What if Anna didn't kum home? She choked back another sob. She checked to make sure their bed was made, then started upstairs.

A door shut, and a floorboard in the kitchen creaked. She froze in fear, even though she told herself it was irrational. Had Henry kum again? When she was alone?

"Esther?" The voice was female. *Rachel?*

Esther sagged in relief. Her knees shook as she went back down-stairs and carried the lantern into the kitchen. "What are you doing here?" She stared at her cousin.

"Viktor stopped and asked me to stay with you so you wouldn't be alone. He told me about Anna. And he gave strict orders that Lily is not welkum to stay if she comes while he's gone. I do have to work tomorrow, but I'll kum by when I get off and see if the Petersheims have returned."

So, Viktor was overriding Reuben's concerns about her reputa-tion and wouldn't allow her to be sent away?

"Stay with me? To-nacht, you mean?"

Rachel shrugged. "It sounded to me as if it'd be until Anna is released from the hospital. He mentioned the overcrowding at your haus and how his grossdaedi needs you as much as his mammi."

Esther caught her breath. Such a sweet man, looking after her, even when their relationship had been destroyed.

By her own doing.

Why was it she could stand her ground around Viktor and Reuben, but she was afraid around Daed and Henry?

Of course, Daed wouldn't hesitate to administer the strap. Maybe she had the same fear of Henry. Esther shook her head. She'd think about it later. Maybe after she went to bed. It'd be strange sleeping beside Rachel. They hadn't had a sleepover in years.

After Rachel drifted off, Esther would stay awake to plan how to tell Viktor she'd changed her mind and wanted to wait. For him. If she could.

And there she was, thinking about it again.

She turned to Rachel. "Want some tea?"

"Chocolate milk." Rachel pulled a small plastic container of chocolate powder out of her pocket. "Want some?"

Ach, jah. It'd been forever since she'd had chocolate.

Right now, it was a "must-have."

⌒

It seemed to Viktor that they'd arrived at the hospital weeks ago instead of mere hours. Grossmammi had been whisked off to some examination room, leaving Viktor and Grossdaedi pacing the waiting room. All the chairs were occupied.

After a while, the double doors leading to the emergency wing opened, and a woman wearing light blue scrubs came out. She looked around the room. Her gaze centered on Grossdaedi, and she approached. "Petersheim family?"

Grossdaedi stood a bit straighter. "Yes." He motioned to Viktor.

"Come with me." She led the way to a smaller room. "The doctor will be with you shortly." She shut the door behind Viktor.

This room was windowless. It contained a long conference table and coordinating chairs. It wasn't designed for comfort. Just business.

Viktor sighed. If he and Grossdaedi had been allowed back into the emergency wing, there wouldn't be the need for this formality. He sighed again, more loudly.

Grossdaedi looked at him. "Glad you're home, sohn. Gott knew we needed you."

Viktor grunted and turned away, trying to ignore the additional subliminal message. *Kum home for gut.*

He needed time. It would mean a lot of change. Before he committed, he'd have to spend hours in prayer. *Wow.* Something had changed. He smiled, remembering the strange sense of peace that had washed over him after talking with Josh at the pond, filling some longing deep inside. Giving him something he hadn't known was missing.

Gott.

Overflowing his heart—or soul—and spreading from side to side. *Joy.* His smile widened.

The door opened again, and this time, a doctor walked in, trailed by a woman in pink and black floral scrubs. She carried a clipboard.

"Family of Petersheim?" the doctor asked.

"Yes." Grossdaedi answered.

The doctor's eyes flickered to Viktor, and he nodded once, apparently satisfied that he also belonged. Then he set his gaze on Grossdaedi. "The bad news is, your wife broke her hip bone. The good news is, a simple hip replacement will repair the damage much faster than waiting for the bone to mend. After she recovers, the stability and lack of pain in the joint will be a welcome relief. If it isn't repaired immediately, further damage could occur. If you'll sign the release, we'll do it first thing in the morning. I've already obtained your wife's consent."

Viktor frowned. "A hip replacement? How could this happen? She's been in a wheelchair for...." He shrugged and looked at Grossdaedi.

The doctor took the clipboard from the nurse and placed it on the table, near Grossdaedi. "Sometimes it's the inactivity of the joint that results in the deterioration. If you don't use it, you lose it. Sometimes just getting up wrong can cause it to snap. She'll be fine. These surgeries are routine. Of course, with any surgery, there are some risks." And he went on to elaborate for several minutes.

When the doctor finished speaking, Grossdaedi narrowed his eyes as he studied the paper, then glanced at Viktor. He raised his eyebrow in a silent question. Should they risk it?

Viktor nodded. What other choice did they have?

Grossdaedi picked up the pen and signed his name.

"Good, good." The doctor reached for the clipboard. "Another nurse will show you to another waiting room, and we'll notify you when Mrs. Petersheim is settled so you can visit her in her room." He and the nurse left the room, leaving the door open.

A few minutes later, another nurse reappeared. "If you'll follow me...."

She led Viktor and Grossdaedi down the hall. Viktor spied the doctor and his nurse standing at the other end of the hallway, talking with another man, but the nurse they followed turned down a different corridor and approached an elevator, chatting the whole time about the hot, humid weather.

What did she expect from July?

Viktor tuned her out.

The waiting room they were taken to was as large as the one outside the emergency wing, but it was more comfortable and not as crowded. There were plenty of couches, soft-looking chairs, and coffee tables piled with magazines, and in the corner, a TV played a movie. Several people were sprawled on one of the couches, staring at the screen.

After the nurse left, Grossdaedi lowered himself wearily into a chair. "The waiting, it isn't so pleasant." He sighed.

"How's your back?" Viktor studied him. His lips were pinched together.

Grossdaedi shrugged. "I didn't do it any favors, trying to lift your grossmammi."

"Do I need to get you into the chiropractor again?"

He grunted.

"But you did feel better for a few hours, ain't so?"

"Not worth it."

"A matter of opinion. I'll make an appointment. Tomorrow, after the surgery."

Grossdaedi grunted again.

Viktor fell silent. He sat next to Grossdaedi, then reached for a magazine. His gaze landed on a Gideon Bible. He glanced at Grossdaedi and, seeing that his attention was focused on the nurses' station on the other side of the open hallway, reached for the tome. He opened it, thumbing through the stiff pages, until he found the book of Ephesians. He couldn't remember the references Josh had showed him, so he started reading at chapter one.

He read through the first fifteen verses twice. Verses five through seven especially stuck out. He'd accepted Christ that afternoon, newly confident in *"redemption through his blood, the forgiveness of sins, according to the riches of his grace."* It was thrilling to read. Gott's grace amazed him. He hungered to learn everything about der Herr.

Grossdaedi's hand moved into his line of vision. Viktor looked up.

"What are you doing, sohn?" Grossdaedi's gaze rested on the Bible, then rose to Viktor's face. Hope lit his eyes.

Viktor swallowed. "Josh met Gott on the Appalachian Trail. And he…he introduced Him to me."

Tears welled in Grossdaedi's eyes. "Really?"

"Jah. But…well, I'm still processing, trying to understand. I never heard some of the stuff Josh talked about. Like this." He held the Bible out and pointed to the words, then read them out loud: *"'Having predestinated us unto the adoption of children by Jesus Christ to himself, according to the good pleasure of his will, to the praise of the glory of his grace, wherein he hath made us accepted in the beloved.'"* His voice cracked. He cleared his throat. *"'In whom we have redemption through his blood, the forgiveness of sins, according to the riches of his grace.'"* He pulled the Bible back. "You know what that means?" His throat clogged with emotion. "It…it means that Gott forgives me, through Jesus, for killing my family." His voice broke. "I'm accepted in the beloved."

Grossdaedi blinked multiple times. "You…you blamed yourself? But…it was a firecracker. And—"

"And I was out in the back field with my friends. We were drinking, and we shot off that firecracker."

"Ach, Viktor." Grossdaedi patted his hand. He opened his mouth, then shut it. His brow furrowed. "You were home before it started. I heard you kum in."

Viktor shrugged. "Who knows how long it took for the fire to start? I was home. It might've been smoldering when I got there. All I know is that it was a firecracker, and my friends and I were shooting them off."

"That doesn't mean it was you. Others set off fireworks that nacht, too. Maybe one of your brothers lit one of those sparklers in the bedroom. I saw Isaiah with some."

Was there really a chance it hadn't been him? He imagined Isaiah's childish, ornery face.

"But if it was you—and I don't think it was—then I forgive you. Gott has forgiven you." Grossdaedi tapped the Bible. "You said it yourself. In the district in Pennsylvania where your grossmammi and I lived, there was one preacher who was different from most others. He never talked this way from the pulpit, unfortunately, but he would speak privately with people, when he felt their minds were open. Your grossmammi and I were both saved, as were your daed and mamm. But here, I've never heard that message mentioned. Not once." He frowned. "I've been afraid to talk much, seeing how Gott never called me to be a preacher."

Viktor sighed. "By lot, Grossdaedi. They call preachers by lot."

Grossdaedi shrugged. "Jah. And I wouldn't want the responsibility. It's a great weight for a man, being responsible for an entire district. Besides, as Anna always said, it's easier to infiltrate from the inside than the outside." He rubbed his jaw. "And maybe so. I've started bringing things into the Bible reading at nacht. Sharing with Esther." He grinned. "Infiltrating from the inside."

"Is Esther receptive?" Viktor whispered. His heart clenched.

"She hasn't questioned anything yet. But Anna thinks Esther's searching. She's seen things in her expression that have led her to believe she's curious. Struggling. And not just because of you."

Viktor's mouth quirked. "She needed to think about Henry. He's just a bad choice, all around."

Grossdaedi expelled a breath of air. "You understand how it is, sohn. Girls are raised to do as they are told and not to think for themselves. She was told from an early age that she'd marry Henry. He took the necessary steps. It's a done deal."

"She deserves better."

"And normally, she would have that right to choose better. To refuse Henry. Not sure what makes this different." Grossdaedi started to lean back, then grimaced and straightened. "What makes you think you're better?"

Viktor looked away. "I'm nowhere near worthy of her." *Or of Gott.* And yet, Gott loved him anyway.

He looked back down at the Bible and remembered the first verse Josh had shared with him. "*For by grace are ye saved through faith....*"

"*Accepted in the beloved.*"

Grossdaedi reached over and grasped his hand.

Tears burned Viktor's eyes. Was this what freedom felt like?

～

Esther rolled over and looked at the dim light on the clock. Time to get up. She'd slept fitfully, despite Rachel's comforting presence, listening for Viktor and Reuben to return. She'd never heard them kum in. Hopefully, someone would send news today.

She slipped out of bed, trying not to make noise as she dressed and left the room.

Viktor's door was shut. She hesitated in front of it, listening. It'd been open when she'd gone to bed. Hadn't it?

Something creaked inside the room, followed by a bump. Esther backed away, then hurried downstairs to the kitchen. They were home! She started oatmeal and put bacon in a frying pan, then went to Anna's room to help her get ready for the day—if she was awake. They must've gotten in really late.

She cracked open the door to the first-floor bedroom. Reuben snored, the pillow next to him empty. Anna was still in the hospital? Esther shut the door and headed back to the kitchen.

So...did Reuben's orders still stand? Was she to spend the day cooking *many* meals, then go home? Or should she take Rachel's word that Viktor had sent her to stay until Anna came home? Who was the boss, Reuben or Viktor? And would Rachel's presence be enough to make it acceptable for Esther to remain?

She'd have to wait until she talked to either Viktor or Reuben. In the meantime, she'd start bread. It needed to be done either way.

She was elbow-deep in bread dough when Viktor came downstairs. His hair was wet, as if he'd just taken a shower. It'd be wunderbaar seeing that sight for years to kum. He'd be worth the wait. He glanced at Esther and nodded. "Morgen." Then he grabbed his shoes and opened the door.

"I'll wait for you...if you still want me to. Ich liebe dich." She said the words in a rush. Not exactly the way she'd planned. But at least they were out in the open. And hopefully they undid the damage of yesterday's "Nein."

He froze, his hand on the knob. After a moment, he turned back to face her. A slow grin spread across his face and lit his eyes. She smiled in return. "Gut." He nodded. "I'll try to make sure you're allowed to. Ich liebe—" He took a step in her direction, then hesitated, his gaze moving beyond her.

A sound behind Esther caught her attention. She glanced over her shoulder as her cousin came into the kitchen. Then she looked back at Viktor. Had he almost declared his love for her? If only Rachel would go back upstairs for a few minutes. Esther swallowed her disappointment. "Rachel said she's staying with me until Anna comes home?"

Viktor nodded. "Jah. You stay here. Grossdaedi needs you as much as Grossmammi. Rachel will be here at nacht."

Which meant nein more meeting Viktor at the pond. Probably a gut thing. Still, disappointment coursed through her, warring with relief that she wouldn't be sent home.

Viktor expelled a breath. "I promised Bishop Joe I'd help with the barn raising, but with Grossmammi in the hospital...." He shook his head. "I'm going to do the chores, call the chiropractor for Grossdaedi when the office opens, and then take you and him both to the hospital to see Grossmammi. Plan on sandwiches for lunch. Roast beef with horseradish sauce, like you made for Sunday, will be fine." His gaze moved to Rachel. "Danki for coming on such short notice." He nodded once before heading outside.

"How can I help?" Rachel came farther into the room. "And may I take a sandwich with me to work?"

Esther nodded. "You can either make sandwiches or slice up peaches for the oatmeal. I need to can the rest. They're getting overripe."

Rachel glanced toward the screen door. Esther followed her gaze. Viktor had slipped his shoes on and was halfway to the barn.

"'Ich liebe dich'? Really?" Rachel giggled as she looked at Esther. "Though, he's a much better man than *Henry*." Her lips curled as she said his name. "But Viktor jumped the fence."

Esther's face heated. She should've known someone would hear. But he'd called her "my love." Twice. Even if he hadn't actually said the three words, it showed in his eyes, his kisses, his care for her, his defending her honor to Henry, his asking for her to wait....

"He'll be coming back to take care of his großeltern, sooner or later. And with the recent turn of events, it's looking like sooner."

"And joining the church?"

Esther swallowed. "I think so."

Rachel giggled again. "Is he always so bossy? Telling you what to make for lunch? Telling you what you're going to do today?" She picked several peaches out of the bowl. "He really didn't give me the option of saying 'nein.' Not that I would have. He just said, 'I need you to stay with Esther until Anna gets home.' And I dropped everything and came."

Esther smiled. "Sometimes he's bossy. Not usually. Usually, he's—"

"He's used to being obeyed on the riverboat. He's over the crew. In charge of making decisions in the wheelhouse." Reuben came into the room, a bit hunched over, his right hand pressed against his back. "Esther, I hate to ask, but would you mind helping me with my shoes? I need to go help Viktor with the chores." He lowered himself into a chair with a slight moan.

Esther shook her head. "You need to stay inside and let Viktor handle the chores. Breakfast will be ready in a few minutes."

Reuben sighed but then nodded. "They are going to do a hip replacement on Anna this morgen. They said it snapped. Not sure how that could happen, but it did."

Esther said a silent prayer for a successful surgery as she stirred the oatmeal and flipped the bacon. She put two pieces on a plate, along with a leftover biscuit, and set it on the table, then gathered the butter and jam from the refrigerator. "Oatmeal will be another minute or two." She would keep the pan on the stove for Viktor. Chores would take a while, especially with his having to do Reuben's in addition to his own.

Gravel crunched as a white van pulled into the driveway. Why was the driver here? Viktor had said he'd take her and Reuben to the hospital. She glanced at Reuben. "Did you call for a driver?"

He shook his head. "I wonder who it is."

Esther went outside on the porch, followed by Rachel.

The driver opened the door and got out. "Hello."

She murmured a greeting as he went around to the back and unloaded a couple of suitcases. Then he opened the side door.

A lump lodged in her stomach and settled there.

Lily.

Chapter 28

I'm here!"

The high-pitched scream so closely following the arrival of the Amish driver caused Viktor's stomach to roil. He hesitated in the shadows just inside the barn doors, tempted to disappear into the dark recesses of the highest loft and leave Rachel and Esther to carry out his orders to send Lily—if it was indeed to her that the obnoxious voice belonged—away.

But that would be the coward's way out. And he wasn't a coward. But it was kind of unsettling to know that a girl he couldn't even remember had bragged about going behind the barn with him. That she was back, with the idea she'd be helping Esther as a caregiver. Or replacing her. He shuddered. Besides, that high-pitched voice would give him a headache. He couldn't subject his großeltern to it, either.

He wouldn't let that happen. Esther was the nucleus of their family. The one who kept it running smoothly. Grossmammi and Grossdaedi loved her...and so did he. Nobody would ever—could ever—replace her.

He gulped at the knot in his throat and stepped out of the barn. "Wait!" He waved his arms at the driver to stop, but apparently the driver didn't notice him. Either that, or the driver didn't desire Lily's presence in his vehicle any longer. The van picked up speed, leaving as fast as it had arrived.

Viktor would be forced to tolerate her at breakfast.

The churning in his stomach turned into a full-fledged riot.

He swallowed down the nausea and stopped his advance toward the farmhaus. Nein point in dealing with Lily any sooner than he had to. He'd wait until he went in for the morgen meal. Then he'd take her home. With Esther along to give directions so he wouldn't end up on a secluded back road somewhere with a woman in his arms.

His stomach clenched, and not because of Lily this time.

"Viktor! Ach, look at you. I missed you so much." A whirlwind blew across the small clearing between the haus and the barn and wrapped her tentacles around his neck in a stranglehold.

He staggered a bit and got a blurred view of a pair of black-rimmed brown eyes before lips were pressed to his. Hard lips. Not soft and pliable, like Esther's.

Ugh. He blinked, then grabbed her upper arms and pushed her away.

Her hair was more auburn than red. The freckles were faintly visible, covered by a heavy layer of makeup. He failed to see the resemblance to anyone he'd known in the past.

He preferred Esther's un-made-up innocence.

Her brown eyes glistened with...something. Her lips curled into a pout. "Aren't you going to kiss me? Ach, probably not with an audience, ain't so?" She waved a hand over her shoulder in a dismissive manner. "Go on inside, girls. I'll be in later."

Viktor searched for his voice. It'd gotten lost somewhere during the unexpected attack.

"Let's disappear for a while." Her voice had dropped to a husky level, and she batted her impossibly thick eyelashes as her hand grasped his. She tugged, taking a couple of steps to the side.

His eyes widened in shock. Surely, an Amish girl wouldn't be so bold. He moved away, jerking his hand free. Then he pulled in much-needed air with a gasp, letting it out in a whoosh. "Uh...Lily, I presume?"

"Don't you remember me?" Her lower lip protruded further.

Not even a little. He never would've been able to pick her out in a crowd. His gaze moved beyond her to Esther and Rachel, standing still, their mouths hanging open in shock. Hurt shone in Esther's eyes. Grossdaedi stood behind them in the doorway, a frown marring his features.

"You can't stay here." Viktor barely kept from growling. Or maybe he had growled. He didn't much care.

Relief washed over Esther's expression. She closed her mouth and turned away, heading back inside. Grossdaedi stepped aside to let her in.

"Of course, I can. I already cleared it with my parents." Lily planted her fists on her hips.

Rachel followed Esther.

"Nein, you can't. I'll take you home after breakfast. Grossmammi is in the hospital, and even if she weren't, you wouldn't be needed."

"If your grossmammi is in the hospital, then Esther won't be needed either, ain't so? Are you taking her home?" Lily sounded accusing. "Besides, you could send Esther home for gut and keep me on as caregiver." A wide smile appeared. His stomach turned again. "I'm the only one you'll ever need." Her eyebrow quirked with the double entendre.

Grossdaedi waited on the porch, a silent observer.

"Seems all the Beachy women have trouble with submission." The words had slipped out without thought. And Esther worried about her "lack" of it. Viktor shook his head. Compared to Lily, she was a model citizen.

"Well?" Lily's fists went back to her hips.

"Grossdaedi needs care, too." Viktor didn't dare glance at him. "Rachel is staying here with Esther, to make sure everything is above reproach."

"Not that you'd be interested in Esther anyway." Lily did a little body wiggle involving the chest and hips. "Or in Rachel. Besides, they both are being courted. Unbelievable, but true." She gave a flick of her wrist. "I guess it might be best if I went home. We'd have more privacy then. I'll wait up for you tonight. My bedroom window is the one nearest the road on the east side." She smiled and turned on her heel, heading for the haus.

Didn't matter. He had nein idea where she lived. He did an about-face and strode back to the barn.

She'd have a long wait.

~~~

The oatmeal bubbled vigorously on the stove. Esther stirred it, glad it hadn't stuck to the bottom of the almost-forgotten pan. She divided the hot cereal among five bowls and set four of them around the table, along with a platter piled with leftover biscuits and a plate of bacon.

Her appetite had fled. Probably catching a ride with the Amish driver, since it had abandoned her with Lily's arrival.

Esther blinked back tears. Nausea rose in her throat, threatening to choke her.

Her cousin sashayed into the kitchen. That was the only word Esther could think of to describe the exaggerated sway of Lily's hips. Esther glanced outside but didn't see Viktor standing there watching the show. Of course, he might be in the shadows of the barn, just out of sight. She shut her eyes against the burn. Lily would win the man, of course. She always did.

Esther nodded toward the table. "Breakfast...is...ready." She swallowed the bile, but it came right back up.

Lily wrapped her in a hug that reminded her of a boa constrictor. "So gut to see you, Cousin." She backed up and smirked at Rachel. "Babysitting Esther to make sure she behaves herself, jah? Viktor said you were."

Babysitting? To make sure she behaved herself? The words didn't sound as if they'd kum from Viktor, but they brought to mind her brash behavior and Henry's wagging tongue. The tears Esther fought started to win the battle. Several leaked out of the corners of her eyes. She turned away, hurried upstairs to the bathroom, and shut the door. She slid down against the wall, hugged her knees to her chest, and tried to forget the memory of Lily flinging herself into Viktor's arms. As if she had a right to be there. Kissing him. Pressing herself close.

Was that how Lily had expected Esther to behave when she'd given her the directive *"Kiss Viktor for me"*?

And she had. Except that it hadn't been for Lily. And she'd obviously made a fool out of herself, being so wanton. Clinging to him.

Even worse, telling him she'd wait. *For nothing*. Nein promises. Nein commitment. Just a few words that might have meant something but were never said in completion.

Had he responded to Lily before pushing her away?

Never mind tears "escaping." They poured out in mass amounts.

And the lump in her throat insisted on following. She crawled over to the toilet, heaves mixing with the tears.

Afterward, she scrubbed her face and brushed her teeth. She took a deep breath, squared her shoulders, and returned to the kitchen.

Lily had settled in Esther's chair, a smug expression on her face. Not that it mattered where she sat. As long as it wasn't in Viktor's lap.

Reuben stood in the doorway, his hand on his lower back again. His eyes sought Esther's, and he held her gaze as he shook his head, slowly, as if he wouldn't believe it if he hadn't seen it. *Jah.* She wouldn't have, either.

Nice to know she had an ally. And Viktor had said Lily couldn't stay. Esther straightened her spine.

Reuben's lips were set in a flat line. Maybe from pain. Or anger. He expelled a long breath, moved to the table, and sat. After the silent prayer, he peered at Lily. "So, Lily Beachy. What brings you back to Jamesport? How was Pennsylvania?"

Lily reached for the bacon and took several slices. She left only two on the plate. One for Rachel, one for Viktor. Esther opened the refrigerator and retrieved the white-wrapped butcher's package again. She'd fry up the rest rather than save it for potato soup, as she'd planned.

"I returned for Viktor, of course. I'm here to bring him back into the fold."

Esther bit her bottom lip and stared at the stove.

Reuben made a weird sound. Not quite a grunt, not quite a cough. More of a strangled harrumph. "Is that so? I heard you were engaged to a man out in Lancaster County."

Really? A spark of hope flared, flickered—and then died. Esther rewrapped the bacon in the butcher paper and returned it to the refrigerator. Rachel never ate a big breakfast, and Viktor never ate more than two pieces of bacon. She grabbed the coffeepot and headed for the table.

Lily waved her hand dismissively. "Viktor and I love each other. We're meant to be. You'll see."

Reuben's brow furrowed, his frown deepening. "So...he knew you were coming? The two of you have been communicating?"

Ach, nein. Esther's hand shook. She missed Reuben's mug, forming a mud-colored puddle on the table.

"I told Esther to tell him I was coming. Told her to tell you I'd be helping as caregiver to your frau, though it seems I won't be needed." She shot a glare at Esther. "Viktor...well, I didn't have his address, exactly, and he didn't have mine. Besides, men aren't much for writing letters. And neither am I, really. Better to interact in person, ain't so?"

So, they hadn't been communicating. Viktor had even claimed not to know who she was.

Reuben made the weird sound again as he pushed away his plate of untouched food. "Help me with my shoes, Esther." It wasn't a request. It was a direct order. And spoken in a tone that allowed *nein* argument.

She set down the coffeepot and obeyed without question. Her mind was numb, confused, shaken up. She didn't understand Lily. She sounded like a pack of nonsense half of the time. But Esther knew her track record with men. And the odds weren't in Esther's favor.

Rachel raised her finger to ear level and made a circular motion. *Crazy.*

That certainly described Esther's emotions.

~

"Where are you?" Grossdaedi's faint voice broke the stillness.

Viktor raised his head from the bovine's flank. "Cow barn."

A few moments later, Grossdaedi labored his way down the six concrete steps. He opened the door at the end of the room, letting in a breath of fresh air. "She's a piece of work."

"For sure," Viktor muttered.

"She says she came back to marry you. That you love each other."

Viktor snorted. "A half hour ago, I wouldn't have been able to pick her out from a half dozen of Esther's cousins. Now, she's permanently etched in my mind, and when I see her, I'll be tempted to head the opposite direction."

"Wise. Very wise." Grossdaedi hesitated. "She also said she wanted to stay here as caregiver."

"I won't have her." And he meant that in every way possible.

Grossdaedi smiled. "How can I help?"

Viktor sighed. "You shouldn't even be out here, Grossdaedi. But considering who's in the haus, I can't blame you. I'm almost done. There are only a couple eggs, since it's too hot for laying. They're in the bowl right there on the ledge. I'll get the milk pails and let the cows out, if you want to get the eggs."

Grossdaedi nodded. "I'd like to be at the hospital for your grossmammi's surgery...."

Viktor pulled out his cell phone and checked the time. "I'll finish up and then we'll go. But I'll need to take Lily home first."

"Rachel has to pass right by Lily's parents' haus on the way to work." Grossdaedi winked.

Viktor grinned. "Problem solved." He let the cows out, grabbed the two pails of milk, and headed for the haus, whistling. He set the milk down on the counter and turned. "Esther, if you want to go to the hospital with Grossdaedi and me, then you'll need to be ready in ten minutes. Rachel, take Lily home on the way to work." He didn't look at either woman as he grabbed his bowl of cold oatmeal and started eating. He moved over to stand by the stove. Close to Esther.

As if Lily would understand the nonverbal message he wanted to convey. Especially since she hadn't understood the direct ones.

Neither Rachel nor Lily responded to his directives. Or if they did, he didn't notice.

Esther got out the strainer. Her lips were pressed so tight, they'd lost most of their color. Her cheeks were pale. She silently poured the milk into empty gallon jars and moved them to the refrigerator. As soon as she'd finished, she put on her shoes. "I'll do the dishes when I return, if it's okay."

"I'll do them." Rachel glanced at the wall clock. "I have a little while before I have to leave. Lily, you can dry."

"I don't know where anything goes." Viktor heard the whine in Lily's voice.

"It won't be hard to figure out. Appreciate the help." Viktor attempted to sound civil. He turned to Esther. "Let's go, then. You ready, Grossdaedi?"

"More than ready."

Viktor couldn't keep from grinning. "All right. I'll get the truck and drive it around."

It would be nice, traveling to town and back with Esther pressed up against his side. Maybe he could slide his arm around her shoulders and—

Nein. Grossdaedi would be with them. And Esther was skittish in the cab of the truck.

Still, it'd be a date, of sorts. With a chaperone.

He opened the door and took a step outside.

"See you tonight, Viktor," Lily cooed in an overly sweet, sexy voice.

"In your dreams." Viktor shut the door behind him.

Wow. Grossdaedi was right—she was a piece of work.

Chapter 29

Esther sucked in a deep breath. *"In your dreams"*? What did that mean, exactly? She didn't even want them dreaming about each other. She inhaled the piney scent of the truck cab as she slid across the bench seat, then pulled her skirt out of the way and adjusted it as Reuben eased into the vehicle. Viktor shut the passenger door, then jogged around the front of his pickup and climbed in next to her. His thigh pressed against hers, his upper arm brushing her shoulder as he grasped the steering wheel.

He positioned his right foot on the gas pedal. "Everyone buckled?" He glanced over at them as Grossdaedi snapped his seat belt. "That means you, süße." With a heart-stopping grin, he reached over Esther and grabbed the lap belt between her and Reuben. He pulled it across her waist, his fingers grazing her in the process.

She inhaled sharply as he snapped the metal closure into the lock. "Middle seat included." His gaze darkened.

His touch and his look encouraged her. She stared into the chocolate depths of his eyes, wishing she could snuggle in his strong arms and let his kisses whisk her away from the queasy uncertainty that had invaded her world with Henry's recent behavior and Lily's arrival.

She'd never had issues with either of them before Viktor had entered the picture. She and Lily had enjoyed many gut times together. And she and Henry had shared some times that were tolerable, if not gut. She shifted a bit closer to Viktor, as if for protection.

His eyes darkened more, his gaze dropping to her mouth. Her heart rate quickened.

Reuben cleared his throat, breaking the almost magnetic spell between her and Viktor. She jerked her gaze away and glanced at her hands folded in her lap, heat rising in her cheeks.

Viktor shifted the truck into gear, and it rolled over the gravel. His foot pressed on the pedal, the rocks crunching under the tires as he sped down the drive to the dirt road. He made a sharp turn without so much as a pause.

Esther reached for something to grab as she fell against Viktor, but there was nothing to hang on to—unless she grabbed each man by the arm. The heat in her cheeks turned to fire as she straightened.

Viktor let go of the wheel with his right hand and wiped it over his mouth and chin in a downward motion. A muscle jumped in his jaw. He moved his hand back to the steering wheel.

She tried to focus on the tingling from the continuous brushing of his arm against hers. The pressure of his leg. And not on the speed of the truck or the other drivers on the road. It never seemed scary in the middle seat of a driver's van. The front seat of a truck, on the other hand—would she ever get used to it? She wouldn't need to, if he returned to the Amish and to the saner pace they kept, traveling by buggy. Her breath came in rapid spurts as she struggled to get enough air.

"Breathe slowly, süße." Viktor's tone was touched with humor, as if he realized she was close to hyperventilating. His hand left the steering wheel and rested on her knee, a bold move that both comforted her and scared her at the same time.

Finally, they arrived at the hospital. Viktor pulled under an overhang by the entrance to let them out, then drove off to park in the lot.

The wide halls of the hospital smelled of antiseptic and other things Esther couldn't identify. Reuben kept his hand against his back as he slowly walked beside her toward the reception desk adjacent to a wall. "Anna Petersheim."

The woman behind the desk typed something on the keyboard and looked at her computer screen. After a moment, she read off a number.

"Thank you." Reuben nodded at her, then turned away.

"I'll take you." The older, gray-haired man who'd been standing behind the woman came around from behind the desk. "Follow me."

He led the way to an elevator and pushed a button. When the metal doors slid open, he ushered them inside.

As they approached the room, a couple of nurses wheeled Anna out on a gurney. Reuben quickened his steps and grasped Anna's hand.

The nurses didn't stop their rapid strides. "Follow us. We'll take you to the waiting room outside surgery."

Reuben kept hold of Anna's hand. He'd probably pay for it with pain afterward. Esther winced as she watched him.

The nurses pointed them to a waiting room. "Here."

"Stop a moment." Reuben bent over and brushed a kiss across Anna's forehead. "Ich liebe dich. I'll be waiting."

Anna reached up and stroked his bearded chin. "Ich liebe dich."

Such a tender scene.

Esther blinked back tears.

Someday, she wanted her ehemann to love her like that.

Viktor stopped at a refreshment kiosk and ordered three cups of plain koffee. He eyed the muffins on display, but they didn't look appetizing. After eating gourmet meals on the riverboat and then getting used to Esther's cooking, he didn't want a pricy substitute for the real thing.

He took the tray of koffees up to Grossmammi's room but found it empty, the bed stripped, and an aide fitting it with fresh sheets. He winced. He'd hoped Grossdaedi hadn't missed Grossmammi's surgery. But they had been a little late arriving, nein thanks to Lily and to heavy traffic.

The aide looked up. "May I help you?"

"Jah—yes. Looking for Anna Petersheim."

"They took her to surgery. Give me a moment, and I'll show you how to get there." She quickly finished making the bed, then led him through a maze of hallways and into an elevator. Finally, they arrived at the waiting room.

He thanked the aide, then entered the small room. It was empty, except for Esther and Grossdaedi. A different waiting room from yesterday.

He handed them each a koffee, trying to ignore the grayness of Grossdaedi's face, then settled down next to Esther. To wait. As soon as the surgery was over, he'd call the chiropractor. He'd do it now, except he didn't have any idea how long the surgery might take.

Viktor thumbed through a magazine, then picked up a Bible similar to the one he'd read yesterday. A snore came from Grossdaedi. He glanced over at him, then met Esther's gaze and grinned. He slid an arm around her shoulder and hugged her close.

She stiffened a moment, then relaxed in his embrace. He could still see questions in her eyes: What would they do about Lily? What about Henry? How would a relationship between them work, even if she waited?

He didn't have answers.

He bent his head and brushed his lips against hers. He was leaning in for a second kiss when the door opened and a volunteer ushered in his aenties and onkels, as well as Bishop Joe.

Viktor pulled back, his face heating. Caught. By the bishop. He turned his attention back to the Bible, but guilt ate at him, both for the kiss and the Book. It was Englisch, not High German. And he didn't have any idea whether it was the approved text or not.

Grossdaedi still slept, his chin resting on his chest, though he did stir.

The words of the text swam. Viktor looked up at the intruders. "Why are you here?" He addressed the bishop, avoiding his aenties' eyes. He should've informed them about Grossmammi's surgery. They would've wanted to be there for their mamm. But then, when would he have found the time, between their late nacht and Lily's early-morgen arrival?

Grossdaedi straightened, blinked, and opened his eyes.

"Rachel stopped by to tell us," Bishop Joe explained. "I considered sending a preacher to sit with you but then felt that maybe I should kum instead."

"But your barn raising is today."

"Your grossmammi is more important than my barn."

Maybe Bishop Joe would be sympathetic to his cause. The whole thing, from reading an Englisch Bible to discussing salvation to permitting Esther's freedom.

"And I needed to see to some things myself." The bishop's eyes narrowed on him and Esther.

Aenti Nancy frowned at him. "Don't you think you should've told us?"

Aenties Sandy and Elisabeth nodded.

Viktor winced, the guilt gnawing at him. "It was…last-minute. We came home from singing last nacht to find Grossmammi had fallen, and it was in the wee hours of the morgen when we arrived home after taking her to the hospital." He'd never been close to his aenties ever since his family's death. Hadn't even thought of contacting them.

Grossdaedi cleared his throat. "Nice of you to kum, though. We appreciate it." His voice still sounded raspy.

"We'll bring meals by while Mamm is hospitalized." Aenti Sandy glanced at her sisters, then looked at her daed. "Since Esther will be going home."

Esther inched closer to Viktor's side.

"Esther won't be going home," Viktor stated. "Grossdaedi needs her, and—"

"He won't need her if we bring meals by," Aenti Nancy interrupted.

Esther caught her breath.

The bishop speared Viktor with a look. "And under the circumstances, it'll be best if she returns home. Permanently. Until she marries Henry."

Esther's knuckles whitened around her apron.

So, Henry had talked. And Viktor had been judged and found guilty without a trial. He clamped his mouth shut to keep his thoughts from spewing forth.

"Nein." Grossdaedi frowned. "Esther is the one I want helping. She and Anna have a relationship. They love each other. And she knows our needs. Maybe Viktor could stay elsewhere at nacht."

Rejected by his grossdaedi, too, in favor of Esther. But then, he'd suggested that very arrangement a couple of days ago. To protect Esther. And at least this inconvenience would keep her with them and not with her family, who might pressure her to marry Henry.

"He can stay with me until Esther marries, or he returns to the riverboat." Aenti Sandy smiled at him. "He'll be close enough to get home easily to do the chores."

He would rather sleep in the barn or down by the pond. Then he'd be close enough to be summoned if there were another accident. Close to Esther. And not feeling awkward and out of place with relatives he didn't really know. Besides, he'd already arranged for Rachel to stay.

He glanced at Esther. She sat in silence, hands folded in her lap, staring down. But a couple of tears made tracks down her cheeks.

"Bishop, walk with me." Viktor shot to his feet. But the door opened again, and this time the doctor came in.

"Petersheim family?" He looked around the room.

They were all family. Except for Esther and the bishop, but they might as well be. Viktor nodded. As did Grossdaedi.

"It went well. She'll be in recovery awhile, and then we'll return her to her room. She'll probably be sleeping most of the day, due to the pain meds."

Viktor's phone buzzed. He ignored it, since the doctor was still talking. But he couldn't focus on anything other than the woman beside him.

As the doctor left the room, the bishop stood, as well. "Kum, then. We'll talk. But since the surgery went well, we'll need to be going pretty quick." He directed his last comment to the others.

Viktor sighed and followed Bishop Joe from the room. They stopped maybe a hundred yards down the hall.

"Aren't you going to ask me about anything, or do you plan to just take Henry Beiler's word?" Viktor tried not to glare at him.

"Henry said that you admitted Esther wasn't a virgin—by your doing. Lily told us she's been throwing up. That means she's probably with child. There's nothing more to be said. She needs to be married. Immediately. Henry's still willing to marry her, despite this shame. I won't discuss this further."

Viktor blinked. "Whoa. Esther and I have never.... She.... I.... Nein." He took a second to compose his thoughts. "What I said was that she wouldn't be a virgin when she married Henry because she would marry me, instead. That was not an admission of any wrongdoing."

"I saw you kissing her when we walked in." The bishop's gaze sharpened. "She'll marry Henry. As soon as they complete classes. End of discussion." He turned and stalked off.

And that was that.

⁓

Esther wiped her eyes, hoping Viktor's relatives didn't notice as they chatted among themselves.

Bishop Joe came back in the room. "I found the driver," he announced. "He's getting the van, and anyone who's going needs to kum now."

"You'll be okay, right, Daed?" Viktor's aenti Sandy asked Reuben.

Reuben reached for Esther's hand and patted it. "I'll be just fine. You go on. We'll update you when we know more."

The others filed out, following the bishop, then Viktor returned to the room. "I called the chiropractor," he told his grossdaedi. "He has an opening, but we need to go right away. I'll bring you back to the hospital afterward." A muscle jerked in his jaw, and his mouth was firmly set. Anger shadowed his eyes.

Esther stood to her feet. Whatever he'd said to the bishop, he'd been refused. The judgment had been handed down. Nobody disobeyed the bishop.

A heavy weight descended over her, threatening to cut off her breath. She walked over to Viktor. "Can I go with you?" To the chiropractor or to the river. Both, preferably.

A small smile flashed, then vanished. "You bet. We won't be gone long. And Grossmammi won't even miss us if she's sleeping." His fingers grazed Esther's hand, then fell away.

If only she could've grabbed hold and clung for dear life.

She and Reuben followed Viktor to the exit. Reuben's strides were labored, his hand pressed to his back. He must've really hurt it this time.

"I'll pick you up." Viktor's gaze slid over Reuben before he strode out into the oppressive heat.

The chiropractor's clinic was located in an area of the city zoned as both business and residential, an older neighborhood, with tall, old-fashioned houses probably built in the late 1800s or early 1900s. They were close together, separated by narrow tire-tracked lanes.

Viktor pulled into an alley behind the building and parked. They walked up a narrow sidewalk to the front.

There was a rummage sale at the haus next door. Esther glanced at the tables as they walked past.

"You can look if you'd like, Esther," Viktor told her. "I'll sign Grossdaedi in, and then I'll join you."

"Esther." Not "süße."

She wordlessly veered off into the yard and started looking around at the various items on display. A snow globe caught her eye, one that had a red covered bridge and a horse and buggy inside.

Anna would love it. And she had a birthday coming up. Esther turned it upside down to check the price. "Snow" fell from the bottom to the top of the globe. There was a knob at the bottom. A music box? Esther turned it, but she didn't recognize the tinkling tune. At least it still played. And it was within her price range.

"Grossdaedi's with the chiropractor," Viktor said, joining her. "He didn't even get seated before they called him." He looked around. "Might be able to find a bikini here."

Her face flamed. "Not that I'd wear one." But her heart leapt at the thought of being with Viktor in the water—and out.

"Let's look anyway." He walked over to a table of clothes and started sorting through them. A few minutes later, he unearthed a hot pink swimsuit top—nothing but two small triangles and strings. He held it up for her with a rakish grin. A second later, his other hand brandished matching bottoms.

Esther's underwear covered more. She shook her head, sure that her face matched the hue of the swimsuit.

"Speechless, sü—Esther?" He dropped them back on the table with a scowl. "Wouldn't want you to wear this for Henry."

She gripped the snow globe tighter and turned away, her earlier bout of nausea returning. He came up beside her. "What'd you find?"

"A snow globe. For Anna's birthday."

Something flashed in his eyes, but it disappeared before she could identify it, sadness taking its place. He looked away. "I'm…I'm going to look at the…the books. Let me know when you're ready to go." He walked off, his spine straight.

Esther turned over the snow globe and wound up the music box once more. The same haunting melody played. When she held it upright again, the tiny snow flurries scattered this way and that. She watched, fascinated.

And mournful.

She glanced at Viktor.

The bishop had decreed that she would marry Henry. He wouldn't change his mind.

She looked back down at the snow globe. Interesting how it was so much prettier when shaken than settled and still.

Her life was about to go back to its unshaken state of normal, and she couldn't do a thing to stop it.

Chapter 30

Viktor stared at the road, unseeing. Somehow he managed to get the pickup back home. Grossmammi would be in the hospital one more day. He pulled the truck into the drive and put it in park. "All ashore." He tried to keep his voice cheerful but wasn't sure he succeeded.

Esther clutched the plastic bag holding the snow globe from the yard sale, carefully wrapped in newspaper. She slid out after Grossdaedi and glanced back at Viktor. The corners of her mouth drooped. Tears glittered in her eyes.

He watched her go, his heart heavy. Judged and found guilty for something he hadn't done. Fresh pain shot through him.

Gott, I know I'm new to knowing You, but this is going to be the hardest thing I've ever done. Help me through it. Help her through it.

He waited until Grossdaedi and Esther had disappeared inside, then pulled out of the driveway and drove to the bishop's haus. The newly finished barn stood in place of the old one. Viktor got out of his truck and shut the door.

Bishop Joe came out of the barn.

"We need to talk." Viktor strode around the front of the truck.

The bishop shook his head. "Henry gave me her kapp—the one you removed at the pond. Told me about her disheveled appearance." His gaze hardened. "There's nothing to say."

Viktor flexed his jaw. His fists closed by his sides. It wasn't true. Esther had found the kapp in the folded quilt. "I'm innocent of the charges. I haven't touched her." *In that way.* "Besides, I think Henry is abus—"

"I won't listen to gossip. And I won't change my mind." The bishop turned his back.

"You mean, you won't listen to me. You listened to Henry's gossip."

Nein reply came. The bishop headed for the barn.

Viktor pulled in a deep breath and then expelled it. "I'm leaving. Tomorrow morgen. I was called back to the river because someone had to take emergency family leave." He hadn't told his großeltern. It pained him to leave in the middle of his own family emergency, but with Esther's capable hands, and with other men helping, they should manage. "Thing is, Grossdaedi needs me. But I'll be back in September. Can you have someone take care of the farm work for him? His back is bad."

Bishop Joe stopped walking and turned around. "I'll talk to your onkels and the other men. Reuben will be cared for until September."

"Esther can stay and take care of him and Grossmammi?"

He nodded. "Jah, Esther can stay. But not you. And I'll make sure she's married before you return."

Right. He'd expected that, but it still hurt. He dug his short fingernails into his palms. "I'll sleep at the pond tonight, in case you change your mind."

"I won't."

He hadn't expected him to.

Viktor climbed back into his truck. He had one last nacht with Esther, assuming she even showed up. Unlikely, since Rachel was staying with her, for appearances' sake.

He'd tried so hard to protect her reputation.

All for naught.

A bleary gloom had settled over the farmhaus ever since the bishop had announced his decision. Reuben sat in a hard-backed chair in the kitchen, a mug of hot tea in front of him, a frown on his face.

Viktor returned, parked behind the barn, and disappeared into the shadows of the building. Probably to do chores.

Esther wanted to go to the barn and be with him. Spend a few more verboden moments in his embrace before those had to end permanently. Instead, she moved around the kitchen, fixing a simple supper of hamburgers with cabbage and fried potatoes. Jell-O salad already chilled in the refrigerator.

She didn't think she'd be able to eat a bite.

A horse and buggy clip-clopped into the drive, and Esther glanced outside. Rachel started to unhitch her horse, but Viktor appeared, finished the job, and then led the horse into the barn. Rachel came inside, slipped off her shoes, and headed to the kitchen sink. "Viktor said he'd care for Buttons." She turned the water on and soaped up. "How can I help?" She dried her hands on a dishtowel, then looked at Esther and then Reuben. "Who died? Viktor's moping, too."

My dreams died. That sounded selfish, Esther realized.

Their dreams. Hers and Viktor's. She bit back the words. "It's been a hard day." She set down the spatula. "Keep an eye on supper, please. I'll be right back."

"Jah." Rachel took her place by the stove as Esther put on her shoes.

She went outside, crossed the yard, and stepped into the dimness of the barn, smelling the strong odors of animals and hay. She sneezed.

A second later, Viktor moved out of the shadows of the hayloft and stared down at her.

"I thought you'd be caring for Buttons."

"Is that the horse? Jah, I will." He started down the ladder. "What are you doing out here, Esther?"

"Can we still see each other? If I go to the pond?" She regretted the words immediately after blurting them out. Did it make her a lesser person, begging to sneak around with a man she'd never be allowed to marry?

He stepped off the ladder and approached her. A few moments later, his trembling fingers brushed her cheek. "I'm not so sure we should." He pulled away and wiped his hands roughly over his face. "We'd be asking for trouble, süße."

Her shoulders slumped. She gazed at him, silent. She wanted to throw herself into his arms and never let go. Instead, she forced herself to turn away. Somehow she walked out of the barn. To the haus. Into the kitchen. And to the stove.

She tried to still the quivering lips. To keep the tears at bay. She'd known what he would say, but it hadn't made hearing it any easier.

Rachel glanced at her, looked away, and then studied her again. She turned the burners to low and steered Esther out of the kitchen. "Okay, talk to me. What happened?"

⌒

Viktor skipped supper. He didn't go to the pond, either, even though he'd told the bishop that he'd be there. Instead, he made a bed in the hayloft and lay there listening to the mice.

Esther. Another reason that future homecomings would be difficult.

He gave a bitter chuckle, remembering how he'd resented her presence in their home and had even tried to talk his großeltern into hiring another caregiver. Anyone but Esther. And then he'd gone and fallen in love with her.

Well, going back to the river would bring one blessing: He'd be able to avoid Lily. Easily.

Maybe two blessings. He wouldn't have to watch Esther marry Henry. She wouldn't be working for Grossmammi after she married, so if he stayed away from church and from frolics, he'd be able to avoid her. Eventually, his heart would heal.

Maybe.

He gave up on sleep in the wee hours of the morgen. He quietly did the chores, left the milk on the table, and went to get his bag.

He scribbled a note on a piece of paper. A tear dropped onto the page.

He folded the note and tucked it under one of the milk pails.

Then he loaded his things into his truck, pushing aside memories of trying to drown his grief on the river five years ago. *Gott, please watch over my loved ones while I'm gone,* came his silent prayer. *Including Esther.*

Long before the rooster crowed, he was headed for the Mississippi River.

Chapter 31

Esther stumbled into the bathroom and peered at her reflection in the tiny mirror above the sink. She winced. If ever there was a time to hide behind makeup, this was it. Her eyes were bloodshot and sore, the skin beneath them puffy. But she shouldn't have expected anything else after crying herself to sleep.

Still, she didn't want to face Viktor looking like this.

She scrubbed her face with soap and water, then patted it dry, pinched her cheeks, and squared her shoulders. Not much else would improve her appearance. Maybe he wouldn't look her in the eye. Wouldn't notice the redness.

Right.

His bedroom door was open, the bed made. It looked as if he hadn't slept in it. He must be downstairs already. Maybe in the barn.

With a sigh, she went to the kitchen to start breakfast. There *had* to be a way to get around the bishop's decree. But neither she nor Rachel had been able to think of one, even though they'd stayed up talking—Esther crying—for hours.

Nein wonder she hadn't heard Viktor kum in.

Why was the bishop forcing this marriage to Henry, anyway? Why couldn't she wait for Viktor to join the church? Bishop Joe's words replayed in her memory, as did his harsh look. *"Under the circumstances, it'll be best if she returns home. Permanently. Until she marries Henry."*

What circumstances? Had someone seen her and Viktor kissing and run to the preachers with the news? Was the decision based on the too-brief peck Viktor had given her in the waiting room at the hospital when the bishop had walked in?

Or, had Henry taken the news of her missing kapp and started spreading rumors?

Wait.

219

Her blood chilled. Viktor had said that Henry had made some claim about her "anticipating her wedding vows."

Dizziness washed over her. She gripped the back of a chair to steady herself.

This was worse that she'd thought. It meant more than she'd initially imagined. And Henry had spread it around? How could she marry him after this?

But if her suspicions were correct, why weren't they forcing her to marry Viktor instead of Henry? Was it because he hadn't joined the church, so they felt they had nein control over him? Or because even though he planned to return, he hadn't started classes and wouldn't be able to until next year—and she'd have to wait?

Though waiting would prove she wasn't with child.

Would it make a difference if she went to Bishop Joe and told him that she wanted to wait for Viktor?

Would it make a difference if *she* dropped out of baptism classes? That way, they wouldn't be able to force her to marry Henry. Right?

She smiled. That might solve everything. If she didn't attend classes, if she didn't kneel for baptism, then she couldn't marry in the church...and she'd be able to wait for Viktor.

She turned on a gas light in the kitchen. The milk buckets were on the table already, along with a handwritten note.

Why would Viktor leave a note? Unless....

Prickles of unease shot through her. She stared at it, scared of what it might say. Finally, with trembling fingers, she picked it up. Unfolded it.

> *I was called back to the Mississippi River because someone had a family emergency. Sorry for leaving without warning. I'll see you in September.*
>
> *Grossdaedi, I asked Bishop Joe to provide help. Let him. Please, let your back heal. I also contacted the driver and asked him to take you to the hospital when Grossmammi is released.*

*Esther, I'm sorry. So sorry. I never meant to hurt you. I wish
you all the best in your marriage.*

Don't let Grossdaedi overwork himself.

Love always,
Viktor

A drop of moisture had blurred one of the lines. Had it been a
tear?

And was the "love always" meant for her or for his großeltern? Or
had it been used merely as a general closing?

Why hadn't he told them he was leaving last nacht? He must've
known then, if he'd already talked to the bishop and made plans. She
remembered how his fingers had trembled as he'd touched her cheek
in the barn. Was that his way of saying good-bye?

Quick tears burned her eyes, and she slumped. Trying to get out
of marrying Henry seemed pointless. Viktor had gone to the bishop.
Twice, apparently.

She didn't know what had been said in their private conversations, only that the answer had been a firm nein.

And he'd left—with nein plans to return until after she married.
But he'd be back in September. Could she hold off until then?

Why had Gott allowed Viktor to kum in her life, allowed her to
fall in love with him, only to take him away?

It wasn't fair.

Viktor boarded the riverboat in Burlington, Iowa. As he
descended the steps, he inhaled the strong odor of diesel—and the
scent of food. Something with a tomato base. His stomach rumbled.
He hadn't eaten anything since noon yesterday, and even then, he'd
taken just a few bites only to humor his grossdaedi.

He carried his bags below deck to his room. It was a tiny space,
about as plain as his bedroom at home, with a full-sized bed and a

small dresser. Unlike at home, he didn't have to clean it. The deck-hands would pick up after him. The scent of the food followed him, and his stomach growled again. He left the room and went to the kitchen to see what smelled so tantalizing.

The cook, Lis, stirred something in a pot. He peeked over her shoulder at the long spaghetti noodles and miniature meatballs simmering in tomato sauce. A German chocolate cake cooled on the counter. He pointed to the spaghetti. "Worms?" He forced a chuckle so she'd know he was teasing. He didn't want his friends to see his broken heart. Better they think he was glad to be back.

Fake it until he could make it.

Lis swung around. A hardly noticeable hairnet covered her short, graying head. Her hazel eyes widened when they lit on him. "Viktor!" She slapped his arm. "You scared me. Glad you're here. Kyle left because his wife was in an accident."

He sobered. "I heard. I hope she'll be all right. Wasn't she expecting a baby?"

Lis nodded, her mouth set. "It was all Kyle could talk about. I haven't heard any updates."

"Looking forward to lunch. I'm starved." He winked at her, then headed up the ladderlike steps to the wheelhouse. Hopefully, he could avoid questions and not be reminded of home.

"Viktor, good to see you!" The mate slapped his arm. "How's life in Amish country?"

Viktor cringed. "Work, as usual." He tried to answer as he normally would. Usually, he enjoyed returning to the river.

"How are the grandparents?"

"They should be fine until September, if my grandfather takes care of himself." He'd reevaluate the situation then. And the new help, whoever it was, to see if she would be gut as a caregiver for them.

Nobody would be as gut as Esther. Tears stung his eyes. He blinked, struggling to keep his emotions under control.

They would've discovered his absence by now. Wondered at his cowardly behavior, sneaking off without saying good-bye. Without

The Snow Globe 223

warning. But he didn't think he'd be able to handle saying farewell—
for gut—to Esther.

Fresh pain singed his heart.

He swallowed the lump in his throat and stared—unseeing—at
the controls.

Marriage with Esther had been something to dream of.

Now he had nothing.

⌒

Esther stepped outside as the Amish driver's van pulled into
the driveway for the third time in as many days. This time, Reuben
headed toward the back, probably to unload the wheelchair, while the
driver went around to the other side to bring Anna out. They must've
planned it in advance.

Esther hurried to join Reuben at the back of the van. She wasn't
sure whether lifting the back hatch of the vehicle and taking out the
wheelchair fell under the chiropractor's order of "absolutely no lifting," or whether that was a gray area that could technically be okay.
But just to be safe, she would help.

"I'll get that for you."

"I don't need help." But he stepped aside.

She reached for the handle of the hatch and squeezed, causing
the lock to disengage. Amazing that she'd figured out an Englisch
contraption on her own. For a moment, she allowed herself to bask in
the pride of self-discovery before she raised the handle high overhead.
She watched it a second, to make sure it would stay put and not fall
on her, and then she reached inside and lifted out the wheelchair,
unfolded it, and wheeled it around to the side of the van.

The driver—she never did learn his name—lifted Anna in his
arms and lowered her into the wheelchair. Reuben positioned the
footrests, and Anna slowly lifted her feet. Esther wheeled the chair
over to the porch and up the ramp. It wasn't easy, given the rocky
ground and the slight incline of the ramp, but she couldn't let Reuben
do it with his sore back.

Reuben's sohn-in-law Lucas had kum by earlier while Esther was picking green beans in the garden and told her he'd be back that evening to do the chores. Apparently Viktor had completed all the morgen work before leaving.

She swallowed a sob.

At least she wouldn't have to worry about seeing Henry until Sunday. Six more days of freedom. If she could get out of it, she'd skip the singing. But Rachel's brother Sam would be picking her up, as usual. And with Anna recovering from surgery, and Reuben suffering from a bad back, then she'd have an excuse to decline.

She straightened, hope surging through her veins. Now to get out of baptism classes. Even though it seemed pointless, Viktor had asked her to wait, and she'd agreed. He'd never told her not to bother.

She'd try this tactic and see if it would work a miracle.

If only it would.

She wheeled Anna to the kitchen table.

"We ate lunch at the hospital, süße." Anna peered up at her, love lighting her eyes. It was so nice to have her home again and to see her color almost normal. "Not as gut as anything you would have fixed, though. Just Jell-O, something that might've passed for meat loaf, mashed potatoes, and some overcooked peas. They were plain mush." She wrinkled her nose. "But I'd love an iced tea. I'll join you and Viktor while you eat."

Reuben hadn't told her that Viktor had left? Esther glanced at the older man as she opened the cabinet door.

He set his mouth in a firm line. "He went back to the river."

Anna blinked. "Ach, nein. He wasn't supposed to go back for"— she glanced at the wall calendar—"another week and a half. Why'd he go early?"

Esther filled a glass with iced tea and set it on the table in front of Anna.

"He said someone had a family emergency." Reuben's glance skittered to Esther before he looked back at Anna. "But the bishop has ordered Esther to marry Henry due to...some unfortunate rumors.

There may be a bit of broken heart involved in his decision to leave early."

Esther realized that if Viktor were forced to marry another, she'd run away, too, rather than stand by and watch.

Anna grasped her hand. "Ach, süße. What are we going to do?"

Esther liked her use of the first-person plural pronoun. The way she included Esther in the problem-solving.

She shrugged, her eyes burning with tears. "I don't know." Her voice broke. "I thought maybe I'd quit going to baptism classes. Do you think that'd work?"

Anna exchanged a glance with her ehemann, then looked back at Esther. "Süße, did I ever tell you about the bu who courted me before Reuben?"

Chapter 32

Viktor was assigned to the night shift, since he was filling in for Kyle. Nothing bad about that. It would afford plenty of opportunities for stargazing, so long as the boat was far from the bright lights of cities along the shore.

But then again, stargazing would remind him of time spent with Esther at the pond. And it also might give him too much time to think.

He blew out a frustrated breath and looked out the window. A gentle breeze stirred the branches of the trees as the motor of the boat chugged slowly down the river, heading from Iowa waters southward to Missouri and eventually farther south, to Louisiana.

He glanced at the logbook to calculate how much grain was on board. A single barge carried the equivalent of 147 semitrucks piled full of grain, keeping a lot of traffic off highways. Sometimes it seemed the interstates had too many trucks, even with this arrangement.

That reminded him of all the farm wagons used to harvest this grain, and an unexpected pang of homesickness hit him. Sharp tears sprang to his eyes. He blinked them away, along with his thoughts of the quiet dirt road where his haus was located and the quiet family of three—Esther included—who waited there for him.

He couldn't think about her. About them. About home. He blinked again and turned his blurry gaze back to the logbook, trying to listen to the man briefing him on various details, such as river levels and channel reports. Most of them went unheard, despite his attempts to focus.

Nein matter. He'd figure it out. If he could keep his mind from wandering back to where he wanted to be. Funny—when he'd first gone home, he'd longed for the Mississippi River.

Somehow, somewhere, sometime, his desires had shifted.

He glanced at his cell phone to check the time. Soon he'd duck into his private room and get some sleep. He would kum on duty in about six hours, so was free to get a little shut-eye.

After he'd finished catching up with the two men in the wheel-house, he headed downstairs and dropped into a chair in front of the television where a few off-duty guys were watching a movie. He'd seen it before, but the action of the spaceship landing in an alternate universe pulled his mind away from Esther and his großeltern.

But soon he fantasized about starting an Amish community in another galaxy far away, where he and Esther could be together and not be forced apart by some dictator posing as a bishop.

He must've dozed off, because he woke up as the credits were rolling. His head pounded, and his neck hurt. He went in search of painkillers and food.

"Must've been some dream." One of the deckhands looked up from his meal with a smirk. "You kept calling out for someone named 'Süße.'"

Wait for me, süße.

⁓

Esther settled in the chair next to Anna. Reuben hung his hat on a hook by the door, then sat at the end of the table and reached for an apple in the red bowl.

"I was sixteen," Anna began. "I was so excited when Mark started paying attention to me. I thought he was the most exciting bu in Pennsylvania."

"More exciting than me?" Reuben winked and bit into the apple.

Anna waved her hand. "You know better."

He chuckled.

"And he was the most handsome. He knew it, too."

"Makes you wonder why she settled for me, doesn't it?" Reuben winked at Esther.

"You two are cute." Esther took a sip of her tea. What did this have to do with anything?

"I decided I wanted to marry Mark," Anna continued, "and I was going to do all I could to get what I wanted. I became something I wasn't, to get his attention, and I started putting up with his... garbage."

"And that's what it was." Reuben expelled a sigh.

Anna looked down. "To make a long story short, he became verbally abusive. Said unkind things, spread untruths, and then, on the eve of our wedding, he hit me. Multiple times."

Reuben's knuckles whitened. A muscle jumped in his jaw.

"Reuben witnessed it. He convinced me to go away and hide, and not marry Mark, saying that if he did that before marriage, he'd be even worse afterward. Reuben arranged for me to visit some distant cousins here in Missouri. I resurfaced at home several weeks after the wedding was supposed to have taken place. Even though Mark said he loved me and forgave me for running away, I allowed Reuben to court me. Secretly. Well, his friends knew. I didn't tell mine, afraid they'd accidentally spill the secret to Mark. He never did know until after the bishop announced it."

"He never forgave me." Reuben looked down and swallowed. "He's the reason we left Pennsylvania. Soon as we married, we left, and didn't look back."

"I got the better man." Anna smiled at her ehemann.

Reuben glanced at Esther again. "I loved her since the first time I saw her, sitting in the front seat in the one-room schoolhaus. Hated the day I was too old for school and wouldn't see her all the time. Anxiously waited for her to grow up and notice me." He exhaled a heavy sigh. "And...Mark knew it. I don't know for sure, but I think that's why he was abusive. He was jealous."

"That's sad." Esther's eyes burned. How could anyone hurt sweet Anna?

"Just saying, if you have a reason you need to escape from Henry, even if it's the eve of your wedding, I might be able to make it happen." Reuben slapped the table with the palm of his hand.

"Reuben's not saying that he had to move into a relative's haus, because his brother—did I mention that Mark is his brother?—threatened to kill him when he found out he'd helped me escape." Anna's look issued a warning.

Reuben would be nein protection against Henry, because he was old with a weak back. But it didn't matter. Henry had never abused her physically. However, he was verbally abusive, spreading untruths, and he had a horrible temper. Esther supposed it could escalate. But, as things stood, wouldn't his falsehoods about her character be enough reason to escape marriage to him? Didn't it matter what she wanted?

Daed had told her many times, "Wanting something doesn't always mean you should have it." Of course, that had usually been after she'd begged for a piece of candy or another sweet.

This was bigger than a piece of candy.

Esther sighed.

Daed and Mamm would both disregard her love for Viktor—as they did her love for sweets—and order her to honor her promise to Henry.

Rather, the promise they had made for her.

Anna and Reuben were the only ones in favor of her marrying Viktor.

Of course, her cousins Rachel and Greta both disliked Henry. Greta didn't know about Viktor, but Rachel liked him...with some reservations.

She sighed again.

Anna reached out and patted her hand. "It'll all work out, süße. I feel peace."

Reuben nodded. "We need to pray."

The water of the Mississippi River closed over Viktor as he plummeted thirty or forty feet. River catfish stared at him, the alien invading their habitat. He probably looked like one, since he wore goggles and a faded orange life jacket. It was nice to dive in and swim in the deep river. Someday, he'd like to swim in the ocean.

Maybe on his honeymoon. Or maybe he could take his großeltern to Pinecraft, Florida. They'd rent one of those little cottages. Grossdaedi and Grossmammi would enjoy seeing their friends who vacationed or retired there, and he and Esther could—

Nein. His heart twisted. He wouldn't go there. Couldn't. Nein honeymoon in his foreseeable future.

The weather had gotten increasingly hotter the farther south they'd gone. They'd stopped in Memphis with a load of grain products before heading down almost as far as the Gulf of Mexico.

Now they were docked for inspection. They'd head north as soon as the inspector left.

As he neared to the surface of the water, Viktor began to hear the muffled shouts and calls of the other crewmates who played in the river or hung over the sides of the boat. He surfaced and sucked in air, then dove under again.

Esther really needed to learn to swim.

Fresh pain shot through him. She wouldn't need to if she married Henry. She wouldn't be allowed to partake of such frivolous activities as stargazing, playing in the pond, or taking long walks to talk about hopes and dreams.

Ach, Esther. He surfaced again, struck with the sudden desire to go back on board and write her a letter telling her about his trip so far. About the bald eagles he'd seen diving down and snatching fish churned up behind the boat. About what he'd seen on shore, about the metal bridges they'd passed under....

It wouldn't do any gut. Unless he wrote it so she could share it with her travel-hungry cousin, Rachel. But then he wouldn't be able to record any of the things on his heart. Such as a suggestion for her to run away and meet him in New Orleans, Memphis, St. Louis...any city on the river route.

That would leave his großeltern alone, unattended. Uncared for.

He blew out a frustrated breath.

Too bad his aenties wouldn't step in for a while. But then, Grossmammi and Grossdaedi were his responsibility. He was the one who had killed their only sohn. He couldn't put the blame on his younger brother Isaiah, despite Grossdaedi's willingness to do so. He was the one who needed to take care of them.

The familiar guilt filled him, along with the depressing refrains about how he should've died instead. He tried to push the thoughts away as he swam to the boat and climbed aboard.

Instead of writing Esther a letter, he needed to read the letters Gott had written him in the Bible, to refresh his memory about Gott's forgiveness.

It was gut he'd brought his along.

On his way past the kitchen, he snagged a couple of cranberry-white-chocolate-macadamia cookies. A combination he never would've dreamed of, but Lis was an adventurous cook. And they tasted wunderbaar. Maybe he should get the recipe for Esther.

Nein.

He slipped into his room, shut the door, and dried off. He draped his wet suit over the back of a chair, pulled on a pair of lounge pants, and then dropped down on the bed and reached for his Bible.

He opened it to the book of John and started reading where he'd last left off, in chapter eight.

> *Then said Jesus to those Jews which believed on him, If ye continue in my word, then are ye my disciples indeed; and ye shall know the truth, and the truth shall make you free. They answered him, We be Abraham's seed, and were never in bondage to any man: how sayest thou, Ye shall be made free? Jesus answered them, Verily, verily, I say unto you, whosoever committeth sin is the servant of sin. And the servant abideth not in the house for ever: but the Son abideth ever. If the Son therefore shall make you free, ye shall be free indeed.*

He read over those verses again and leaned back against his pillow.

Wow.

The engines rumbled to life, and the boat started moving.

He let the familiar motion relax him as he lay back, considering the verses.

"Gott, help me to be free," he whispered. "And, while You're at it, free Esther, too. She's about to be in bondage to a man because the bishop won't believe the truth. Help me to trust that You're in control."

Chapter 33

Esther stared out the window, willing Viktor's truck to appear in the driveway. Instead of a vehicle, a horse and buggy pulled into the drive.

Lily.

Her cousin Greta made a disgusted snort and dropped the tongs she'd been using to lift the canning jars of green beans from the hot-water bath. "I'll be back."

Esther frowned, wishing Rachel were there for her steadfast support. Greta tended to vanish when Lily came around. Greta liked quiet people, and Lily's drama drained her. It fatigued Esther, as well. She took a deep breath and slipped outside to the porch. She wouldn't invite Lily inside. She needed to protect Greta...and Anna. Besides, she wasn't sure how she'd evict Lily if she managed to get through the door.

Lily sashayed up to the porch, taking frequent glances behind her in the direction of the barn, probably to see if Viktor would kum out. News of his departure must not have made it to her haus. Strange, since he'd been gone a while. Almost two weeks.

"Hallo, Esther. I haven't seen anyone in ever so long. There's nothing going on around here." Lily glanced over her shoulder again. "Where is everyone?"

It was none of Lily's business, but she didn't want her barging inside to discover the answers for herself. "Anna is supposed to be taking a nap. The therapists just left. And Reuben's in the barn. Preacher Zeke came by to help with the chores."

"Where's Viktor? I *need* to talk to him."

"He...he was called back to the Mississippi. Said he'd be back in September." And it hadn't gotten any easier. She missed him more every day.

Lily stomped her foot—a wasted effort, since the packed dirt made nein sound. Anger flushed her cheeks. "How could he do that? I came home especially for him, you know."

"I know." And it hurt to admit it. But at the same time, she was glad Viktor was far away from her cousin's feminine wiles.

"I heard some vicious stories about you." Lily's gaze swept over Esther's abdomen, as if checking her waist size under her loose dress and apron.

Goose pimples appeared on Esther's arms. She didn't want to know.

"Pregnant, Esther? Really?"

"What?" The word spluttered out at a louder than necessary volume.

"I never would've guessed Miss Goody-goody Esther Beachy would get pregnant before she married."

Esther's mouth gaped. She forced it shut. "That's *not* true. Actually, it's impossible, because I haven't done anything...with anyone. Who's saying such things?" But she could guess. *How dare he!* At least she knew the circumstances Bishop Joe was referring to.

"Henry told me. He said he got permission to marry you quickly because of it. Sounded right proud, too. He says you'll be married when you finish baptism classes." Lily planted her fists on her hips.

Esther reached for the porch rail for support. She wouldn't marry Henry. *Couldn't.* "Nein. I—"

"I heard the *river rat* is the father. That's Viktor, ain't so? Henry didn't tell me that. I heard people whispering about it." Lily narrowed her eyes. "When I told you to kiss Viktor for me, I didn't mean anything further. You shock me. My parents are questioning whether you're such a gut influence."

And they weren't questioning their dochter's coming over here to spend time with said "river rat"?

Lily shook her head. "I heard Henry's mamm is as mad as a disturbed beehive. I bet you'll be paying."

Esther didn't even want to imagine how Henry's mamm would make her pay. But...wow. Henry had spread wild rumors, for sure.

And this was going around the community? Well, that explained all the sideways looks she'd gotten in town the last time she'd gone grocery shopping. All the whispers behind cupped hands. The pursed lips and disapproving glares.

Tears stung Esther's eyes. Was that why Viktor had left so quickly? Was he afraid they'd force *him* to marry her?

But nein—he'd been upset with Bishop Joe. Hurt. His fingers had touched her cheek so tenderly that nacht in the barn….

It had to be a broken heart, as Anna and Reuben had said.

"You're going to have to kneel and confess."

She had nothing to confess. Except for falling in love with the wrong man. Disobeying her parents—and the bishop.

"I missed the last baptism class," Esther blurted out. Nobody had called her on it yet. But she imagined someone would when she missed the second. And it would be missed, for sure.

"You know, you'll be shunned for six weeks, too, if you don't marry Henry," Lily pointed out.

Shunned…and shamed. Either way, she'd eventually be forced to leave Anna and Reuben. At least she'd be free from Henry. That alone would be worth it, even if she had nowhere to go.

"I'm really furious at Viktor for leaving." Lily stomped her foot again. "You don't happen to have his address, do you?"

Esther shook her head at the sudden switch in topic. "He's on the river." Were they even able to get mail there?

"He never came by to see me at all." Lily pursed her lips. "I don't know what's wrong with him. Unless he heard the rumors about Peter refusing to marry me."

Esther tightened her grip on the railing Viktor had installed. "What rumors? And why would Peter refuse to marry you?"

Lily rolled her eyes. "You and I are in the same situation. Are you really so dense? Peter said I'm easy, and he's not the father. Since he lives there, they take his word over mine. But I figured Viktor would marry me, if…well…."

If she put him in a compromised position? *Danki, Gott, that he's gone.*

Lily sighed. "But then he left you high and dry, ain't so? At least you have Henry to absorb your...." She bit her lip. "Dishonor."

"I am not—" Esther bit off the word "pregnant." She'd denied it before, and Lily had ignored her. And it seemed as if it'd be a slap in the face to insist on it following Lily's revelation. Esther glanced at Lily's waistline. She didn't notice any difference. She raised her gaze again and caught Lily wiping away a tear.

Out of the corner of her eye, she saw movement in the barn doorway. Reuben and Preacher Zeke appeared. Viktor would be glad to see his grossdaedi's improvement. Reuben walked straight and had resumed doing some simple chores, freeing the men of the community from having to spend so much time away from their own farms. The "unnecessary" work, as it had been deemed by the preachers, went undone, waiting for Viktor's return.

As she did.

Wait for me, süße.

She heard the words in her dreams and at random times in her subconscious, and they reignited her determination to do just that. She couldn't wait to see him. To fall into his arms. To tell him she'd waited.

Both men looked toward them. Lily spun around and went to meet them. Maybe to see if Reuben knew of a way she could contact Viktor.

Esther turned to go back inside. Her stomach churned. She couldn't believe Henry had told people she was pregnant without first coming to confirm it with her. She hadn't seen him since Viktor's return to the river. Seemed he was content to revert to his usual mode of courtship—doing virtually nothing at all. He hadn't even kum by to check on her after she'd missed a singing or frolic.

Unlike before, being ignored suited Esther just fine.

Except for the horrible rumors.

And there'd be nein way to stop the rumors from circulating through the grapevine.

It was strange that Daed hadn't kum over demanding an explanation. Ordering her home. Or maybe he couldn't bear to look on her in her supposed shame. Wouldn't he push to get her married and have this problem taken care of? Or was it possible he doubted Henry's account?

She peeked out the open window just as Lily shouted, "I need to talk to him!" before stalking off. She climbed into the buggy and cracked the whip over the horse's head. Preacher Zeke frowned as he watched her go.

Esther set out a plate of cookies and put some koffee on, just in case Reuben invited the preacher to kum in and sit a spell.

The door opened and closed quietly. She glanced over her shoulder. Reuben entered, trailed by Preacher Zeke.

The preacher hung up his hat, then tugged on his beard as he faced Esther. "Do you have a moment?"

She pulled in a breath for courage. "Jah."

Did this have something to do with her missing the most recent baptism class? Or about the rumors flying around? Maybe there'd be a chance Preacher Zeke would believe her—and she wouldn't have to marry Henry. She removed two mugs from the cabinet and checked the koffee. Almost ready. She filled a pitcher with cream and set out the sugar bowl.

When the men sat, she poured them each a cup of koffee, then sat in her place at the table, head bowed, hands clasped. She drew another breath. *Gott, please…let me get my miracle.*

"We've heard some disturbing things," Preacher Zeke began. "Henry Beiler informed Bishop Joe that you and Viktor…." He cleared his throat. "Are you in the family way?"

Esther shook her head, tears burning her eyes. "Nein. Lies. All lies."

He nodded. "That's what Reuben said. But I hear you've been suffering a bit from morgen sickness. Henry said Lily told him you've been vomiting."

Esther blinked. The only time she could remember was the day of Lily's arrival, and that had been due to stress. She shook her head. "Nein." And Lily had told Henry stories? Fueled his lies?

"Henry presented Bishop Joe with your kapp, which he found at the Petersheims' pond, and told a wild tale of how Viktor attacked him when he confronted him. Can you explain that?"

Esther shook her head. "I don't know who started the fight at the pond. And he can't be sure the kapp is mine, since they're all the same. I'm not missing any." Which was true. The one she'd lost at the pond had been found in the folds of Viktor's quilt when she'd washed it, and Viktor and Reuben both knew it.

Which meant Henry had lied further, to damage her reputation. Had he taken one of his sister's kapps? Or had he really found one at the pond? If so, whose was it?

The preacher nodded again. "Reuben told me that, as well. I believe you, Esther. I'll report back to Bishop Joe. Danki for talking with me. Gott go with you."

Esther nodded, blinking back tears of relief. Someone believed her. Reuben had vouched for her again. "Danki," she whispered. The word was meant for them both.

She went outside and watered the garden while the men talked.

Would she finally clear her name? Free herself from Henry and his lies?

Viktor took a sip of the steaming, strong koffee as he headed up to the bridge. Even though he'd been gone almost two weeks, the homesickness hadn't eased. Esther would be closer to her forced marriage to Henry. Grossdaedi's back was either healing or needing another treatment, depending on whether he'd been taking it easy or not. And Grossmammi—how was she doing after her hip replacement?

Maybe he could leave a message at the phone shanty, asking after everyone. He'd never done that before, but they might appreciate it. Usually, he wrote. But mailing and receiving letters took time. Precious time. He pulled out his cell phone and checked the signal. Service was always spotty on the river.

He dialed the number for the shanty by the road outside Rachel's haus. It rang three times...four...five...six.... He waited for the answering machine to kick on.

Before the seventh ring, a breathless-sounding female answered the phone. "Hallo?"

He blinked, surprised that someone had answered. "This is Viktor Petersheim. I'm calling to check on my family."

"Ach, Viktor. This is Rachel. I can run to get Esther or Reuben, if you want to call back."

"I can't talk; I'm getting ready to start work. Just checking."

"I'll tell them you called. Reuben is getting around much better. The other men aren't having to help so much. I haven't heard anything on Anna. Mamm hasn't been out to see her. Esther is staying pretty secluded, too. I've heard rumors that she's expecting your boppli." She sounded curious. Maybe a bit critical.

Viktor winced. He'd expected that gossip to spread, but it still hurt to hear a confirmation. Henry seemed determined to hurt Esther. Or him. "It's not true."

"I didn't think you'd leave her if it were." She paused, then let out a noisy huff of air. "I heard Lily is expecting, too."

"I don't know anything about Lily's situation, but if she is, I'm not the father." *Danki, Gott.* "Listen, I need to go. Tell Esther that if she can get away, I'll try to call her Sunday around two to check on Grossmammi. That's assuming I have service. If I don't call, she shouldn't worry."

"We have a frolic tomorrow nacht. I'll tell her then."

"Danki, Rachel." He wanted to say more. Ask more. But it was enough to know Esther wasn't married yet. And a relief that he'd removed himself from Lily when he had. She couldn't pin her pregnancy on him, if it was true she was expecting.

The way the rumor mill worked, especially where he was concerned, he couldn't be sure of anything. Guilty, regardless of the evidence or lack thereof. Because he was the "bad bu." Always had been. And Henry was from one of the *important* families of the community. A pillar. A gut bu.

Even if Viktor were to return, kneel in confession and repentance, and join the church, the people would look at him with suspicion, wondering how long it would be before he left. Again. For gut.

Gott, be with my family. Be with Esther.

Wait for me, süße.

~

Esther didn't want to go to the frolic. It'd be nice to see her cousins and her friends, play volleyball, and spend time with others her age. But with all the horrible things being said about her, she didn't want to face anyone. Wouldn't be able to look anyone in the eye. And Henry would be there. How could she face him?

She'd meant to send a letter to Rachel to tell her and her brother, Sam, not to kum pick her up, but she'd forgotten to. In mere minutes, Sam would be pulling into the drive. She needed to get ready.

When she realized that she'd be expected to ride home with Henry, a chill shot through her. She still hadn't seen him, other than across the barn at church, since Viktor's departure. She'd skipped the baptism class and the singing that evening. Skipped the frolics the next weekend. And still he hadn't cared enough to kum by to check on her.

Or maybe she'd accidentally fed his lies by not going. *Morgen sickness....*

Her stomach churned.

There'd been nein word from the bishop or the preachers since her conversation with Preacher Zeke several days ago. Nein word of apology from Henry. Not that she was surprised. And nein word from her parents. Nothing.

Reuben would tell her to go to the frolic. To walk tall and face the rumors head-on. But maybe she could pretend to have a headache. It'd be a lie, but she wasn't ready to resume being Henry's girl. Not after what he'd done. And not with her heart committed to wait for Viktor.

She might've gone along with it in the past, when she hadn't known any better. But now that she'd fallen in love with Viktor, she'd be reentering the relationship on the rebound. Unwillingly, because of an obligation. And if Henry would lie about her being pregnant after she'd tried to break up with him, to what other depths would he stoop in order to get his way?

Reuben's dochter Sandy drove up in her buggy. She climbed out, tied the horse to a post, and came to the door. Esther opened it for her. "Hallo."

"Daed told me you would be going to a frolic tonight." She sounded a bit gruff, as if she were bitter that she had to fill in for Esther just so she could attend a social event. To be fair, she took care of her ehemann's parents, and Esther had heard that her father-in-law suffered from dementia. He didn't get out much.

"I don't think I'll be going. I'm not feeling so well." Esther pressed her hand to her temple and winced, as if it throbbed with a headache. She hated to lie. But then, the thought of being with Henry really did make her head hurt.

"I hope it's nothing contagious. We don't need them getting sick on top of everything else." Sandy came inside. "I'll say hi, since I'm here, and then I'll head home. By the way, you do a fantastic job, Esther. If Mamm and Daed didn't need you, I'd hire you."

Esther closed the door behind her. "Danki."

"Heard a few things about you, but I have to say, I don't believe any of it. I know Daed checked you out thoroughly before he approached your daed about hiring you. I heard your daed is pretty angry about the rumors, too. He believes Henry is spreading lies because he's jealous."

Really? Daed had said that? Something inside Esther warmed.

She followed Sandy to the living room, where Anna and Reuben sat at a card table working on a puzzle of a Pennsylvania covered bridge. Anna had commented that it reminded her of the days when Reuben had courted her. It reminded Esther of the snow globe hidden away in her room for Anna's birthday, just a couple of days away. She needed to take it out of its newspaper packing and make sure it was clean. Maybe listen to the music one more time.

Sandy pulled a straight chair to the table and picked up a puzzle piece while she chatted with her parents. Esther tuned her out as she studied the cozy threesome.

It was wunderbaar that Reuben had married Anna, the girl he'd always loved. Even if they'd had to leave Pennsylvania, they'd had a gut life. But it was sad that they'd had to flee the land they loved to escape from Reuben's brother.

If Anna and Reuben could have a happy-ever-after, maybe she and Viktor could, too.

But the scenario was entirely different. Nobody had ever tried to force Anna to marry Mark, and Henry had never hit Esther. How could he? That would involve physical touch. Her lip curled involuntarily.

Buggy wheels crunched in the driveway. Esther turned and went back to the door. This time, it was Sam and Rachel. Esther stepped onto the porch. "I have a bit of a headache, so I'm not going tonight. Sorry I didn't tell you ahead of time."

"I'll be praying you feel better, Esther," Rachel said with a wave.

"Me, too," Sam put in. "I'll tell Henry you're sick."

"Ach, and Viktor called last nacht," Rachel added. "He said he'd call back tomorrow at two, if you're free."

She'd be free, for a chance to talk with Viktor. Anna and Reuben would let her go for a few minutes. She smiled, already looking forward to it.

Sam clicked at the horse. It trotted off as Esther shut the door again.

She turned to find Reuben standing behind her. "You aren't going to the frolic?" He frowned. "I know you don't really have a headache."

Esther shook her head. "I…I just can't. I can't pretend to be happy when I'm not. I can't pretend to want to be with Henry when I don't. I can't—" *Can't risk being trapped in a buggy with him on the way home.*

"Jah. But didn't our conversation the other day show you that Gott will work things out? That He will make a way of escape?"

Esther nodded. Gulped. "Sometimes I feel like some toy that's randomly played with and forgotten about the rest of the time." She caught a tear trickling out of her left eye. "I feel like Gott doesn't love me after all." If He did, He wouldn't have made her suffer by bringing Viktor into her life, only to yank him away. A mean trick, like her older siblings' cruelly jerking her favorite toy out of her grasp just to make her cry when they were kinner.

"Ach, Esther. That isn't true. Gott loves you very much." Reuben turned to the cupboard, brought out two glasses, and filled them with iced tea. He set them on the table. "Kum. Sit. Let me get the Bible, and I'll show you how much He cares."

Chapter 34

Viktor paced around the boat, going from end to end, stopping routinely to check his phone. It didn't do any gut. Nein signal.

He sighed. So much for hearing Esther's sweet voice today. To hear firsthand how his family fared—how she was doing. If there'd been any changes in their circumstances.

Because if one person believed them, then maybe more did, too. Grossdaedi and Grossmammi believed him. And Rachel had indicated that she thought he was telling the truth. That made three. Did he dare hope there might be four?

His stomach ached. He hoped he wasn't getting an ulcer dealing with this unwanted stress.

Who said the plain life was simple?

He climbed up to the wheelhouse and stood right outside to check his phone again. Still nein signal.

Reluctantly, he slid the phone back inside his pocket and went down to his room. He pulled out a piece of lined paper and a black pen.

Dear Grossdaedi, Grossmammi, and Esther,

Not sure where we are, exactly. Somewhere south of Cairo, Illinois, but not sure how far south. I haven't checked the log recently. An empty barge travels about 10 mph upriver. Loaded, it's much slower. And we're carrying coal.

I wanted to call today and see how everyone was doing, but I had nein cell-phone signal. Esther, I'm sorry if I made you wait by the phone shanty for the call that never came. I wanted to tell you about some of the sights we've seen on this trip. About the bald eagle in Burlington, Iowa, diving down to get some fish churned up by the boat. The seagulls we saw further south as we neared the Gulf of Mexico. We tossed bread to them. Some of the guys dipped the bread in hot sauce when the birds got into a feeding frenzy. It was funny watching them dive into the water for a drink.

I will try to call again soon, and if I get an answer, I'll have someone run to get you. I'm sorry I didn't do that when I called Friday nacht.

Miss you all, more than I can say.

Happy birthday, Grossmammi.

Love,
Viktor

He folded the sheet of paper in half lengthwise and slid it into the envelope, leaving it unsealed, in case he thought of something more to say before he had a chance to mail it. Then he stepped out of his room. Lis wasn't in the kitchen, but the oven was preheating. He lifted the lid of the cookie jar, glad to see that it was almost full. He grabbed a handful of chocolate chip cookies. Nein nuts, because one of the guys who'd just kum on board had an allergy. Too bad. He enjoyed the walnuts Esther put in hers. Then he headed for the TV to see what movie they had playing.

"Man overboard!"

⁓

On Sunday nacht, Anna and Reuben were already in bed when Esther set the snow globe by Anna's place at the kitchen table for her to find when she came in for breakfast in the morgen. She'd made Anna's favorite cinnamon rolls, which she would bake in the morgen.

If she'd gone to the singing, she'd probably be heading home around now. Instead, despite its being Sunday, she'd been busy, if preparing cinnamon rolls counted as work. Esther stared out the kitchen window at the stars. If Viktor were home, she'd slip on her shoes and run out the door to meet him at the pond so they could stargaze. She'd asked Rachel to order her a book about stars on the Internet.

It had kum in yesterday's mail. But she hadn't read about stars last nacht. Instead, she'd sat with Reuben at the table, reading Scripture after Scripture, as he showed her how important she was to Gott.

How Gott loved her enough to send His Son to die for her. How she could know for sure she was saved. Unbelievable, freeing, and beyond wunderbaar. She couldn't believe the joy and peace that had filled her. Why hadn't she heard this message in church? Hadn't she been paying attention?

Instead of studying the sky and thinking of Viktor, she'd cried and prayed, asking Gott to forgive her. Inviting Him into her heart. And promising her life to Him. Best decision ever.

To-nacht, instead of lying beside Viktor on a quilt and staring up at the sky, she would read a book about the stars, contemplate the Gott who had made them, and how much He cared. And she would pray for Viktor's safe return.

Esther stepped out on the front porch. Did he see the same stars, wherever he was?

Something cracked, and Esther turned toward the sound. A dark figure approached on foot, up the driveway. He must've parked his horse and buggy along the road. Maybe his horse had thrown a shoe.

"Esther? That you?"

Henry. Her breath lodged in her throat. "Why are you here?" She kept her voice hushed, not wanting to disturb Reuben and Anna. Their bedroom window was open.

"Why'd you miss singing? Two church Sundays in a row. And you've missed the last two baptism classes. What are you thinking?" His voice was harsh and not very quiet. "They won't allow us to marry if you don't join the church."

That was the idea.

She pressed her forefinger to her lips, then used the other to point toward the open window.

Henry responded by reaching out and grabbing her wrist—the first time he'd ever touched her—and yanking her off the porch. Not down the steps, just off. She landed hard, but at least she was on her feet.

She didn't feel any sparks. At least, not the gut kind. Instead, her temper flared to life as he tightened his grip. He gave another jerk, and she stumbled against him. He twisted her arm up behind her back, painfully high.

Maybe she shouldn't have pointed out the open window. Reuben might've heard and kum to her rescue.

Henry's hot breath blew in her face. It smelled like garlic.

Esther gasped, blinking back tears.

"You *will* attend the next baptism class." Impossibly, he twisted her arm higher, as if he were trying to break it. "Bad enough you shame me this way, trying to refuse me for a *river rat*, but I will not have you disobey me. Got it?"

She managed a mute nod, afraid that if she opened her mouth, a scream would emerge. She couldn't let Reuben see this. If he did, he'd try to protect her; and there was nein telling what Henry would do to him, given his bad back.

"You wanted to be touched, you tramp. How do you like it? Huh?"

He released her with a shove. She fell back against the porch rail with a thud. Her head hit the edge, and she slid down into the dirt, crushing the flowers she'd planted. The scent of mums rose around her. She sat in a numb daze. Her head pounded.

Somehow, she had to placate him. But she didn't know how.

"How dare you get pregnant by *him*?"

Did he really believe the lie of his own creation?

"I'm not," she whimpered. "It's not true."

He bent down, and his palm connected with her face hard enough that her head jerked to the side. Tears sprang to her eyes. *Gott, help. Please.*

"Liar!" His roar might've rattled the windows.

Nein hope of Reuben and Anna sleeping through this.

Sure enough, she heard muffled sounds through the open window.

"You will learn to respect me, or you can expect more of this." He kicked her shin with his booted foot.

She cried out and automatically reached for her throbbing leg.

"You'll be at the next frolic and baptism class, jah?"

Her tears escaped, running unhampered down her cheeks. She managed a nod. Hopefully, that would end the abuse and prompt him to leave.

"Your brat can expect the same treatment." Henry added a few foul words before disappearing back into the darkness.

The kitchen door opened and shut. Steps sounded above her, but she couldn't bring herself to move. Shock warred with despair. What should she do? Where could she go to get away without leaving Reuben and Anna subject to harm?

A few seconds later, Reuben knelt beside her. "Are you okay?"

She whimpered.

He reached out and patted her shoulder. Slid his arm awkwardly around her. She huddled against him, sniffling. "Shhhh. He's gone now, süße."

The whispered endearment didn't help. She wanted Viktor's arms around her. His voice whispering the word.

Her throat closed up as she choked on her tears.

⁓

Viktor strode onto solid ground. St. Louis at nacht. They'd stopped to refuel and to check on the man who'd fallen overboard. The Coast Guard had made sure he'd gotten to a hospital. He'd almost drowned before being rescued. He'd gotten caught in the fast current and hadn't been wearing a life vest.

Viktor saw the illuminated Arch and all the tall buildings with lights on in different windows. He remembered the crowded streets from when he'd wandered them as a teen running away to the river. Who knew it would be so hard to find? He chuckled at the memory.

He pulled his phone out of his pocket to check for missed calls. The signal was always strong in cities.

There was one missed call from the nearby phone shanty. There was a voice mail. He entered the password.

"Viktor. This is Grossdaedi. You…." And that was all he could make out. It was as if Grossdaedi had spoken away from the receiver.

Was there a problem? Did Grossdaedi need him for something?

His truck was in Iowa, and it would be a while before he reached it. Viktor shut his eyes, weighing his options. And he still had three weeks left before he could leave. Unless it was an emergency.

Ach, Lord. Let them be okay.

He dialed the number for the shanty. It rang eight times, and then he heard the answering machine. *Figures.*

He was back on the river, in the middle of a lock, before the return call came.

"Kum home." Grossdaedi sounded disjointed.

"What happened?" Viktor nearly shouted. "Is she okay?" It had to be a "she," whether Grossmammi or Esther.

The reply was jumbled, broken. He heard one word: "Hurt."

"I'll kum as soon as I can."

When they got out of the lock and were in the river again, he could order the boat to the side and leave, but he'd have nein way home without his truck—unless he rented a vehicle. But in the middle of nowhere, who knew where the nearest rental place would be. Like it or not, he'd stay on board until Iowa.

Yet he sensed an urgency that he couldn't shake. He decided to call for a driver to meet him by the river.

Grossdaedi wouldn't have called unless….

He shuddered.

This was an emergency.

Chapter 35

Esther washed the dishes from the noon meal. Her leg ached terribly, but at least she could walk. Her arm hurt to move in certain ways, but she was functioning. Her headache was managed by a couple of pain pills. And the bruising—would it be wrong to tell the truth if anyone asked what had happened? Would anyone believe her?

Her parents did, according to Sandy. Rachel did. Preacher Zeke. Reuben and Anna. She wasn't alone in this, after all. *Danki, Gott.*

She would get better. Slowly.

But she had nein guarantee that Henry wouldn't do this again. If she was forced to marry him, what would keep him from hurting her? And she'd have nein protection.

She couldn't allow it to happen. She'd fight for her freedom.

She turned to the table and spied the snow globe still sitting there. Anna had asked her to place it somewhere they all could enjoy it. Esther picked it up and wound the key to play the tune. The glittery snow swirled around the buggy and the covered bridge. So pretty.

"Praise Gott from Whom All Blessings Flow" played like a hundred little bells tinkling. The doxology, Reuben had said. She'd known she recognized it from somewhere; she'd just never heard an instrumental version. It was a song they sang every church Sunday. *Ach, derr Herr. I'm sorry for doubting.* She still doubted. *Help me believe that You will help me.*

Would Reuben be able to hide her? Would she be able to protect them from the danger Henry posed if she allowed him to spirit her away? What if Henry threatened to kill them, like Mark had Reuben all those years ago?

Esther dried the final dish and was putting it away when she heard gravel crunching. She looked out the window. A white van. The familiar driver.

She wasn't expecting anyone. Neither was Reuben, as far as she knew.

She didn't want to go to meet whoever it was. Not with the side of her face still red and bruised.

The vehicle door slammed. Footsteps sounded on the wooden porch. Then the screen door opened.

She swiveled around, scared that it might be Henry again. Or Lily.

Viktor stood in the doorway. Was she dreaming? She blinked a couple times, then pinched her arm. It hurt. He was here? Really? She stared at him, her hand automatically going to cover her cheek, trying to hide it from him.

If only she could run into his arms and hang on for dear life.

"Ach, Viktor." Her voice broke with a sob.

"Grossmammi okay?"

She managed a nod. "She's sleeping."

"Grossdaedi?"

She nodded again.

"Then it's you." His voice broke. He crossed the room with long strides. "What happened?" His hand caught hers and gently pulled it away from her face. With the fingertips of his other hand, he traced over the discoloration. His jaw firmed. "Henry?"

Tears filled her eyes. She wanted to fling herself into his arms. Instead, she pulled away, angling her head to study his feet, ashamed that he'd seen her like this.

His fingers caught beneath her chin and gently raised it again. "You aren't married, are you?" His gaze was piercing. "Is that why you're looking away?"

"Nein." Little more than a whisper.

His gaze searched hers. " Where's Grossdaedi? I need to talk to him."

"He's gone to get the bishop. Did he call you?"

Viktor hesitated. "Last nacht. I got here as soon as I could." A muscle worked in his jaw. "You're not marrying him, süße. You can't."

She looked down again. "I don't know how to escape."

"Do you want to?"

She managed a nod. *More than anything.*

"Then you have a choice. Marry me, süße. Today."

"Can we do that?" Hope flared. She dared to raise her eyes to meet his gaze.

"Jah, we can do that. If you want to. Missouri has a no-wait law." He pulled in a breath and caught her hands in his as he dropped to one knee. "Ich liebe dich, süße. Will you marry me? Today?"

Her eyes brimmed. "Jah." She squealed, then remembered Anna, supposedly sleeping in the bedroom. "Ich liebe dich. And…ach, Viktor."

He smiled and rose.

She threw herself in his arms, kissing him on his nose, his cheeks, his eyes, his lips. He wrapped his arms around her waist and returned her kisses, then chuckled as he pulled away. "Kum. The driver is waiting."

In the next second, he scooped her up and held her, close to his heart. She could feel it throbbing beneath her fingers. Viktor was here. He had her. He was taking charge. It would be all right.

She wrapped her arms around his neck as he carried her out of the haus to the waiting van and gently deposited her in the backseat.

Viktor glanced at the driver. "Take us to the courthaus." He settled next to Esther and slid the door shut.

A horse and buggy pulled into the driveway, followed by another.

The driver raised his eyebrows at them in the rearview mirror. Esther cringed, sinking lower in the seat when she recognized the stern face of the bishop.

Viktor reached for her hand, intertwining his fingers with hers, but a frown marred his features. He didn't look at her, instead meeting the driver's gaze.

"Go."

⌒

Mission accomplished. Viktor signed his name with a flourish, right underneath hers. *Esther Anne Beachy. Viktor Steven Petersheim.*

The judge signed the paper, followed by the witnesses—one of them their driver.

And they were married. Nein muss, nein fuss. And the best thing: Bishop Joe couldn't do a thing about it. Viktor grinned at Esther.

She smiled back, a light shining in her eyes. The defeat he'd seen when he'd arrived had vanished.

"Congratulations!" said the judge.

Viktor did the Englisch thing and pulled Esther into his arms for an ardent kiss. Then he bent her backward, as the heroes did in some of the old movies he'd seen on board the boat. She squealed and clung to him but kissed him back with every bit of the passion he'd remembered and dreamed about.

The witnesses clapped as Viktor straightened and helped her regain her footing. A delicious-looking blush colored her cheeks, staining even the bruise.

He held her hand as they left the room.

As the driver went to get the van, Viktor leaned close. "I can't wait to stargaze with you tonight."

A sense of heaviness weighed on Esther when the driver stopped in front of the farmhaus, where the bishop's buggy still waited in the driveway. The horse had been unhitched. If he had waited hours for her return, then it couldn't be gut. But then, what could he do? She was married. She wasn't yet a church member, so she couldn't be shunned. He could do nothing.

But still.

She watched as Viktor paid the driver, both men still wearing wide grins. Then he turned and helped Esther out. He boldly pulled her into his arms and kissed her. "Nein matter what is said, remember, ich liebe dich. He can do nothing now. Don't worry, süße." He held her gaze until she nodded. Then he grasped her hand, and together they climbed the porch steps and entered the kitchen.

Anna and Reuben sat at opposite ends of the table. Bishop Joe sat between them, in Viktor's place. In the middle of the table was a mostly empty pie pan, as well as Anna's precious snow globe. Two pieces of pie remained—one for each of them. Or two to share between the four of them for supper. Maybe she should make another pie. It would give her something to do besides sit and worry.

She glanced at Viktor. *Nothing to worry about.*

Bishop Joe hitched his brow, and his normally stern expression grew...sterner.

Esther's courage fled. She dropped into a chair. *Nothing to worry about.* Just some unpleasantness. Anna reached for her hand.

Reuben nodded at Viktor. "Glad you made it back. But you took off in a hurry. Where'd you go?"

Viktor glanced at Esther with a smile, his eyes gentle and full of love, before looking at Reuben. He leaned closer, as if preparing to let him in on a juicy secret. "I married Esther." Then he straightened, folded his arms across his chest, and leaned against the countertop with a smirk as he looked at the bishop. "Legally."

Esther's face heated. *Married. To Viktor. A wunderbaar thing.*

"Married!" Anna gasped. "Ach, Viktor. Praise Gott."

A smile appeared on Reuben's face and quickly widened.

Bishop Joe inhaled and exhaled loudly, then slowly rose to his feet. Was it to assume a position of authority? Or maybe to make a hasty exit after he handed down his decree?

He glanced at Esther, then at Viktor. "I've had several visits over the past few days. Samuel's Rachel came by with Andy's Greta to tell me about Henry's temper. About a flour bag exploding in the store." A slight smile played on his lips. "That, I think I might've liked to have seen."

Esther wasn't fond of drama, but the thought of poor Greta covered in flour.... She couldn't help but smile back. Besides, her cousins had dared to approach the bishop in her defense. What a blessing.

Bishop Joe took a step toward Viktor. "Then I had additional visits from these same girls, and from others in the community, including Preacher Zeke, claiming that Henry had lied about many things to force the situation to go his way. Apparently his design was to keep Esther from marrying you."

He'd failed. Joy bubbled up inside Esther as she met Viktor's eyes again.

"Esther's daed even came by, and though he admitted he knew nothing about what had transpired between Esther and you, he said he could vouch for his dochter's character—and for Henry's temper and lies. He also said he trusted Reuben completely with Esther's care." The bishop sobered as he turned to Reuben. "This morgen, Reuben came over, demanding that I kum see what Henry had done to Esther." He sighed and looked at her. "I am not blind. And I will have words with Henry. The Beilers' will be my next stop."

Viktor shifted as he hitched an eyebrow. "So then, I—we— might expect an apology?"

A smile flickered on the bishop's lips. "You've been among the Englisch too long, sohn. A bit arrogant, ain't so?"

Viktor shrugged.

The bishop patted his shoulder. "I'm sorry I judged you wrongly. And I will work to right this situation in the community. I will deal with Henry." He turned to face Esther, his expression grim. "I should've known better. You, of all maidals."

She straightened her shoulders. After days and weeks of rumors and mistreatment, harsh looks of condemnation, and accusations, she'd been vindicated. She smiled as peace flooded her heart.

Bishop Joe took his hat off the hook and glanced back at Viktor. "You might be joining baptism classes, then?"

Viktor made a clicking sound with his tongue and winked at Esther. "Jah. You bet."

Her smile grew. He was back for gut.

The bishop chuckled and walked out the door.

Esther picked up the snow globe, now a depiction of the reality of her own life. *Praise Gott from whom all blessings flow.*

Indeed.

About the Author

Amember of the American Christian Fiction Writers, Laura V. Hilton is a professional book reviewer for the Christian market, with more than a thousand reviews published on the Web.

Her first series with Whitaker House, The Amish of Seymour, comprises *Patchwork Dreams*, *A Harvest of Hearts*, and *Promised to Another*. In 2012, *A Harvest of Hearts* received a Laurel Award, placing first in the Amish Genre Clash. Her second series, The Amish of Webster County, comprises *Healing Love*, *Surrendered Love*, and *Awakened Love*. A stand-alone title, *A White Christmas in Webster County*, was released in September 2014. *The Snow Globe* is book one in Laura's latest series, The Amish of Jamesport.

Previously, Laura published two novels with Treble Heart Books, *Hot Chocolate* and *Shadows of the Past*, as well as several devotionals. Laura and her husband, Steve, have five children, whom Laura home-schools. The family makes their home in Arkansas. To learn more about Laura, read her reviews, and find out about her upcoming releases, readers may visit her blog at http://lighthouse-academy.blogspot.com/.